No Turning Back

Best Wishes
Iris　　　5·10·2015

Iris Button

First published in Great Britain

All paper used in the printing of this book has been made
from wood grown in managed, sustainable forests.

ISBN 978-1-78003-851-3

Printed and bound in the UK

Pen Press is an imprint of
Author Essentials
4 The Courtyard
South Street
Falmer
East Sussex
BN1 9PQ

I should like to dedicate this book to my daughter Julia.
Always in touch and always helpful. Always there.

CHAPTER ONE

It was the night of the year, the Hollywood Academy Awards, and the red carpet was alive and buzzing with excitement as cameras flashed on the rich and famous. The most gorgeous top designer evening gowns were worn by the most glamorous women with the most flattering figures and elegant jewellery shimmered and sparkled under the brightness of the lights, but of course all had been loaned just for the evening and armed security men hovered in the background. Famous stars paraded before the cameras with confidence, while new young starlets paraded with wide excited smiles and flashing eyes, hoping to get really noticed, each one trying to outshine the other. The beautiful people were out in force, the men immaculately attired in black tie, very stylish and equally handsome. Some were perfectly dressed right down to their white trainers, a very modern-day trend, thinking that they were stylish but actually looking tacky and showing their ignorance.

Male and female flaunted in the limelight as the cameras continually flashed and the reporters shouted, 'TURN THIS WAY! HELLO! LOOK HERE!' Some reporters with microphones were interviewing and asking questions about the magnificent gowns and designer labels. This was going live on television, and also the next day all would be revealed in the papers and glossy magazines. Some of the designer gowns, hastily worked on overnight, would be copied and appear the next morning in the chain stores much reduced in price.

The pavement was crowded with onlookers and fans, and as the cars drew up outside the hotel the porters opened the doors and the news cameramen surged forward. The crowds gathered with excited shouts and hoorays and amateur photographs lifted cameras high above their heads, hoping to be pointing the camera in the right direction, seeing nothing, but straining their necks to get a good look. There were shouts and clapping and whistles, and the policemen on duty, keeping order, had the best view.

A black Rolls-Royce pulled up, the door opened by a porter. There was a lot of noise from the crowd as Amber De Carla stepped out, and then there was an excited uproar as the name, 'Amber De Carla, it's Amber De Carla, it's Amber,' passed from lips to lips, and the crowded spectators pressed forward.

Amber De Carla, just twenty-three years old, was British and at the top of her career, having just finished a blockbuster film called *Love to Kill*. She was beautiful and oozed glamour, her skin delicately golden and flawless, although much of it was professional makeup. Her blue eyes were heavy with black mascara, and her long silver-blonde hair, originally mousy brown, had tonight been piled up into silver curls on top of her head. She looked gorgeous in a white and silver crystal-beaded silk evening gown that clung to her slim figure as if it had been sprayed onto her naked body, and there was a long split up the side showing the length of her shapely leg as she walked in silver kid platforms with four-inch stiletto heels. She was five feet six inches tall, but the shoes made her much taller. Diamonds sparkled at her throat, her ears and her wrists, of course all loaned by Van Cleef & Arpels especially for the evening. She moved elegantly with raised shoulders, turning this way and that for the cameras; the bright red lips protruded as she blew kisses to the crowd, and the voices of the cameramen called above the commotion, 'Amber! Amber! Look this way, Miss De Carla! Look this way.' And she turned for their pleasure, swinging her slim hips this way and that, holding the small beaded clutch bag with slender hands and long red fingernails. The long black lashes fluttered and the blue eyes shone with an innocent shyness and her shoulders lifted, almost touching her ears, as her head turned before the cameras with the beautiful wide red-lipped smile, following the instructions of her first manager Max Milner. It was all good publicity and the crowd missed nothing.

Her escort for this evening was Steve Salvettini, which happened to be his real name, and he was equally as popular, and every bit as handsome. He was every woman's dream, at six feet six inches tall, slim and athletic-looking, with deep golden suntanned skin, black wavy hair, dark brown flashing eyes and a white dazzling smile. Although he looked dark and continental he was actually an all-American boy from California, and before becoming an actor, he had been a basketball player. He had done some sports advertising and eventually got into acting. His voice was deep and masterful; when he played a love scene all women went into raptures, almost fainting with the joy of just watching. Steve was serious-minded; he of course enjoyed the attention, but fame had not gone to his head. He was very level-headed, the quiet type: as Americans would put it, 'a real regular Joe'. His manner was polite, friendly and very down-to-earth and although he enjoyed the limelight he was a complete contrast to the bold and hard-headed Amber. He sometimes wondered now how he had stayed with her for a whole year. He had liked her, she had style, but although they'd had a lot of fun together she was the last girl he would ever want to spend the rest of his life with; in fact he was happy to be a bachelor.

They had met on a film set and were both the most popular and the most in-demand couple in the theatrical world at this time. Their last film together was a big box-office hit, *Kiss of the Raven*, a fast-moving detective story that no one had dared to miss, he playing Larry Raven, handsome suave murderer and romantic lover. They looked so good together and she was the envy of every woman from nine to ninety.

Some of the guests tonight knew of their hate relationship, but it was all about show business. They were both good actors, and the smiles they gave to each other tonight were all false. They had been lovers once, until *he* had been caught in a hotel room with a young starlet by the paparazzi and the next day it had been displayed on the front page of every newspaper. Show business was all about being seen with the right people. Amber had felt secure in knowing that he was a solid guy, but now she had lost her trust in him, even though she now knew the truth that the young starlet had arranged it all for her own publicity. The whole affair really had ruined Amber and Steve's image as a solid couple. But they were such good actors that the waiting crowd saw only love in their eyes.

They moved on into the reception and the crowd outside simmered down. Then they surged forward again as the next car came to a standstill. All those at the back could see was the silver-grey hair of Elliot Stirling the film director and his wife Elaine as they alighted; they were not known to most of the public, and a whisper went through the crowd of 'Who is it?' And then one could hear the *aaah* of disappointment go through the crowd.

Elaine was short and grey-haired and although well into her sixties she looked elegant wearing midnight-blue silk. Of course her once-slim figure had gained a few pounds, but her diamond bracelet and the expensive real pearls at her throat and ears were all her own. The cameras flashed, but the crowd had quietened down.

Inside the hotel the cameras still flashed and the cameramen still called, 'Look this way, Amber!' and she twisted and turned at each request to please them, giving a loving smile as if for that one cameraman alone, the bright red lips blowing quiet kisses, and the long black false eyelashes fluttering. Her blonde head moved from side to side, almost touching her raised shoulders, as she preened in front of them in a shy and innocent way as if it were the first time that she had ever been photographed.

After the red-carpet entrance the evening started with the beautiful people gathered in small groups sipping champagne; Amber was standing with Steve Salvettini and Elliot and Elaine Stirling. Elliot had particularly asked Amber and Steve to arrive together just for this evening, knowing of course that they were not friendly but saying that it would look good for the film awards. Meanwhile Jerome Howard, Amber's current conquest, had escorted Stacey Devlin, who had taken the supporting role in tonight's nominated film, *Love to Kill*. Neither of them had agreed with this, but Elliot had insisted it would be good publicity for Stacey Devlin, and when Elliot insisted, Elliot insisted.

Jerome, feeling disappointed at not being able to escort Amber, had picked Stacey up on the way, or she would have arrived alone. She looked beautiful in orange silk. She was a good actress and Elliot had thought her on her way to stardom. And seeing her now, Jerome was stunned and proud to have her on his arm. Elliot had said that it would boost Stacey's popularity to be seen on the arm of a popular actor; that had also pleased Jerome, being called a popular actor. He had made a lot of films but had never quite made it to the top.

Jerome smiled for the cameras, pulling himself up to his full height, six feet two inches, and holding his head very erect as Stacey Devlin was interviewed about her designer label gown, and then he felt very proud as he was being questioned about his Brioni suit. Jerome in a rugged sort of way was more attractive than handsome, tall and well-built and fit. His face could be described as large with a square chin and a sharp nose; his eyes were blue, his hair straight, thick and blonde. He had a pleasant but serious nature; he didn't smile a lot. He gave the impression of jealousy and of wanting to hog the limelight. Most of the parts he played were the villainous type, the hitman or sometimes hard-headed policeman; these roles suited him, but never the romantic lover. In real life, he was quite romantic and generous. Although he looked forceful he was really of a quieter nature, and this was why he liked to be seen with Amber De Carla; it boosted his ego. He felt handsome and masterful in her company but had not got the suave stature of Salvettini.

And now, each with a glass of champagne in one hand, he and Stacey joined the group. Jerome stood close to Amber and put his arm around her very slim waist, then glanced at Steve Salvettini before kissing Amber on the cheek and squeezing her close, in a sort of claiming attitude. Amber looked up at him with a sweet smile; they touched glasses, making a big show of their fondness for each other, and said, 'Cheers,' and smiled lovingly at each other for all to see, but Steve knew better. Jerome Howard was getting good publicity out of being seen with Amber, but Steve knew that Amber only really loved Amber.

It was then that the loud and booming voice of the red-coated Master of Ceremonies announced that 'Dinner is served!' and the two hundred guests began gradually making their way with a buzz of noisy chatter into the magnificent dining hall. They took their places under bright chandeliers of glittering glass and fabulous floral arrangements that wafted a delicate perfume through the vast room, the tables set with snow-white cloths and silver and sparkling cut glass.

The stage at the end of the hall was set with a deep purple background of velvet drapes, four pedestals of white roses, and a dais and lectern in the centre.

The round table seated ten; Amber sat between Steve Salvettini on her right and Jerome Howard to her left. Jerome squeezed her hand in a friendly manner and she gave him a look of daggers, a look of *unhand me, sir*, her chin lifted high as if it were a sin to touch her. She looked around the table like a queen looking down on her subjects. That was Amber's problem; she was toploftical.

Next to Jerome was Elaine, then the producer Ronald Tappener, the young Stacey Devlin, then the director Elliot Stirling. Ronald Tappener, being a widower since his wife had passed away last year with breast cancer, had this evening brought along his daughter Marlene, who was beautiful, with long raven hair and olive skin, very expensively dressed and dripping in diamonds. She had nothing to do with acting; she was a lawyer, but the pressure to dress up and be seen was upon every woman in the room.

Stacey Devlin looked a little nervous tonight, sitting at a top table for the first time ever; Elliot Stirling touched her hand to reassure her, knowing that she felt inferior having the great and very confident Amber De Carla sitting opposite. Stacey was a beautiful Irish redhead, and Elliot felt that there must be a little competition there.

Amber was intimidating and talked a lot with her shoulders raised and her chin high and mighty, her eyelashes fluttering as she waved her hands about as if in command. She spoke loudly and very precisely as if addressing the whole room, and most of the time talked down to the other guests. Of course they were all used to her overdramatic theatrical ways; even Stacey Devlin had got used to her after they had worked together, but Stacey had never socialised with Amber before tonight. It seemed that Amber had no time for the lesser creatures, and Stacey had found her hard to work with, as did everyone else; Amber made *everyone* feel inferior. Still, being in the company of the great De Carla, Stacey felt, like Jerome, that it helped her image. Although the cameras were focused around the vast room, most of the time their table would be the one on the television.

Elliot touched Stacey's hand again and Amber noticed that she gave him a false shy smile.

Ronald Tappener had made a great deal of money on the stock market and in the last twelve years had put money into film producing. He wasn't very social, but sat with a satisfied feeling inside for tonight's nominated film. It wasn't the first time; it had all happened before. He had now found another script which he had given to Elliot earlier that morning, and Elliot was to present it to the same cast tomorrow morning. Tappener knew that he couldn't go wrong with De Carla and Salvettini; it would be another blockbuster, there was no doubt, and it would add millions to the millions he already had.

Elliot Stirling had once been a small-time actor; he had now been directing for ten years and had been very successful. His wife Elaine had starred in several films in her younger days and had been a good actress. She had appeared mostly in secondary parts, never having been a great beauty, but had made a good name for herself as Elaine Sherman.

Jonah Lombardo and his wife came to the table, apologising for being a little late; he said that they had been chatting. Jonah had co-starred in tonight's nominated film. His wife Louise was a makeup artist. Louise was small and very delicate, a very beautiful black girl with light skin and shoulder-length silky black hair. She looked stunning tonight in a scarlet off-the-shoulder gown. Of course her makeup was perfect and her wide brown eyes had natural lashes curling with black mascara, her lips full with a deep dark shiny red lipstick. Tonight she wore a heavy gold chain with diamonds around her slender neck, and large round gold earrings that almost touched her shoulders.

Jonah was a huge black African with broad shoulders and huge muscled arms; he spent a lot of time in the gym lifting weights. He had been in America since he was two years old. He had joined a theatrical group while in college, and then had spent many hours waiting around the studios for extra parts, and eventually he had made it; since then he'd made many films. In tonight's nominated film, *Love to Kill*, he had portrayed a rough, cruel and dangerous murderer running from the police. But in real life he was the gentlest and kindest man, quietly spoken in a shy and masculine way. He and Louise had been happily married for five years; they had no children.

The table now complete, they all lifted and touched glasses, saying cheers, before enjoying a delicious meal.

After the dinner the lights were lowered and the award ceremony began, while waiters mingled among the tables in the shadows, very quietly replenishing glasses. There were a few jokes from the popular talk-show host Lawrence Granger, who was now at the dais. He went on to read from a card the nominees from three films as excerpts of each film came up on a large screen for all to see, and then introduced a popular actress, Pauline O'Grady, who was to present the statuette for the best supporting actress.

Granger opened a white envelope with great flair and style, smiling and taking his time and keeping the audience in suspense. He pretended that he couldn't get the card out of the envelope, and then held his breath and smiled even wider, while some whispered to their partners who they thought it would be, and then Lawrence Granger was announcing, '*And* the *winner is...* for Best Supporting Actress... Anna Southland, for *Diamond Sky.*'

Anna, a beautiful American girl dressed in black sequins, went up onto the stage to loud applause, to collect her award. She held it close to her heart and made a short vote of thanks, and then left the stage to clapping again.

Several other films were shown and the actors and actresses given honours for their hard work, and each made the appropriate speeches to thank producers, directors and fellow actors, the audience clapping, whooping and whistling and laughing at comical comments, knowing that the whole thing was an act anyway.

Then from the next card, three films were shown for Best Actress. '*The Western Way*, nominee is Tina Malaren, *Home Grown*, Mellissa Greenstone, and then *Love to Kill*, Amber De Carla, and the winner is...' Again Granger took his time with the white envelope, smiling at the audience, but everyone already knew that it was a foregone conclusion. He suddenly announced, 'Amber De Carla!'

The clapping was loud and enthusiastic as she stood up, turning slowly and waving her hand in a delicate motion with all the grace and panache of a queen greeting her subjects. She moved through the tables as if on air as the spotlight played on the snow-white and silver gown shimmering with crystals, following her and keeping her central as she moved her body sensually to continuous applause, bowing her head and fluttering the long black eyelashes. Looking shy and surprised, she stepped onto the stage and turned to face the audience, *her subjects*, so far beneath her. A lot of her fellow actors would be thinking it was all a lot of show, but then that was what show business was all about: show!

She oozed glamour; you could almost smell the glamour as she received a kiss from Lawrence Granger, and then Larry Warner, a famous older actor who got even more applause as he came onto the stage, was handing her the golden statue with a wide smile and a lot of flamboyance, arms wide and enclosing her with a kiss on both cheeks, almost worshipping her with a bow as he would a queen. If they could have read his mind, the audience would have known he was thinking what a cantankerous bitch she was, but nevertheless, after working on a film with her some time ago, he had to give her credit; her acting was superb. She fully deserved an award, but he had vowed that he would never take on any film part with her again.

She smiled, thanking him as he left the stage to more applause, and then she turned to the audience. The red lips curled in a false smile as she gave a shy cringe and a shrug of her bare right shoulder, the sequins and rhinestones glittering under the lights as she moved her voluptuous breasts, as if it were the first time that this great event had ever happened, and she was overwhelmed.

She waited for a pause in the applause, then nervously cleared her throat and gave her vote of thanks to everyone who had made it possible; she mentioned Ronald Tappener, the producer, and '*darling*' Elliot Stirling, whose 'expert direction' had 'made all *this* possible'. She always called him 'darling', but it was not an endearment and it sounded so false. She smiled in the direction of the table. 'And, of course, the *gorgeous* Steve Salvettini.'

She waited while the exuberant applause calmed down, and Steve at the mention of his name half-stood and took a bow, raising his eyebrows with a nonchalant smile. Amber then give a little girlish giggle, shrugging her bare shoulders again and moving her head shyly to one side, knowing that every woman in the room envied her that long and sensual screen kiss, but thinking in her mind that *she* had hated every second of it. She smiled, making them even more envious, as she heard a frustrated exhalation from the ladies.

She and Steve had met on a previous film set, and had started out as real-life lovers. Having been happy together for over a year, they had been so glad to be working together again on *Love to Kill*. He had moved into her luxurious house in Beverly Hills; Bessie had not approved, but of course she had to get used to it. They had been seen as the glamorous couple, the king and queen of Hollywood, and were followed and filmed everywhere they went, until one night he was caught on camera in bed with a young actress. Someone had sent the photos to the press and the word was that the great Amber De Carla, screen goddess, could not hold a man. She had felt very hurt to think that he had made such a fool of her, and of course it had all ended right there!

The screen kiss had looked so passionate but of course now she loathed the very sight of him, and after the cameras had stopped rolling she had pushed him away in disgust. But *that* was show business.

Now she was hugging the statue as if it were solid gold, a little excited and genuinely a little emotional; some of it *did* come naturally, but it was mostly show. She could see Max Milner, her very first manager, sitting at a table, and she heard his voice in her head, as he had told her so many times back in the UK and that very first time she'd had a magazine shoot: 'Make them love you. Let the tears fall; let the eye makeup run; get all the publicity you can get.' It was really through Max and that very first shoot that she had come to where she was today. And he had come all the way from London just for this special night, as he had done several times before. She had a new manager now, James Avery, a New Yorker, who was loudly spoken, rough and no-nonsense.

Amber had danced with several partners and it had been a wonderful evening. Jerome's driver had taken them to her home and Jerome had come in for coffee that Bessie made; she had been waiting up for them and had been watching the whole show on the television. Jerome was by now very drunk, and he wanted to stay the night. But Amber sent him home; she was tired and irritable now, and she knew that *he* had to be in the studio early in the morning.

CHAPTER TWO

Amber awoke with a start as Bessie came into the bedroom and pulled back the long drapes, letting in a burst of bright Beverly Hills sunshine.

'What the hell's the matter with you? Close those curtains, it's too bright, and get out of here!' Amber stretched in the pink satin sheets, and sleepily and irritably asked, 'What's the time?'

'Eleven thirty!' Bessie was just as blunt. 'Time you were up! Mr Stirling called, twice! Wants you to be in his office by lunchtime. And Mary Anne is waiting downstairs for your notes and instructions for the day.'

'Oh, all right, all right, don't keep on!' Amber shouted back sleepily, angry at Bessie's sharp tongue; she felt a little hung over, and the sun hurt her eyes, and she had a headache.

She lazily eased herself up and smoothed the pink satin sheet in front of her as Delilah, a small and pretty black girl, came in with her breakfast of orange juice, coffee, fruit and toast set beside a folded snow-white linen napkin. She set the gilt tray before her. 'Good morning, Miss De Carla.' The girl smiled and almost curtsied.

Amber didn't acknowledge her; she frowned deeply, trying to focus her eyes on the tray. 'Send Mary Anne up!' It was a command; she was addressing Bessie, who was just going out of the door.

Bessie grimaced and rolled her eyes upwards at the irritable aggression, then closed the door with a bang, and Amber looked up with annoyance and breathed hard down her nose. Bessie stood for a moment outside the door, her lips bunched hard together. 'Too many late nights,' she mumbled to herself.

Downstairs Bessie poked her head around the office door, where she knew that Mary Anne, Amber's PA, was at her desk working. 'Her *ladyship* is awake and wants you upstairs!' She rolled her eyes again. 'And it's about time; she's not the only one who had a late night. *I* was makin' coffee for *that drunken bloke* at three o'clock 'smornin', and *she's* jest 'aving breakfast.' She glanced at her wristwatch. 'An' it's nearly bloody lunchtime!' Bessie grimaced in disgust and shut the door with a bang and walked off down the hall to the kitchen, where she found Bella Hammond, the cook, preparing the lunch.

'What's the matter with you?' Bella raised her eyebrows, seeing the fuming look on Bessie's face.

'Bloody *Lady Muck* again. Demanding! Giving 'er bloody orders. Only just opened her eyes, and she bloody starts.'

Bella smiled; she'd heard it all before. 'Sit down, have a cup of coffee, relax.' She poured a black coffee and pushed it across the kitchen counter, and Bessie sat on a high and uncomfortable stool and rested her chin on her hand.

Bessie was a London cockney; normally she was kindly and willing to help. And she was efficient; she knew that! She had known Amber for years, but Amber had changed since she had found fame, and she annoyed Bessie with her aggressive and fancy ways. She had come from nothing, but since coming to the States, well...

Bessie clenched her hands, rubbing them hard together with annoyance. Her thoughts were that *Kitty* now treated everyone like dirt, as if they were beneath her. *Where would she be without any of us, eh? Bloody runnin' around after 'er every bloody minute she's in the 'ouse!* She bunched her lips. *Thinks she's the bloody queen of bloody 'ollywood!*

Mary Anne had picked up her notebook and gone up the stairs; she was a young and vibrant American girl, and had been PA to Amber De Carla for almost nine months. Her college friends envied her; it sounded a glamorous job working for a great star like Amber De Carla, but after the first month she had found Amber so tiresome and too demanding. Still, the pay was good, and so she was still there.

She tapped on the door and pushed it open. The room was bright, the sunlight playing on the ivory-coloured walls that had just a hint of soft blushed pink.

Amber lazed in the pink satin sheets and yawned. Her head felt muggy and her eyes felt a little sticky after last night's partying at the awards event; her dyed very white blonde hair was untidily scuffed up in a rubber band; behind her the pink satin pillows were propped up against the headboard, which was fan-shaped and ivory-coloured with golden stripes representing the rising sun. As the door opened she sat bolt upright, squaring her shoulders, her breast full and heavy under white satin and lace as she took a deep breath, her chin rising haughtily as usual. Her face was still shiny from last night's cream. Amber was naturally a very good-looking woman with high cheekbones and full pink lips, her eyes very blue, but without the makeup, she was not the Amber De Carla of the silver screen; she was plain.

Mary Anne came in, always smart in a white silk blouse and grey skirt, her naturally blonde hair tied back in a neat ponytail, her face young and vivacious with only a hint of eyeshadow and pink lipstick. She was a few years younger than Amber, and Amber secretly admired and felt a little jealous of her young beauty and her vibrant and lively attitude towards another busy day that lay ahead. Amber herself had never been good in the mornings; she guessed she was having too many late nights.

'Good morning, Miss De Carla.' Mary Anne smiled brightly with a sing-song approach and a spring in her step; she took a chair from the corner of the room and brought it closer to the bed, pad and pen at the ready.

Amber didn't acknowledge the happy sing-song 'good morning'. 'Bessie said Stirling phoned?' There was irritation in her tone.

'Yes, ma'am, he called twice. He would like you to be in his office at twelve thirty.' She looked at her watch and grimaced, knowing that there was no chance.

'Call him back, and tell him I'll be there at one o'clock!'

Mary Anne made a note.

'And you can take that white evening gown to the cleaners; that drunken idiot Jerome spilt red wine all over it last night! I'm sure they will never get it clean! He hasn't phoned, has he?'

'No, madam. Max Milner phoned.'

'*Max?* What did he want?'

'Didn't say, ma'am. Only that he's still in the country and that he'd phone again later.' Max had come for the film awards as usual, and he had said last night that he intended to leave early this morning. James Avery was now Amber's manager and had been ever since she had arrived in the USA. He guided her well and he was strict, a hard-headed New Yorker. As usual she wanted things her way, and she gave him the snub-nosed treatment like she did everyone, but it didn't always work out.

Amber nodded to Mary Anne, and leaned back lazily on the pink satin pillows. 'Well, that's all; you can go! There not much on today!' Then, just as Mary Anne got to the door, she called, 'Tell Delilah to run me a bath!'

'Yes, ma'am.' She almost closed the door.

'And tell Delilah to come up after the bath, and tell Kelly I want my hair done! And I left some emails on your desk last night; make sure you send them off! Thank you.'

Mary Anne opened the door again and had a double-take. 'Yes, ma'am!' She closed the door quietly and looked back for a moment, arching her eyebrows. To get a 'thank you' was quite an achievement. She never got a 'please' or a 'thank you' from Amber De Carla, and neither did anyone else; it was all just demand. Miss De Carla seemed to be bitter with the world. And yet she had everything. Mary Anne inclined her head. It was probably *because* she had everything, because she had nothing to look forward to, or perhaps it was something she ate?

Bessie was still sitting in the kitchen, still stewing over Amber, rubbing her hands hard together with annoyance.

She got more annoyed every day over Amber's high-handedness. 'She treats me like dirt!'

Bella raised her eyebrows.

'Wouldn't bloody get up at all, if I didn't call 'er!'

'Why do you stay here then?' Bella asked.

'Because I've known *Kitty* too bloody long, that's why!'

'Want some more coffee?'

'Naah, I got some work t'do.' She slid irritably off the high stool and left the kitchen.

With the coffee pot still in her hand, Bella called after her with a frown, 'Who's Kitty?' But Bessie just closed the door and didn't answer.

Bessie made her way to her small office and made a few notes to remind herself about the housekeeping, and then put her elbows on the desk and rested her chin in her hands; she was frustrated. She took a deep breath. Bella was right; who *was* bloody Kitty? And why *did* she stay? *Bloody demanding 'do this, do that,' and telling me to get out as soon as she opens 'er bloody eyes; she wouldn't bloody get up at all if I didn't wake 'er...*

Then, thinking back on her life, yes, she had known Kitty too bloody long, and too well! But Kitty had changed since she'd become famous; she never used to be like this. Kitty had been a good friend, a nice girl, bright, a little forceful but eager to get on, and she had done well. Bessie had to admit she had to be that way... but now she had gone too far.

Then again, it was only through Kitty that Bessie had the luxurious life that she was enjoying right now. She would never have done this on her own; she would still have been sewing in the pokey little back room in the London Theatre, and that was why she would never leave. But Kitty now got under her skin.

Bessie bunched her lips, and shook her head, as her thoughts went way, way back. She sat, elbows on the desk, her chin resting on clasped hands, the pictures still bright in her mind...

She had been a seamstress for the London Theatre. It was a job; it didn't pay very well. She had altered and repaired stage costumes for the actors. That was where she had first met Kitty Hawksenburge, for that was her real name; she was a nobody then. She had been brought up in a back street in the east end of London, having three brothers and a bit of a rough life as her father had left them and her mother struggled to keep them fed and clothed.

Kitty had been about seventeen when they had first met. She'd had a job stacking shelves in the supermarket and a girl she worked with had said she was leaving to pursue her career as a dancer; she had auditioned at the theatre for a musical and had been a couple of times for rehearsals, and that evening they were to sort out the costumes before the first dress rehearsal. Kitty was interested and had gone along to the theatre with her just to watch. She said she'd been standing in the wings, just watching and listening, when someone had begun herding all those who had come for the dress fittings onto the stage, and Kitty had been pushed along with the group of about ten girls and several young men. They were told that they were to go to wardrobe and try on their costumes and, if they were not right, to take them to the seamstress for a fitting; they would need them a week on Friday for a full dress rehearsal.

Kitty had no idea what she was to do; she shouldn't have been there anyway. The costume she was given was a long pink dress, Edwardian-style, and a large hat with flowers and feathers all round the brim, and she had to carry a parasol. Kitty had said that she'd been to dancing classes as a child but she could hardly be called a dancer and, although she could also sing, she had never been on the stage, but it had all turned out all right. Her friend had said that they were just to walk about the stage in a busy street scene twirling the parasol; they were to walk four paces forward and two steps back. It could hardly be called dancing. They would get paid ten pounds a night, and they hoped to run the show for six weeks.

The costume had been too big, and this was where Kitty and Bessie had met. Kitty had to have two fittings and they had chatted while Bessie had been pinning her up. It seemed that they both came from the same part of London and they had become good friends. After working for some weeks in the show, Kitty had got a room nearer the theatre and in the next street to where Bessie lived, so quite often they would get the bus home together, or maybe on occasion they'd have a hamburger and a drink after the show in the Three Whistles.

Bessie was divorced and now lived alone, and was glad to have a friend who was a good listener. She poured her heart out to Kitty about her violent marriage. Her ex-husband Reggie Nichols had knocked her about in his drunken rages; he was a truck driver for a building firm, and was now serving three months in jail for violence and causing bodily harm to a workmate. Kitty had listened night after night and sympathised.

The stage production finished after running for another month, and then they were both out of work. After a few weeks Kitty was informed that another musical production was to be put on, and they were looking for dancers. She and her friend Carol both went for the audition again. Kitty had told Bessie there was to be another show, and Bessie had got the job of seamstress again.

Kitty had enjoyed this show much more than the first show. After about a month or six weeks, Melanie Corfield, the leading lady, was taken ill – well, it turned out that she'd had too much to drink at lunchtime – and the understudy, Judith Painton, just two days before, had received a very nasty black eye from her boyfriend. Makeup had tried everything, but the black eye still showed and the swelling had not gone down.

The director Matt Ryan was beside himself, not knowing what to do, and just two hours before the night's performance he decided to close the show for that evening. It was then that Kitty Hawksenburge stepped forward and said that she knew the part off by heart. Matt Ryan had automatically said, 'No!' but then had second thoughts. Kitty whatever-her-name-was was blonde and beautiful; she was also about the same size as Melanie Corfield. But then, could he take a chance?

He'd had a quick word with the producer Pat Benson, and between the two of them they had decided to take a chance sooner than close the show. A quick rehearsal had been arranged, and that night the show went on. The next morning the paper reviews were good; there was a lot of praise for the performance of Kitty Hawksenburge.

The next afternoon Melanie Corfield had arrived late for rehearsals as usual and smelling of drink, but had gone on to do the performance that night. The morning after, the papers were saying that Melanie Corfield's performance was poor, and that she did not have the feeling for the part, and that the director should consider Kathy Hutchinson, who had given a more polished performance the night before. Even though they'd got the name wrong.

The producer Pat Benson was on the phone to Matt Ryan, and between them they decided to give the part to Kitty Hawksenburge. Of course Melanie was furious, but Matt Ryan said she was quite often the worse for drink, and never on time for a rehearsal. A big shouting argument broke out on stage in front of the whole cast, and ended with Melanie storming off the stage in a rage, full of loud tears, swearing at Matt and shouting that she would be back, on time and sober, for the evening's performance.

Ryan's voice bellowed through the whole auditorium. 'Don't bother; you're fired!'

There was a loud bang and they all heard the glass fall as the inner door shattered, and then a second terrific bang as the outer door was slammed closed.

Bessie and the two other women had heard all this down in the sewing room, which was some distance from the stage. Then all had gone deadly quiet for a few seconds... and then they had heard the strains of music.

Kitty had told Bessie afterwards that Matt had brought everyone back to life by clapping his hands. 'Well, come on, don't just stand there; get moving. We've got a show to put on tonight. Kitty, you're taking the lead from now on.'

He'd raised his hand up, and the music had struck up, and the dancers had gone into action.

The show had continued to be a success for the next two months. A week after it had closed, Kitty had been approached and had got a small part in a film. It was then that they had drifted apart, with Kitty being away for months on location; there had been no time for phone calls, no contact at all.

Bessie had then felt let down and alone; she missed Kitty. It seemed that part of her life had gone. She stayed home in her little house, never going out for a drink and a hamburger, or to the little café where they used to go.

One day, seeing from a poster outside the theatre that another stage production was to be put on, she applied for the job of seamstress. This brightened her days, working in the little back room with two other women, and the young actors and actresses who came in from time to time for fittings and repairs. They were excited and full of hope that someday they would reach stardom, just like Kitty had been.

Bessie took a deep breath and sat back, thinking on that chilly afternoon about a year later, as she and Jenny Maxwell were sitting quietly working in the theatre sewing room. Jenny had suddenly said, 'Oh, I've got something to show you; I found this.' She had then pulled a magazine from her bag; there was a photo. 'I found this last night,' said Jenny. 'That looks like Kitty Hawksenburge, doesn't it? You knew her quite well, didn't you?'

Under the photograph the write-up said, *Kathy Hutchinson, young up-and-coming starlet*, but there was no doubt that it was a photograph of Kitty with her head thrown back in a wide smile and her long blonde hair, now whiter than white, flowing over a cushion. She was lying on a couch and showing a lot of leg. She'd obviously changed her name. The write-up went on, saying that she had given an outstanding performance, having a small part in a big film production called *Barkers Hill*, and that Kathy Hutchinson was set for stardom...

That evening after work, Bessie had phoned Kitty's very small flat, so small it was virtually a room and a bathroom, not even knowing if she was still there.

'Hellooo?' The voice was so dainty, she took the phone away from her ear and looked at it.

'Can I speak to Kitty Hawksenburge, please?'

The dainty voice came back. 'Bessie, is that you?'

'*Kitty?*' Her eyes had nearly popped out of her head. 'Kitty, is that *you*?'

'Yes, I just got back this afternoon.'

Pleased to hear each other, they arranged to meet for a drink in the Three Whistles, the pub that they had frequented so often a year before. Kitty had arrived in a taxi. They'd clambered up onto the high bar stools and Bill the barman was pleased to welcome them back.

Kitty had changed. She was expensively dressed, and her speech was now all la-di-dah and posh. They'd laughed about it.

'Well, you can't get to be a star saying, "Oh yeah, mate, that ain't right!" It's much better to say, "*Eoh*, yes! That certainly is not qui*t*e righ*t*!" And one mus*t* always sound the endings, the *tees*.' She had sat for a second with her teeth closed tightly together in a wide smile. 'Mustn'*tt* one?' She'd then leaned forward towards Bessie, arching her eyebrows, and fluttered her long false lashes. 'Mustn'*tt* one?'

'Oh yeah, *mustn'tttt one*?' Bessie had put on a false posh voice, and they had laughed heartily together. Bessie was highly amused at Kitty's posh accent. Kitty's clothes were chic, her makeup more vibrant, although she had always been highly made up anyway. She had style, even in the way she sat, the movement of her hands as she spoke; yes, she certainly had style. Whereas Bessie knew herself to be quite plain; her hair was mousy and cut in a short bob, and she wore only a little discreet makeup. Compared to Kitty, her face was podgy. Smiling, Bessie thought she was always ready with a friendly smile, but she was not outstanding in any way. Never would be, being a few years older than Kitty and more the motherly type...

Leaning hard on her elbows now, Bessie put her hands either side of her face. *Guess I have a very ordinary mundane appearance,* she thought. *I was a typical Londoner in me jeans an' roll-necked jumper an' cheap leather jacket. Being a seamstress, I was overworked and underpaid.* She bunched her lips. She had lived alone then, with a house to run; Reggie had worked but they had never had very much of a life.

She and Kitty had talked of old times in the theatre. And then Kitty had told her what had happened to her in the last year. She'd said that she had been so busy, but she had made good money. The work was hard and she had not had a minute to herself, sometimes starting in makeup at five in the morning and being ready on the set at seven; she had found that very hard. A quick sandwich lunch and sometimes she'd still be there at ten at night. There had also been late-night parties, and she'd had to hire beautiful evening gowns and socialise until the early hours of the morning; she had met some very interesting people.

Kitty's voice sounded in her head, saying, 'It all sounds very glamorous, but after you've worked all day... But it really *is* a case of being in the right place at the right time; it's called being *seen*.' Kitty had then smiled, arching her shapely eyebrows again. 'You can't hope to get work if you're not *seen*... But nevertheless I'm loving it.' She had also said that the next morning she had an appointment to see an agent named Max Milner.

And then, with still so much to catch up on, Kitty had suggested that they have dinner. They had left the Three Whistles and Kitty had taken her to a nice restaurant, and they'd had a bottle of wine, and they'd talked and talked. The time went by quickly and it was late; they'd had a taxi home, Kitty saying there would be no more bus rides for her.

Bessie smiled now, raising her eyebrows and sitting up at the desk, and then leaned forward, remembering what she'd replied: 'Hmm, 'ope you're right. The acting profession can be a bit dodgy, work one minute and then no work for months.'

Kitty had grimaced, then smiled confidently. 'Eoh, I'll be all right.'

Bessie remembered laughing at her accent, 'There yer go agin, *eoh, eoh*,' and they had chuckled together; she found herself now smiling at her own thoughts.

The next morning Kitty Hawksenburge, now Kathy Hutchinson, was in Max Milner's office at ten o'clock. There was quite a lot to be discussed. He was more than pleased with her appearance; she was beautiful, and she had style. He was impressed. And then he suggested they have lunch in a very expensive restaurant, and Kitty had the feeling that she was in the big time already, looking around and hoping that she had been *seen*. After that, when she was back home in her little flat, she couldn't contain herself; bubbling over with excitement, she'd phoned Bessie, telling her with great delight that she had a photo session for several glossy magazines on Wednesday, and since that morning she'd become Amber De Carla!

Bessie remembered feeling pleased for her and saying, 'Blimey! You'll 'ave to keep that posh accent up, wiv a name like tha'. Amber De Carla? *Amber? Fancy!* Ah my Gawd.' They'd chuckled together.

Her thoughts went on. Over a few months she had not heard any more from Kitty, but she had bought the weekly magazines and there were articles and glamorous photos of the beautiful Amber De Carla, who they said was starring in her first big film.

CHAPTER THREE

Bessie had gone with Jenny Maxwell to the cinema to see the film, *Cruise Ship*, and Kitty in her first starring role with actor Michael Lamarra, her name in lights: *AMBER DE CARLA*. She was more beautiful on screen, and although Bessie was thrilled for her friend, the thought of it all made her feel a little embarrassed, seeing her kissing and cuddling and rolling about in bed. Fancy performing in front of thousands of people like that; how could she do it? Anyway, the film was a box office success.

She had tried phoning Kitty the next day, but there was no answer. It was then that she knew that the little Kitty Hawksenburge she had once known, later Kathy Hutchinson, now Amber De Carla, was long gone out of her life...

Amber De Carla was interviewed on the television; she was also interviewed by the press, and photographs of Amber De Carla filled the newspapers. Bessie had sat at home alone in tears of joy, and the same tears filled her eyes now sitting here at the desk just thinking back on the old days; how many young hopefuls had she sewn for? But Kitty had made it. Bessie had been really impressed, and she could tell that Kitty was lapping up the limelight. The girl had style; there was no doubt about that. She was born to be a star...

Bessie sighed, adjusting her chin on her hand, then she shook her head gently, a slight smile on her lips. She took her elbows off the desk and stood up wearily, and made her way to her own apartment; she'd done most of her chores and it was her break time.

She eased herself into a comfortable armchair, opening the sliding glass door wide and looking out to the garden at the swaying palm trees, the flowering shrubs and the beautiful warm sunshine. It wasn't like this in London, but then her thoughts went back to what she called the old days, when she had first met Kitty Hawksenburge in the sewing room, so small and slim. The pink Edwardian dress had been far too big. A smile crossed her lips. Kitty had been an ordinary chatty girl and eager to get on, just like all the rest. She had told Bessie that she would one day be a star. Bessie had smiled; didn't they all say that? Still, they had to have hope. But Kitty had been different...

Her thoughts again drifted off into the past. It had been one evening about a month after the film *Cruise Ship*, and the press had died down. Bessie had been sitting alone in front of the fire. She smiled, imagining her little room and the warmth of the fire; it was not luxurious, but it had been cosy watching the television. The phone had rung and Kitty's posh voice was saying, 'I've bought a flat in Belgravia, and I need a housekeeper; do you want the job?'

She'd been stunned for a moment. She heard her own voice in her head: 'Belgravia! Blimey! You're lashing out a bit, ain'tcha? 'Ousekeeper? Oooh! Yeah, I'd like tha'!' A smile touched her lips again, as her own voice continued, 'Yeah, sounds all right. 'Ow much yer gonna pay me?'

'Tuesday, then.' She'd heard the grin in Kitty's tone. 'I'll pick you up.'

She'd come off the phone feeling a bit stunned. She grinned to herself again at the very thought. *'Ousekeeper*: it had sounded so wonderful.

Her thoughts went back now to her little house, tucked into a row of terraced houses in a scruffy London street, among scruffy neighbours. At the time she had not thought of it or them as scruffy; it had just been a way of life, but after living here it was poor. The house had been small and comfortable but cheaply furnished. She and Reggie had worked, but he'd spent most of his earnings on drinking and gambling on the horses, hoping one day to strike it lucky and make a fortune, which he never did. It was losing the money that made him so frustrated and violent.

She could see herself in her mind's eye, now, frowning. *Belgravia?* She'd pursed her lips, then grinned. 'Belgravia? Blimey!' she'd muttered.

Now, that had been a move. She raised her eyebrows and smiled, thinking back. Yeah, it was on the Tuesday at ten o'clock in the morning, as arranged. She was ready, and wearing jeans and black sweater and her black leather jacket. She had answered the knock on the door expecting Kitty, and had nearly fallen over seeing a guy dressed in a grey chauffeur's uniform standing there.

He had touched his cap politely. 'Morning, madam. Miss De Carla asked me to pick you up.'

She looked up at the luxury that surrounded her now, but in her reverie remembered that moment and the pang that had gone through her head; he must have thought her mad, and he had sort of grimaced as she'd looked at him aghast.

Kitty had sent a *chauffeur*? And *madam*? Blimey! What had Kitty got herself into this time?

Her own voice sounded in her head again. 'Wait a minute, I'm not ready!'

He had looked a classy gent in his grey uniform and cap, with silver-grey hair. Yeah, he must have thought her a right ignorant git, and common. He had said, 'That's all right, madam, I'll wait by the car,' and she had been embarrassed. She screwed her eyes up tight even now, still having that guilty feeling after all this time, as she had already rudely pushed the door almost shut in his face.

Behind the door she'd been flustered; her heart had been racing, she not knowing what to do or to think in her own home. She had first turned to the right and then to the left; she'd felt in a right flap. Here she was in jeans and a jumper, and *him* with a black shiny limousine, waiting at her door.

She had raced upstairs; breathless and confused, she had quickly shed her trainers and jeans and put on her best black skirt, a clean white blouse, her best black leather shoes and her best navy blue coat. She had taken her best black leather bag, which she had not used for years, never having anywhere suitable to use it; she remembered stuffing it quickly with her purse, a pair of glasses, tissues and keys, then she had come back downstairs in a tearing hurry, her heart beating fast.

Before opening the door she had taken a deep and nervous breath. Looking into the hall mirror, she had touched her mousey hair and then looked closer, checking her very pale lipstick. Then she had lifted her chin and pulled back her shoulders, bracing herself for the big ordeal, and tried to look dignified before opening the door and stepping outside.

The grey uniformed figure was standing patiently with his hands behind his back by the car. She remembered that walking down the very short front path her legs had felt unsteady; she couldn't allow herself to trip in shoes with heels. She had turned to close the front gate. She also recalled, while he was opening the door of the shiny black Bentley, looking back and wondering if Doris Fowler, her neighbour, was peeping through the curtains as she normally was; she didn't miss much, that one.

She had got into the car, and she remembered him closing the door with a gentle but solid thud; she was locked in. It was deathly quiet. It smelled of polished leather. He then got in behind the steering wheel; there was an uncomfortable silence. She was alone and shut in with a man she didn't know.

She now recalled the soft purr as he turned the key and the engine sprang into life. 'Would you like the radio on, madam?'

She remembered holding her breath, feeling her breasts hard against her bra, her lips tight. She had just replied, 'Mm,' nodding, then soft string music played and they were off on their way to Belgravia! She *hoped*. He could have driven her anywhere. She wondered if Doris Fowler had seen her go, but she was afraid to turn around and look back.

She had thoughts on her very rigid feelings as she'd sat staring straight ahead, hardly daring to move her eyes to glance out of the window, or to lean back on the creamy beige leather. She remembered clasping her hands tightly around the black leather bag on her lap as if her life depended upon it, every muscle and bone rigid. Holding her breath, she was reliving the terrifying moment even now.

They were driving through parts of London that she had never known existed; the only part of London she knew was the bus route. She had swallowed hard, hoping that he had not heard her nervous gulping; she had never felt so strange and out-of-place in all her life!

And then they turned into a driveway, the house hidden by a high hedge, the tyres crunching on a gravel drive, and the soft purring of the engine stopped. Her ears seemed to cloud deathly quiet and the silence seemed to drag them down. She sat very still, gripping her leather bag tightly, wondering if she should open the door, and then the driver opened it for her and she stepped out quickly, not wanting to keep him waiting. Both her hands in tight fists, clutching the bag in front of her, and a nervous feeling in her stomach, her heart was beating fast as she looked up at the black shiny front door, then mounted the five stone steps, not knowing what to expect and feeling afraid to knock at such a posh house. She was pleased and relieved to see the door open and Kitty was there with a big smile.

She let out her breath now with a slight smile of her own, reliving the whole experience and wondering now why she had been so scared. But then the size of the flat had scared her; it had nearly knocked her sideways. It was enormous; it was a palace. She had never stepped inside a place like this in her life! The hall floor was of pure white tiles. Kitty had greeted her warmly, kissing her on both cheeks, and then showed her into the living room; it was enormous...

Bessie smiled, looking around her now; it had been small compared with this apartment that she had now occupied for the last few years. Her own voice sounded in her head again.

''*Ow*, Kitty?' Her hand went to her breast. ''Ow long 'ave you 'ad *this?*' Her voice had risen to an amazed squeak.

'Amber! Please!' she remembered Kitty correcting her. Kitty had closed her eyes with dignity and pushed forward her shoulder like a model on the front cover of a glossy magazine, smiling. 'It's *Amber* now!' And then she relaxed. 'Well, to *you*, anyway,' – she kind of smiled and winked and wobbled her head – 'and you'll have to get used to it. But to the rest of the staff, it *is... Miss De Carla!*' She raised her eyebrows again comically with a smirk, and the long red fingernails pushed a stray hair back behind her right ear; it was a false ladylike pose, and looked all too superior. Then she'd shrugged with a grin, and they had chuckled easily together... Bessie smiled thoughtfully now, as her daydreaming went on...

She remembered exclaiming, 'Blimey, this place is enormous! 'Ow long you 'ad it, Kit? Will there be other *staff*, then? Do I have to move in 'ere?'

'*Yes!* Oh, yes! Of course,' the posh voice went on, '*that is*, if you want the housekeeper's job, you'll have to move in.' Kitty had sounded so hoity-toity and nodded, raising her eyebrows; her high-handed voice just seemed to go with the lush surroundings, then. Well, as it did now, and the surroundings didn't get any posher than this, but Kitty had changed; she wasn't the same person even then. Fame had really gone to her head; she was now hoity-toity, high-handed, superior, and snobbish.

'I've only been here a week so far, alone.' Kitty had raised her thin and pencilled eyebrows and flashed the long black lashes. 'I've got a maid and a cook starting tomorrow at eight thirty. I should like you to be here!' It had been a command.

''Ere, wait a minute, 'ow much you gonna pay me?'

Kitty had ignored the question and said, 'You can stay the night if you like, and get your things tomorrow? Of course, I'll need a secretary, and there will also be a maintenance man-cum-butler, but I haven't found one yet!'

'*Blimey*, gel! You've done all right for yerself, ain'tcha? I saw you on the telly.' She remembered then swallowing hard and realising that the friendship had gone, and that Kitty was now *Amber*, and a celebrity, and if Bessie wanted this housekeeper's job she would be employed and it really would be way out of her league... But Kitty had given her that look of confidence, knowing her to be honest and trustworthy, and she could see that Kitty wanted her to stay and look after things and be a good housekeeper. Even with all this luxury, Kitty would be far too busy being a celebrity to take care of the place herself. And Bessie had made her mind up there and then that it would be a better way to live, and that she would soon get used to it; she would have to get used to it...

'Come on.' Kitty, changed back almost to her old self, took her by the hand. 'I'll show you round.'

It was soon afterwards that Bessie had moved out of her rented house and moved in to Belgravia, where she had two well-furnished rooms of her very own: a luxury that she had never dared to even dream of... And she had looked after Amber ever since like a mother, waiting up for her at night when there were late-night shows, and sometimes high-class parties or dinner parties, and looking after her very expensive and glamorous wardrobe, as she was still doing now. She had also taken charge of the staff, having a maid and a cook to organise; she had felt very proud. Kitty paid her a good wage and she was able to buy more fashionable clothes, and she had her hair restyled and done every week, a luxury she could never before have afforded. And that was just the beginning; she had never dreamed that she would be living here in America.

It was just about nine months later that Kitty landed a film contract in Hollywood, and the Belgravia flat was closed, much to Bessie's disappointment. They were about to move here, to America, and Bessie had felt a bit frightened; she had only ever been on a plane once, and that was just to Holland with Reggie to see the tulip fields. The flight to the USA would be much longer.

It had been weeks of packing, and there had been just the two of them in the Belgravia flat at that time; both the maid and the cook had been paid off. The driver, on his very last day, was putting the bags in the car, and was to drive them to the airport. Bessie had got used to this high living in Belgravia, but leaving London was a worry; she'd never lived anywhere else and had thoughts on whether she would ever come back.

She twitched her nose now with a slight smile; even though Kitty got on her high horse and it annoyed her, she knew she would never want to go back to her old lifestyle now. Thinking of the advert, *It's the American Way*, she grinned, and nodded, and she had to admit it *was* a good way of life...

Her thoughts went back now to the flight. It had been first-class. It had worried her for weeks, the prospect of flying all the way to America; she hadn't known there were other ways to fly. The Fokker Friendship hadn't been like this; it had hummed and buzzed until they had landed in Holland and then a bus had taken them to the tulip fields. It had been a most luxurious weekend for her and Reggie. The thought of leaving London for another country back then had seemed like something out-of-this-world. But then, on landing here in the States, it was another world; a chauffeur-driven car was there to meet them, and she almost fainted away when she saw *this house* in Beverly Hills. The name Beverly Hills was a dream, a fairytale; it had only ever existed in films. She had read about it and seen pictures in magazines. Only posh film stars lived in places like this. It was unbelievable; it frightened her. How was she to housekeep a palace?

She smiled, remembering how she and Kitty had stood side by side, shoulder to shoulder, looking up the five white half-moon-shaped front steps to the two tall white pillars before the dark blue painted front door. The door was opened and a tall and well-built man in a smart black jacket, snow-white shirt, red tie and pinstriped trousers was there bowing politely and saying, 'Good afternoon, ladies.'

She remembered muttering, 'Ah my Gawd,' and slapping her hand across her mouth; she even put a hand to her mouth now, as flashes of the scene came to her. Even Kitty had been shocked.

They had stepped into the vast hallway with its glossy pink marbled floor patterned here and there with a black star. Bessie had looked up the sweeping pink marble staircase with the shiny brass handrail to the star-shaped glass skylight high above, and hanging from it was the most beautiful sparkling glass chandelier that she had ever seen; well, at the time it was the *only* one that she had ever seen, apart from in interior magazines. She remembered the look on Kitty's face as they had glanced at each other, taking a breath open-mouthed.

The butler had said, 'Welcome to Sunny Hill House, *ladies*,' and introduced himself as 'Downs. Edward Downs, madam.'

'*Eoh!*' Bessie knew that Kitty had been taken by surprise, but in her high-handed manner, Kitty had said, 'I wasn't expecting *staaaff*,' then added, 'to already be *here!*' She had fluttered her false eyelashes at the man and moved her head as if he were beneath her, and as if he were in the way. Bessie remembered that sinking feeling in her stomach, knowing it was wrong; Kitty shouldn't act like that.

'A Mr Milner engaged us, madam. There is a cook, four maids, and of course John, the driver, whom you have already met; he is also the footman. There are three gardeners; they also look after the pool and the fountains. Can I get you some refreshment, madam, coffee or maybe a cold drink?'

He had put out his arm, indicating that they should follow him, and he'd shown them into the well-furnished modern lounge with a thick Persian carpet and deep and comfortable beige armchairs, such as the one that she now occupied. There were beautiful paintings around the walls and glass and china ornaments and a huge vase of flowers on a coffee table; she remembered feeling mesmerised by it all, and saw it all now in her mind's eye.

The butler had hesitated, and was looking at her; the unasked question was whether he should show her to her quarters, and it was then that she had wondered just who she was, a friend or a servant. But then Kitty had come to the rescue. '*Eoh*, thank you. We'll both have coffee in here. Er, Edward, is it?' The high-handed voice lifted with the chin and long sweeping eyelashes fluttered and the blue eyes had that way of looking down on lesser creatures.

'Downs will do, madam.' He had dipped his head. Bessie's first impression of Downs was tall and well-built with a long thin face and a pleasant smile, ready to please. His hair was a light brown and thinning; he was aged about fifty.

'Downs?' Kitty had said, making a point of sounding the *ouns* with a cultured, rounded voice. 'Thank you, *Douwns*!'

He'd left the room with a slight drop of his head; it was hardly a bow. Bessie could only imagine his impression of the snooty Miss De Carla.

When he had gone they had looked at each other, holding their breath with eyes nearly popping out of their heads, and they had chuckled. Bessie heard her own voice in her head as if it were all happening now. 'Did you know it would be like *this*, Kit?'

Kitty had shaken her head and said, 'No, I expected it to be quite a big house, but *this is amazing*.'

'It's bloody stupid, all this for one person on their own. What was this bloke Milner thinking of?'

'*Eoh*, Bessie, all *stars* have big houses in Hollywood.'

'Oh, come on, Kit, this is a bloody palace. You'll be wearing a bloody crown next.'

'Amber, *pleeeease*, Bessie, and Miss De Carla to the butler.'

'*And* to the four pretty maids all in a row, the cook and the gardeners.' She had smirked. 'And the *footman*! And Uncle Tom Cobley an' all... bloody 'ell.'

'And don't keep saying "bloody".'

'Bloody 'ell,' she'd muttered again, looking sharply at Kitty, amazed by her high-handed manner.

Downs came back with the coffee; he set a tray down on the coffee table. 'Shall I pour, madam?'

'Yes please, Douwns.'

Bessie remembered Kitty resting her elbow on the arm of the chair, and resting her chin on the back of her index finger, the long red fingernails bright and shiny; it was a pose that she so often did, even now, like a model in a glossy magazine, an annoying pose that said that she was *so* superior. It still annoyed Bessie, and she was getting worse.

'Black or white?' Downs had asked.

'Black,' they had both said together.

'Douwns? I should like to see the cook!' Kitty had demanded, with the snooty look and superior lift of the chin.

'Yes, madam.' He nodded. 'I'll send her up right away,' and he left the room.

'Cook? Why do yer wanna see 'er?'

'We have to eat, Bessie.'

There was a tap on the door, and it opened slowly; a short and rounded middle-aged black woman came in. She was wearing a snow-white coat and a cap, her hair wound into a tight bun at the nape of her neck. 'Good afternoon, madam.' She bowed her head, dipping a little; it was almost a curtsey. 'I'm Isabella Springer; they call me just Bella. I can cook anything you want, madam.'

'Bella?' Kitty looked down her nose, as if the name wasn't good enough, and then, with a nod and some sort of a pleasant smile, 'It's very nice to meet you, Bella. I am Amber De Carla! And you will address me as Miss De Carla.'

'Yes, ma'am. Miss De Carla. Ma'am. Yes, ma'am!' She had faltered; Kitty's tone was enough to shake anybody.

'And this is Mrs Elizabeth Nichols, my housekeeper, Mrs Nichols to the staff.'

Bloody 'ell, Bessie was thinking, *what's got into Kitty with all this la-di-dah nonsense? Sounds as if it should cost the woman to speak to 'er.*

Bella nodded; Bessie smiled back.

'I shall want carefully prepared meals, Bella!' Kitty went on in her high-handed manner. 'Mostly salads, non-fattening, and I will be dining alone most evenings. But tonight there will be dinner for two; Mrs Nichols will be joining me this evening. We have not eaten much today with the travelling, and we have a lot to discuss. I think perhaps soup and some roast chicken would be in order?'

'Yes, ma'am, er, Miss De Carla, ma'am.' The woman sounded a bit flummoxed. 'What time would you like to eat, madam?'

Kitty had looked at Bessie. 'I think seven o'clock? *Eoh!* And tell *Douwns* we would like cocktails at six thirty.'

Cocktails? Blimey! Bessie remembered thinking.

Bella nodded with a smile, a little agitated. 'Yes, ma... er... Miss De Carla. Would you like cocktails served on the terrace?'

'*Of course*, Bella! Where else?' As if it were a crime to have suggested anywhere else. 'That would be very nice. Thank you! You may go!'

'Yes, ma'am.' She had nodded nervously, not knowing what to make of the new high-born English mistress; there was almost a curtsey again and she had left the room quickly, a little flustered. Bessie was not bloody surprised, the way Kit was going on.

'Well! What the 'ell was that all abart, Kit?' She'd put on a posh voice. 'Mrs Nichols *will be joining me tonight*?' She raised her eyebrows now, reliving that very first encounter with Bella, who, after all, had turned out to be a kind and friendly person. At the time, Bessie had fluttered her eyelashes. 'A bit la-di-dah, wasn't it? And cocktails on the *terrace*? Where's the bloody terrace anyway?'

'*Doouwns* will show *us*,' Kitty had said, smiling, 'and don't keep saying "bloody"! And I have to start as I mean to go on; I have to show authority. And you won't be dining with me every night; you'll have to eat in the kitchen with the rest of the staff.'

'Ooh-err!'

'And don't call me Kit! It's *Amber*! Well, to *you*, anyway! And Miss De Carla to everyone else!'

'Bloody 'ell...'

Downs had then shown Bessie here, to her quarters; they had also amazed her. She looked around now at the well-appointed apartment: what in England would have been termed 'below stairs', although it was really at ground level, with four rooms and the patio. She had loved living here for now nearly five years. At first she had been flabbergasted, and couldn't wait to tell Kitty to come and look; it was bigger than the whole house that she'd lived in in the east end of London. With marble floors, it was spacious, modern and well-furnished with deep beige armchairs and golden light brackets, table lamps with silk shades, and huge sliding windows that were now slid back and looked out onto her own private patio.

She moved from the armchair and sat now in the white-painted garden chair looking up at the swaying palm trees, across the manicured lawn to the flowering shrubbery, feeling like a queen. The coffee table at her side had an ashtray and a tall white candle in a glass candlestick. She sighed deeply; it was heaven.

It had been early evening when she had first come here, and the sun had still been shining. She couldn't believe it; what had Kitty brought her to? It was a dream and she would wake up and find herself still in London, where it would possibly be pouring with rain. The apartment was at the end of the house and on sneaking a look round the corner she could see the blue water of the swimming pool with a huge shell, and mermaids at a fountain. It had taken her breath away; it was so Hollywood, just like she'd seen in the magazines, and she had never thought that this would ever happen to *her*. She had then unpacked and settled herself in, so stunned by the luxury that she couldn't believe it was real. She took a deep breath; it still was heaven, even though *Kitty* did get on her nerves.

That first evening Downs had shown them to the terrace that overlooked the swimming pool, through a spacious lounge. Bessie was surprised to see a gun hanging above the stone fireplace, and then thought, *Don't all Americans have guns?* They had their cocktails and dined on fine china in the open air and chuckled, saying it was a bit different to the Three Whistles.

The next morning, after a good night's sleep, the sun was still shining and Bessie was introduced to the staff; it was then she realised that *she* was now in charge, but where should she start? Like Kitty, she would have to show some authority. She was nervous; although she'd got used to a bit of authority in London, that had been like a practice run compared to *this*, which was a whole different kettle of fish. She had already met Downs and Bella, and now there was Miss De Carla's PA? Although she really didn't want to show her ignorance, she had to ask Kitty quietly what a PA was. It all seemed like a film set anyway; it just didn't seem real.

Then there was Delilah, Kitty's personal maid, a petite black girl from one of the British Virgin Islands, and then there were Jan and Lucy, the other maids, both white American young women, and Anna, who was the laundress, a plump roundish black woman with a Southern accent. Anna was always very jolly and happy to spend the day in the laundry room, and then have cups of coffee in the staff room when they all had a morning and afternoon break together. Harold, the general handyman, was in charge of the three gardeners, and of course John the driver who had brought them here from the airport. But since that very first morning Bessie had had the job of organising them all, knowing just how Kitty liked things done. Kitty was a perfectionist, strict and to the point, and more so now that she thought she was Lady Muck, with the la-di-dah voice and all her airs and graces. And so Bessie had scribbled out a few notes on what she wanted done and given them to the PA, who used the computer and had work sheets printed out.

From that day onwards, everyone was kept busy with Kitty giving orders right, left and centre. The PA had been rushed off her feet, with piles of paperwork to type out. And as the weeks and months went on, Bessie herself had settled down into a daily routine of keeping the house and got along well with the staff, who never argued with her orders.

Kitty was now spending much more time at the studio, and Bessie had hardly seen her, although she left written orders for Bessie to carry out. There had also been nights when Bessie had dressed her and sent her off all glamorous, like a mother sending a child to a party, and then Kitty would come home in the early hours of the morning, and they would sit with late-night coffee and chat about the events of the evening. Well, that was until Kitty had met the handsome Steve Salvettini, who had brought her home on many occasions, and of course Bessie had not wanted to be in the way and had gone quietly to bed. When she had gone in to wake Kitty early the first morning after, she'd been shocked they were in bed together, and she had felt very embarrassed, but then it had become more regular and she'd got over the embarrassment.

It had really shocked Kitty when he had been caught with that young actress; Bessie had never seen her so disgruntled, so miserable, so bitter. Kitty had kept up the sharp image that she had created from the first day that she had arrived at this house, but after this thing with Salvettini, she had got worse, and she hadn't improved since. After seeing that photo of him, she'd gone off to the studio again in a right huff; Bessie had to agree that Kitty did work hard. And after the Salvettini thing, Bessie had sat up nights waiting for her to come home; some nights Kitty had been working until ten and some until midnight, and Bessie knew that was why she was so irritable in the mornings, not getting enough rest. She had said that the film *Night Ride* was well underway. And this went on and on, and after about nine months or a year, *Night Ride* was finished.

Kitty was now earning millions of dollars, and this was when Kitty *really* changed; she was even more uppity, even more superior, more demanding. It was the Salvettini thing; it had really upset her. Amber De Carla, glamorous queen of Hollywood, or so she thought she was. 'Dropped by the great Salvettini', so the papers had said, and something about a younger woman.

Now Kitty was taking on more staff, her own beauty therapist and a hairdresser, her own trainer, and she had installed a gym. Poor Delilah, her own personal maid, she ordered about like a dog, sit and stand, come and go. Delilah was on the go all day when Amber was there; she was so demanding and now treated them all so badly that no one stayed more than a few months. Bessie now had an almost full-time job training new staff. She loved her position in the house, but Kitty did get under her skin at times.

Bella had asked why she didn't leave, but how could she even think of leaving? It was laughable. She stayed because it was the best life she had ever known, but she wasn't one to be pushed around. She had known Kitty Hawksenburge far too long, and Kitty knew this too, and she also knew just how far to go.

The phone rang, disturbing her train of thought, and she jumped; it was Downs, and she left the apartment to attend to the task in hand.

CHAPTER FOUR

It was 2.55 when Amber finally waltzed nonchalantly into Elliot Stirling's office, dressed in a smart mini-skirted cream suit, a large-brimmed black hat and black platforms with four-inch heels. A black leather Chanel bag slung over her shoulder, she could have been dressed for a wedding.

Elliot looked up from the desk as the door opened; she hadn't knocked. He was a raw New Yorker, and greeted her with a rough tongue. 'What the fucking hell time do you call *this*?' He glanced at his wristwatch, and glared at her over his square spectacles. 'I expected you at twelve thirty!'

'Oh, Elliot! *Darling!*' She jumped back with a childish grin. 'Don't be so cross!' she said, impishly fluttering the long black lashes with a sweet smile and touching her red shiny lips with the long shiny red nails that were all her own, and beautifully manicured. 'I'm here, aren't I? Surely you can wait a few minutes.' Her voice was light and airy as if full of wonderment, and she pouted like a child; what had she done that was so wrong? 'I'm just a little late, that's all.' She glanced around the very modern office with its enormous windows that looked out onto flat rooftops and a thousand windows of a skyscraper that was almost opposite.

'Minutes! Bloody *minutes*!' His eyes were screwed up, his cheekbones raised. He bounced forward in the chair, shouting and scratching his grey hair, a deep frown on his forehead and his lips pulled back; his teeth gnashed in a vicious snarl like that of a wild animal. His heavy tone was heard right through the closed door in the outer office; his secretary Nancy raised her eyes and swallowed hard, and then went back to the computer again.

He frowned, squinting his eyes, and then his eyes got wider as he took a deep breath, expanding his chest; he was flabbergasted. '*Minutes!*' he said again with fury. 'You're fuckin' two and a half *hours late*! I've had Salvettini and Lombardo and Devlin in here, and then put them off for an hour, and *then* had to let them go again.' He furiously slapped his pen down onto the desk and it bounced up from the force. 'Who the hell do you think *you are*? How the hell can I run a business if you just come waltzing in here at any time? Why can't you get your ass in gear like everyone else?'

He took a deep breath, and then sighed, plonking his elbows down heavily on the desk as if he'd lost the battle and all his strength, and realised it was De Carla he was addressing and nothing was going to change her. She was so much in demand, and she knew she had everyone just where she wanted them, and people just pandered to her commands. She knew she could come and go as she pleased, and she did just that! Not only here, but everywhere; her attitude was 'if you want me, you'll wait'.

'Well, Elliot, *darling*.' Her tone was so affected. She put her head on one side, and fluttered the long black eyelashes again. 'It was a very late night, *darling*, wasn't it?' She pouted like a child again, her voice light; she sounded bewildered. 'Now, *darling*,' – it was all so forced – 'what *is* all this *fuss about*? What *is* so important it couldn't wait a few minutes? Couldn't you have phoned?'

51

'*I did!*' He slumped back in the black leather swivel chair, air rushing down his nose; he looked to his left and then to his right in despair, and sighed loudly, giving her an exasperated look. 'I did! *Twice! You* were still in *bed*! While the rest of us have to get up and make a buck!' He breathed air down his nose again in fury, tight-lipped with annoyance and knowing it was quite useless to try to change her; it was like fighting with your hands and feet tied. He leaned forward again and pushed a buff folder with a stack of papers inside across the desk towards her.

'What's this?' She sounded so innocent, of course knowing exactly what it was.

'New script.'

She raised her eyes as if in such surprise. The long red fingernails clasped the wad of papers and she sat her slim frame down in the wide and very modern black leather armchair. Then, with an innocent softness, 'What's it about?'

'Read it! The jungle! Tappener wants you in the part, you can't say no. *Read it!*'

'Oh, not now, *daaarling*, I can't read it now. Come on, what's it about? Tell me what it's about.' She sounded childlike and innocent, as if saying, *Daddy, read me a story.*

It made him want to tear his hair out; it was as if she had never seen a script in her life. He sighed, taking a breath, still feeling furious, as if all were hopeless. Her innocent look seemed to say, *Well, I might consider it,* and the cockiness irritated him even more than he could say, but he knew that it would be a million-dollar deal, and he knew that she would *not* turn it down. Even though she was so aggravating, and pouting like a child as if it were all so tiresome having to read. She sat with wide expectant shining blue eyes, waiting for him to give her some insight into the script. 'It's about getting lost in the jungle.'

'*Oooh!*' She frowned and flinched back in the chair. 'Will there be animals?' Still frowning and pulling a face of distaste.

Elliot leaned back in the chair and folded his arms, his lips bunched hard together, then leaned forward again, his elbows on the desk. She infuriated him, afraid to get a speck of dirt on the soles of her shoes; she was even now brushing her hands together at the disgust of imaginary wild animals. Knowing her finicky ways, he knew he had to convince her there would be no dirty animals, even if, come to think of it, there might be some. He hadn't thought to check on that. Still, he thought now, his hands were tied. If Ronald Tappener wanted her to play the part, it was up to Elliot to convince her it was the right part for her. Ronald was the guy putting up the millions, and he had particularly expressed that he wanted De Carla in the role. They both knew with her starring it would be a success.

And now Elliot took another deep breath, about to convince her that it was a good part. But she was so arrogant, and demanding, and he knew that half the cast would be unhappy working with her anyway.

'Well, it's a jungle film, but no,' he said, 'there won't be wild animals, if that's what you're thinking. Most of it will be filmed in the studio, but you will have to go to Guyana for a couple of days to film the jungle scenes.'

'Guyana?' The black lashes flew up. 'Where's that?'

He flipped his hands haphazardly, and grimaced. 'Somewhere, northern coast of South America. Or somewhere that way.'

'Will it be hot?' Her hand went to her makeup, knowing that on hot sunny days she had to think of her fair complexion and stay out of the sun. She raised her eyebrows and flashed the long black lashes, and, moving her head in her snobbish superior manner, she waited for him to answer.

'Mmm.' He also arched his eyebrows, thinking that it was the jungle, after all. 'Yeah, warmish, I guess.'

She sat thoughtfully, the script on her lap. 'All right, I'll look at it.' She uncrossed her shapely legs, stood up, clutching the script to her breast, and walked to the door, then turned. 'I'll let you know. *Daaarling*.' Her lips twisted in a sarcastic smile.

'Tomorrow!' he shouted. 'I must know!'

She raised her eyebrows at him before closing the door.

Elliot slumped back in his chair with a big hopeless sigh, taking in the Chanel No. 5 that wafted behind her... and mouthing the F-word, but no sound left his lips as he took in another deep breath.

Glancing through the script in the back of the car as John drove her home, she found that the script called for Donald and Eva Harrison – that is, she and Salvettini, whom she now despised – to be honeymooning in Miami, and then to fly to Barbados in the Caribbean and then to Guyana. The trip would be hot and sunny and long on location but sounded interesting. But she knew working with Steve Salvettini it was bound to be... well, *would* be a box office favourite. She guessed he would accept, but *she* had not read through the script yet.

If she took the job, she knew she would earn millions of dollars. They both would, even though they didn't get along, so how could she resist? But since they'd had the break-up it wouldn't be a good working relationship. Still, Jonah Lombardo would be there, and she got along well with him; well, everyone got on well with Jonah, he was so placid and so easy-going. Stacey Devlin, the glamorous young starlet, would also be there, but of course she would not be a threat. Even though Amber had worked with her before, she really hardly knew her; they had not socialised.

Elliot had said that they were all a good team. Well, they had been a good team at one time; they probably still would be if Steve Salvettini had not been caught in bed with a young actress, Dulcie Shand, and it hadn't been splashed across every newspaper, Facebook, Twitter and what-have-you that Amber De Carla had lost her man to a younger and more beautiful actress. The paparazzi had never left her front gate, and there had been questions about her being the older woman, and she had generally been embarrassed. Steve had said that it was all a mistake, but she felt now that she couldn't trust him, and they had parted company.

She waited until late the next evening before phoning Elliot and agreeing to take the part with Salvettini, telling him that she was not happy about it and it would be a strictly working relationship. Elliot had known she would not refuse the part, but he had been on thorns waiting for her call. He didn't really care if it was a working relationship or not; even when they had been on good working terms,

Amber had been a nightmare to direct, and so he knew just what to expect, but he came off the phone with a sigh of relief.

'Well, is she going to take it?' Elaine asked as she heard him sigh.

He took a breath. 'Yeah, I knew she would, but she can be so cantankerous. With her, it'll be hell anyway. I'd better call Ron Tappener.'

CHAPTER FIVE

They had been filming in the Hollywood studio for two months. There had been a few upsets, which Elliot had expected between Amber and Steve, but on the whole things were going reasonably well. The next scenes were to be filmed in Miami, Florida, after a private flight. Amber and Steve, in their roles as Donald and Eva Harrison, were to be honeymooning in Miami, where the script called for bedroom scenes, love scenes on the beautiful white beach and, of course, Amber showing her beautiful figure in an array of bikinis and wraps and Salvettini showing off a bronzed and masculine athletic body. Later they would be in a night club and get mixed up with drug dealers, and then Donald Harrison would be seduced by the beautiful night-club singer Gloria Stoneham, who was really an undercover drugs squad police officer who thought they were involved with drugs; Stacey Devlin would be playing this role. Then the Harrisons were to be chased around the Miami airport by the police detective Albert Tynes, played by Tom Fallen.

Ed Bennett, chief cameraman, had taken a few discreet shots of them hurrying through the busy crowded airport, but the rest of the airport scenes were set up in a disused old hangar apart from the main airport, Elliot having had to get special permission to film there. Here in the hangar they were filmed boarding a plane for Barbados, and Ed would then intermix this with a scene of passengers boarding a real flight. Then in Barbados there were to be more love scenes on the beach, and Elliot again was expecting trouble with Amber and Steve.

Elliot, with permission from Ronald Tappener, had arranged a private jet to transport them all to the tropical Caribbean island of Barbados; they numbered fourteen in all with the artists, the cameras, and the sound and lighting crew. The flight from Miami to Barbados took three hours and forty minutes.

Elliot had also rented a large house that had cottages attached at the side, to provide accommodation for them all. The house included an all-black staff of six maids, a butler named Paul – the crew called him Goliath because he was a big guy – and the chef Sam. The accommodation was very comfortable and the food turned out to be very good.

The house was near a secluded beach on the quiet and almost deserted east coast where, after a day of relaxing, the cameras and sound were then set up and work began again. Most of the tropical love scenes took place in bikinis for Amber, and the healthy bronzed and masculine physique of Steve Salvettini would have the female audience in raptures.

There was one scene where they had to dive naked into the warm blue Caribbean Sea and then in a quick flash the camera just caught a glimpse of them running naked up onto the beach; this they all knew would cause a sensation, and fans would flock to see it. An instant later, they were off-screen and just as quickly towels were waiting to cover them. The scene had actually taken place in the swimming pool, as the sea on the east coast was far too rough for swimming.

There were more love scenes taken on the beach in the crimson sunset that filled the sky most early evenings and later under a black velvet star-studded sky, with magical moonlight that shone like a searchlight across the water, making it sparkle like diamonds, and turned the sand to an ashen yellow powder. The beach was deserted and eerily quiet at midnight, and there were glimpses of the rolling white surf lifting high and crashing and pounding with thunderous force on the beach. The background sound of the many buzzing insects and the whistling frogs and crickets that were all unseen in the daytime came out of the trees, every tropical night filled with their song; it all added to the romantic scene.

As the story went on the police would come into the scene again; Tom Fallen had been flown in to again play police detective Albert Tynes, this time accompanied by Jonathan Hicks, also playing a policeman. Jonah and Louise Lumbardo had also come down on this private flight, and Stacey Devlin arrived to resume her role as Gloria Stoneham, undercover cop. Fallen and Hicks had stayed for just four days of filming; their work done, they had then returned to LA.

In the next scenes, the Harrisons were running from the police again, and this time would escape on a flight to Guyana, Gloria Stoneham having wormed her way into flying with them.

Jonah and Louise Lumbardo, and also Stacey Devlin, were to stay in Barbados for a few weeks, before flying on to Guyana. This was the first time that Jonah was to appear in the film; his part was to play the wild man that the Harrisons encountered in Guyana coming out of the jungle with a spear and terrifying them after the plane crash. The scene for the plane crash had already been filmed weeks ago at a small private airfield near Miami, where arrangements had been made at great expense for a small aircraft to be pushed into the trees and made to look like it had crashed in jungle greenery; a lot of the trees had been flattened or stood up under the wings. The filming of this scene had taken eight weeks. Ronald Tappener had been there and was prepared to pay for any damage.

It was the first time for them all here in Barbados, and they were now all enjoying a break. Elliot, that evening, had arranged a restaurant for dinner for the cast. The crew did their own thing, some staying in the house, the chef cooking for them, and some going to a bar.

Jonah had asked how the filming was going and Elliot had said that he was quite pleased with the results so far, and then said quietly on the side that Amber had not changed. Jonah had smiled knowingly.

Throughout the three weeks spent in Barbados, Amber had been worrying every day about the sun getting to her fair skin. The constant bickering between her and Steve was getting everyone down, especially Elliot, who had thoughts of chucking it all in. Even the camera crew had said that they were willing to leave at any time, as each day it was, 'Are you getting my right side? Do you have to shine that light right into my eyes? This bikini is uncomfortable,' or, 'I'm going to change this bikini; it doesn't flatter my figure. Steve is leaning over me; does he have to do that, Elliot?' or, 'Wait a minute, wait a minute, I need a drink of water! It's far too hot here, Elliot, can't we do this in the shade? And do we need these lights? It's roasting hot enough, with the sunlight. And does he have to hold me so close in this heat? I'm stifled! And this makeup is running, Elliot; can't we stop for a break, *darling*? You have no idea just what it's like out here; you have the shade of an umbrella!' And then there was a break of about five to ten minutes while Annie the choreographer adjusted her script and Louise the beauty therapist fixed the makeup which had no need to be done anyway. The technicians stood around swearing under their breath as these continual breaks just prolonged their time here, on top of having to listen to the nonstop bickering and complaints.

Everyone's nerves were frayed with Amber constantly stopping the production, and when Elliot ordered another break, they were all really a bit relieved to sit around quietly and have a smoke and a cup of coffee, while, in the background, Amber's voice could still be heard raised: 'Well, I don't think so! And does it have to be like that, Elliot? Why can't we change the scene? And those lines are hard to say, *well*, especially to *him*.' She was referring to Salvettini. 'It just doesn't sound right to me.'

'Hmm, *nothing* sounds right to *her*.' George, the man in charge of sound, rolled his eyes and swore under his breath. The camera crew agreed and swore that they would never take on a job again with bloody Amber De Carla. Then Ed Bennett, the chief cameraman, reminded them that they had another week to go through yet, down in Guyana, and then they could pack up and go back home to LA.

But on viewing the videos, even with all the breaks and frustrations and upsets, they had all agreed with Elliot that the love scenes and the smiles were perfect, so loving and so natural, so real, you would never have guessed of the bitter arguments and aggression and the many breaks between scenes.

'She's so beautiful,' said Elliot. 'Every man's dream.'

'Yeah? Only those who don't know 'er!' said George. 'To me, she's a ruddy nightmare.'

Elliot smiled. 'Yeah, I know what you mean, but she's the best nightmare. And Salvettini is the envy of every man! *And* you're getting well paid.'

Elliot then gritted his teeth and turned away. His thoughts were that there were not many who could work with Amber. She knew nothing about photography and filming but she would argue that they were not taking her from good angles, the lighting was not right, the script wasn't right, the lines should be said differently from the way that they were written, the makeup wasn't right, the wardrobe wasn't right. He had known she would be a nightmare right from the start. And this went on every day, and he was sick of it, and knew everyone else was too. But Tappener had insisted that he wanted De Carla to take the part, and he was putting up the millions.

Elliot just shook his head, thinking back on the last week's arguments and the fiery scenes off-set with Amber and Steve. Everyone felt uncomfortable; they were now the worst pair to be acting out love scenes. How Steve put up with it was a wonder. Stacey Devlin, meanwhile, had been reasonably quiet until her Irish temper had got the better of her and she had got into a furious argument with Amber over messing up her lines, and also Amber had accused her of standing in the way of the camera when Amber had been posing for a special shot, and they had to do it all again. It had almost come to blows and then Stacey had gone off in floods of tears. This, of course, again had upset George, who had taken quite a liking to the young girl, and he had tried to calm her down, which of course had stopped the filming yet again for a whole morning.

Elliot had really had enough that day, and was about to phone Tappener and pack it all in, or tell him to find someone else to take the part of Eva Harrison. But then, on reviewing the situation, he knew they would all have to start from scratch, and there were days spent on sunny beaches, and good restaurants, and they had so much strong footage already. They had incorporated a few black actors as extras, and Elliot had paid fishermen with their boats on the shore, and sent the cameras out in boats to film the fishermen with fish in their nets, and then there was a taxi driver who thought himself an actor, and his normal accent and way of displaying his hands just seemed to fit in; it all added to the tropical scene. The driver had been paid and just hung around outside the house, hoping his taxi would be needed again and hoping there was more acting for him to do, with a line to say, like, 'Yeah, maaan!' He had thought himself a star, and he had been disappointed his taxi was not needed again.

Elliot, on second thoughts, had decided to stick with it, knowing that the trip to Guyana for the next scene had already been arranged months ahead; the flights, accommodation and travel arrangements to the jungle were all in place. He was looking for authentic jungle scenes which he had been told by a Guyanese businessman would be ideal; the man had also helped by giving Elliot contacts to call. All now had been arranged, but Elliot didn't really know what to expect; the only real guarantee was that no matter what it was like, good or bad, Amber would be the first to complain.

CHAPTER SIX

Donald and Eva Harrison, the honeymooning couple, were once more on the run from drug smugglers, and Gloria Stoneham, undercover policewoman, had met them in a bar in Barbados, pretending to be on holiday and knowing the smugglers would be close on their tail. The Harrisons had said that they were going to Guyana, and Gloria had fluttered her eyes at Donald Harrison and talked her way into going with them. The script then called for the three of them lost in the jungle, romantic jungle nights and Donald getting involved with the glamorous redhead Gloria, which was to cause a lot of trouble with his wife Eva.

They were to leave the next morning for Guyana. Elliot had advised them all to dress casually; he had suggested they wear shorts and T-shirts, as the weather was extremely warm and they would be in a jungle location. 'Travel light, hand luggage only; it's just for a couple of days. The rest of your luggage will be sent to the hotel in Georgetown where you will be spending the night before going back to Miami and then on to LA.' He nodded to Amber, knowing she would pack a whole wardrobe. 'You girls will only need a toothbrush and a hairbrush; Louise will carry all the makeup you'll need.'

Everyone was assembled in front of the house where a coach awaited to take them to the Grantley Adams airport; they had enjoyed Barbados and were reluctant to leave. The taxi driver, still hovering around the front gate, watched as the equipment was being loaded onto the coach and hoped his taxi would be needed.

The men were wearing beige or white shorts and T-shirts, Louise wearing white shorts and a white T-shirt, Stacey Devlin in white shorts and a green T-shirt. Annie the choreographer and Frank Clayton, a sound technician, both wore blue jeans; they were to depart for Miami and then go on to California to another assignment, as they would not be needed in Guyana.

Some had already boarded the coach and were seated and some were about to board, when Amber appeared through the house's front door; she was the last to arrive, making an entrance with her usual flair, and everything seemed to stop dead as she posed on the front doorstep. They all turned their heads, and gasps and whispers went around; she heard the quick intake of breath and lifted her chin, pushing a stray blonde hair away from her forehead with the red-painted fingernails with an air of grace and charm.

The shortest of shocking pink shorts seemed to sing out, *HERE I AM! LOOK AT ME!* and although she was just standing, it was the way she did it. The tight shocking pink tank top, showing inches of midriff, enhanced her voluptuous bust. All eyes went down her long legs to the silver platform sandals with four-inch stiletto heels; she carried a large matching soft leather silver tote bag over her shoulder, her long silver-blonde hair swept up in a ponytail with an enormous pink ribbon, and there was enough makeup for a command performance. The bright red lips smiled but then changed to a sneer as she noticed the look on all their faces.

Elliot held his breath, put his hand to his mouth and exclaimed quietly, 'Jesus! *This* is casual?' The low whisper escaped from his lips. He glanced at both Steve and Jonah, seeing the amused smirks, then rolled his eyes, taking a breath. 'Come on, Amber.'

She tottered on her high heels to the coach and as she boarded in front of him he was tempted to smack the pink bottom, but thought better of it; she was enough trouble as it was. There were whispered exclamations from the crew as she took a seat in the front near the window and Elliot sat beside her; behind their backs there were twisted lips and rolling eyes and silent titters, and all was unusually quiet. The minibus set off for the Grantley Adams airport, where Elliot had once again arranged a private jet. The taxi driver drove away, disappointed.

They were met by Carol Hollingsworth, an American air hostess who took all their passports to be cleared, and she had organised four porters to transport all their hand luggage and equipment. Louise carried a small zip-up black leather bag, containing the makeup and shampoo and other general toiletries. The jungle scenes would not require too much attention, so the baggage was pretty much all light, but of course Amber had the most.

They then followed the air hostess out onto the runway where the private jet awaited, and they boarded and made themselves comfortable, Amber sitting next to Stacey Devlin; they had not got much conversation and Stacey felt that she had got the short straw, with Amber next to her.

Jonah and Louise sat together and Elliot and Steve Salvettini sat in front of them; the crew all sat to the back.

The flight was not long, and they were soon looking down on a mass of dense green jungle, Ed Barrett, chief cameraman, eagerly filming the very first scenes, as this was what they were supposed to see before the plane ended up on a crash course into the dense trees. Some bits on film were of the pilot struggling with the controls, already filmed in Miami.

They were over the airport now and on their descent, when the captain announced over the intercom that they would have to go around again as there was a problem with the landing gear. Of course this got everyone on edge.

'Well, *do something*!' Amber demanded loudly of Elliot, who of course asked equally loudly what he could do; he couldn't fly the plane. Everyone was silently praying, while Ed took this opportunity to film Amber, Steve and Stacey in their moment of anxiety, which would add to the crash scene, although he kept his fingers crossed that the landing gear *would* come down before they ran out of fuel. He had already filmed this scene weeks ago in a mock aircraft crash when they had been screaming and crying, although now it seemed it was for real everyone was reasonably quiet, until Amber stood up demanding that somebody do something.

Steve Salvettini shouted at her to sit down and pulled her by the shoulder back into the seat. 'Sit down and fasten your seatbelt, you fool; what the hell can any of us do?'

'Don't you shout at me, you *pig*,' Amber screamed, lashing out at him over the back of the seat, but she missed as she flopped clumsily back down again into her own seat, beside Stacey.

'Let's all calm down, shall we?' Elliot had his hands up as if in defence.

Stacey, looking at Amber, had a look of anxious surprise, afraid to even speak.

Jonah, of course, like everyone else, was worried; he took Louise by the hand and squeezed it with a comforting smile. Ed swung the camera around, in a quick sweep of the crew, just as the plane dipped its wing to the right, and everyone gasped out loud.

'This is the captain. Well, we've circled three times around, and the drama seems to be over; the landing gear is now free, and we will be landing shortly.'

Everyone gave a sigh of relief and within a few minutes, the wheels touched the ground.

'Well, that was a bloody scary start,' came a London voice from somewhere at the back; it was Murray Prendagast, who was a sound technician. 'We might have got the bloody film finished for real, right 'ere and now, and all been stuck in the ruddy jungle.'

There were a few chuckles and sighs of relief as some of the guys agreed with him.

Amber's heart was pounding as she looked at Stacey, who was quite white with fright, and they both sighed with relief; that was the closest they'd come to acknowledgement.

'I feel sick,' Stacey said.

Amber rolled her eyes, in an unsaid, *What now?* But luckily Stacey managed to control herself as they taxied to a stop.

The engine was cut and all was exceptionally quiet. There was a clicking of seatbelts, a feeling of relief, and now everyone was talking as they stood up.

The airport was smallish and another plane had landed just before them, and so there were a hundred or more passengers milling about in the terminal. Then, as some of the luggage began to be taken off the carousel, a small brown dog was sniffing around.

Amber, looking alarmed, bent to shoo the dog away from her luggage.

'*Don't!*' said Steve, sharply but quietly.

'Why?' She looked daggers at him with a resentful pout; who was *he* to tell *her* what to do? 'I didn't know they allowed dogs in the airport.'

'It's a sniffer dog.'

'Well, why's it sniffing at my...'

'Drugs!' Steve spoke quietly, and glanced around him in case anyone was listening.

Amber looked very surprised. 'I haven't got any.' She didn't like the idea of some scruffy dog sniffing around her expensive Louis Vuitton bag.

'Well, you've got nothing to worry about, then. It's just doing its job,' said Elliot, overhearing and nodding to the uniformed policeman who was following the dog as it went on to another bag.

The luggage all collected, the whole group moved out of the airport, to where all the equipment was being loaded onto a large and dilapidated minibus. Suddenly they were all surrounded by black youths. Amber smiled, thinking that the reception was for her, but then found that it was *not*, as a dozen or so hands were sticking out under their noses, accompanied by shouts of, 'Give me a dollar! Give a dollar!'

The whole of the film crew backed away and climbed quickly aboard the minibus, and Elliot put a protective arm around Amber, ushering her aboard. Just then, seeing the huge size of Jonah as he pulled himself up to his full height of six foot eight to protect his wife Louise, the youths backed away.

The driver was now closing the sliding door. They were all glad to get away, but then hands came in through the open windows. 'Give me a dollar! Give me a dollar! You rich lady, give me a dollar!'

The driver turned the key and the engine, after spitting and spluttering, turned into a roaring rattling crescendo of life but sounded as if every nut, bolt and screw was loose. They began to move forward but the hands still came through, clinging and clawing at the open windows, then one of the crew threw a handful of coins, and the youths dived and scrambled for them.

The minibus began to pick up speed; it was nice to get a little fresh air from the windows, but with the intense heat of the day the breeze was warm, and now they were picking up more speed and the engine was so noisy they could not hear each other speak.

'*Eoh!* What an ordeal.' Amber cringed and frowned at the back of the grimy seat in front of her, with its cracked and split sickly light blue plastic cover. She blinked her black lashes in disgust at the dark brown spongy stuffing that spilled out. She then had thoughts of her own seat, and leaned a little forward, lifting her silver-blonde ponytail and holding it up on the top of her head; who knew what insects or creepy crawlies lurked in the sponge-like stuffing? She gave Stacey, who was sitting beside her, a look; Stacey also lifted her silky red hair away from the back of the seat.

'Why*ever* did you bring us *here* to such a place, *Elliot*?' Amber sounded exhausted and frustrated as usual, as she flicked at the jagged blue plastic on the back of the seat in front of her, grimacing with distaste. She turned to Elliot sitting across the aisle, to her left. 'Haven't we got enough jungle-like trees in America?'

Elliot just grimaced without commenting; he couldn't hold a conversation with the loud rattling and bumping of the minibus that shuddered all their cheeks and had them hanging on to anything and everything that was solid.

Sitting behind her, Steve grinned across to Elliot, which of course Amber did not see. They were all used to her la-di-dah pretentious and aggressive attitude to everything, no matter what it was! She always had something to complain about. Although she was right; the minibus *was* really tatty, and they were all feeling hot and uncomfortable. The only air conditioning was the warm breeze coming through the opened windows.

The minibus was now racing along at breakneck speed, and the road was rough, and they were shaken and bumped around and had to hang on to the seat in front for support. Then suddenly they were jerked to a stop that threw them all forward and then back again as the minibus started up again. Ed had his hand on the seat opposite, to keep himself steady, and the video camera in the other hand and resting on his shoulder; he was sitting next to Jonah Lombardo's great bulk, which took up most of the seat and part of the centre aisle. The camera jumped and jolted before his eyes, then there was a sharp stop as a car in front squealed its brakes. Ed just managed to capture people crossing the road; it all seemed a jumble, but he was hoping that he would get something worth the while to show.

They soon reached a fast speed again; the driver was swerving and dodging in and out of traffic, then he slowed and shot them all forward again, and then picked up speed, and then another quick jerk as he swerved around a cow that was sitting in the middle of the busy road. One of the technicians shouted, 'Hey, has this guy got a licence?' They all gasped, wondering if they would ever live long enough to find out.

The speed continued; everyone sat holding their breath, waiting any minute for the inevitable crash. Then another emergency stop, as another cow that had been lying in the road just suddenly got up and walked lazily across the busy main road right in front of them, oblivious to the danger it was in, or the danger that it caused. Without a care in the world it just stood there, stopping all the traffic. Ed managed to get a shot of the cow walking just before the driver put his foot down again, driving around it and jerking all their heads back, and they were off on another hair-raising ride.

'Why don't they stop those cows from coming onto the road?' asked Stacey.

The driver half-turned; both Steve and Elliot exchanged glances, hoping that he would soon concentrate on the driving again. 'They are sacred cows, mistress; they are allowed to go anywhere.'

Stacey glanced around, rolling her eyes in wonder.

They then came to an almost-halt, and the minibus was turning left, and the whole thing tipped and lurched to the left; it could have been up on two wheels for all they knew. They all shouted, it was so scary, and then it bumped and righted itself again; everyone gasped, their hearts racing.

They had now entered a very narrow lane, and luckily were a little slower, but then they found themselves dodging away from the open windows as the twigs and branches poked through on both sides as they passed. Between small gaps in the wild hedgerow to the right they glimpsed the river.

Having driven on through the narrow lane for about fifteen to twenty minutes, they then came to a jerking stop. Everyone took a breath, wondering what was to happen next. Even the engine when cut seemed to sigh with relief. The driver got out and slid the door back.

They got out slowly, one after the other, on the right-hand side of the minibus, all relieved but no one complaining of broken bones. There was a large gap in the high hedge and they now stood on the riverbank. Ed had the video camera rolling again.

The driver, helped by some of the crew, got the luggage out and left it on the riverbank. The river was fast-running and a sandy brown in colour with white peaks, and extremely wide; it was like looking out on the horizon.

The driver then informed them, 'This is the famous Demerara River.'

'Famous?' Jonah asked.

'Yes, *sir*.' He grinned, showing a set of strong yellowing teeth. 'This is where all the Caribbean shrimp comes from.'

The grin still there, he was feeling pleased to have given this information. But to Jonah it didn't mean very much.

Elliot glanced at Jonah and grinned on hearing this as he was carefully counting out the money to pay the driver some exorbitant price for the rough ride; it had taken an hour, and it certainly had been a scary experience. The driver nodded and smiled as he pocketed the money, knowing that he'd caught them for a few hundred extra, then waved them goodbye and got back into the minibus, and there was more roaring and rattling as he backed fast up the narrow track.

They stood looking down at two boats. *Well...* Steve inclined his head with a silent thought; he guessed they *had* been boats, *once*. He arched his eyebrows, comically glancing at Elliot, who had obviously had the same thought.

Elliot grimaced. 'Well, they *are* in the water.' He twitched his lips into a smirk.

'Do yer think we'll make it?' Jonah raised his thick black eyebrows comically at both Elliot and Steve.

The second boat was bigger, but they both looked dilapidated. Elliot suggested that all the camera equipment go in the second boat, with the technicians and their personal hand luggage. 'All the other personal luggage goes in the first boat, with Amber, Stacey and Louise, Jonah, Steve, and myself. Ed, you'd better come with us and you can film all this; we might be able to use it somewhere in the script later.' He nodded to Amber to go ahead, then looked down. 'Better take those shoes off, or you'll be spiking holes in the, uh...' He hesitated, swallowed and said, 'Er, boat.'

Steve grinned.

Amber, shoes in hand and silver tote bag on her shoulder, reluctantly stepped down the steep bank and reached out her long red polished fingernails to grip the grubby black hand offered by the boatman, his grizzled grey beard half-parted in an admiring grin on seeing the shocking pink shorts and the long shapely legs. He showed a set of yellowed broken teeth, the short cigar stub still held firmly in the corner of his mouth amongst the grizzled grey whiskers. He steadied her as the boat wobbled, and indicated that she should sit down on the wooden seat that went all around the bow, but with a look of distaste and a slight lifting of her right shoulder, with an *oh my goodness* sort of attitude, she managed to stay standing, the boatman keeping her balanced.

Steve, seeing her plight and knowing her finicky ways, stepped in behind her and held her arm, relieving the boatman, as the boat wobbled again. Steve ran his large bronzed hand over the grimy seat and she sat down, flicking her fingers, trying to rid them of the boatman's touch. Then Steve and the boatman also helped Stacey, and then Louise, who was still held by one arm by Jonah from the bank until he could see that Steve had a secure hold on her arm.

Now all three girls were seated, there was a big 'Oooh!' from them all as Jonah's great bulk made the boat dip dangerously. Then Ed took a last-minute shot from the bank of all the actors before getting into the boat, and Elliot was the last to board.

The boatman, wearing khaki shorts and a grubby white T-shirt, called to his equally grubby friend, 'Hey, Colly, yer ready?'

Colly waved back. 'Sure, Jago,' and both boat engines started up, with a rumble and deep rhythmic throb that shivered their very timbers. Steve grinned at Jonah as both boats turned into the fast-running Demerara River, wondering if they'd make it.

Crossing the wide stretch of the water needed skill; it was not easy. It was like riding the rapids. The sandy brown water rushed at the port side of the boat fast and hard enough to crush the old wood; it squirmed a bit but the boatman managed to keep it in line. A little water splashed over the side, making Amber move a little closer to Steve, and then, realising what she had done, she moved back again. Steve gave a slight smirk.

As they got further away from the riverbank and more into open water, a strong breeze blew downstream.

Elliot told Ed to get some shots of them leaving the riverbank; Ed also got more shots of the stars sitting in the boat.

Elliot turned to open his briefcase, thinking that he might make a few adjustments to the script while they were here, or he would forget about it. A boat hadn't been written into the script, but he could have the Harrisons finding an old boat on the riverside, while fighting their way through the jungle after the plane crash. He also thought that the minibus ride could be incorporated into the script somewhere; right now he didn't know where, but he wanted to jot it down before he forgot.

He took out the script, a thick pile of loose papers in a buff folder. Holding it in one hand, he was now feeling for a pen which he usually carried in the top pocket of his suit, but today, of course, wearing shorts and a T-shirt, there was no pocket. 'Here,' he said to Stacey, who was the nearest, 'hold this.' He handed her the folder, and went for his briefcase again.

Just at that very moment a strong gust of wind blew open the folder and some pages flew out and over the side. Stacey automatically in a quick movement stood up and tried to grab them, dropping the whole folder onto the bottom of the boat, the wind taking more pages as Steve stuck his foot out to hold them down. Stacey, leaning out, was trying to grab the loose pages that were flying through the air when the boat suddenly dipped to the right under her weight and she lost her balance. She screamed as she went over the side head-first into the fast-running brown and murky water and disappeared, and then her head bobbed up, and she was quickly swept away by the strong current.

Everybody shouted as Jonah's quick action and great bulk dived in after her, tipping the boat at a very dangerous angle and shipping a little water, and Louise squealed in alarm as Jonah's foot caught the black leather case beside her on the seat with all the stage makeup in it; it lifted into the air and plopped into the water, disappearing beneath the rushing white peaks before she could grab it.

They all watched with anxious gasps as Jonah's strong muscled arms plunged through the rapid rushing water. Stacey could swim but the current was so strong and she was fighting against it, and each time that Jonah came near enough to grab her the current whisked her away again, and they were now some distance from the boat. When he finally managed to catch her outstretched hand the second boat was now nearer and Colly was trying to steer even closer, but the current was so strong he was struggling to hold the boat steady. And then Jonah managed to grab the side of the boat, and many willing hands pulled Stacey into the boat and to safety.

By now Jago was coming nearer and Jonah swam the few strong strokes against the current, grabbing the side. The boat dipped dangerously again as both Steve and Ed pulled him in, bringing with him a deluge of water that splashed them all and had the script folder that still lay in the bottom of the boat floating.

Elliot called anxiously across to George the sound technician, concerned at seeing Stacey lying there in his arms. George called back, 'She's out cold; I can't bring her round.' One of the other guys was gently slapping her face, but she lay limp in George's arms, so exhausted she had just let go.

Elliot could see that they were trying to bring her round. He told Jago to bring the boat closer; he wanted to get into the other boat, which he did, with some difficulty and a lot of help from the guys as he fell in amongst them, tipping the boat dangerously and almost falling into the rushing rapids himself. Both the boatmen were struggling with the strong current and trying to keep reasonably close without touching, but the boats collided with a loud bump.

Stacey had come round, but of course was cold and wet and badly shaken. Even though she insisted that she was all right, Elliot decided he would take no chances out here in the middle of nowhere, and she had most probably swallowed a lot of the dirty water. He called across, telling the actors to go on ahead; he was going to turn back and take Stacey to a hospital, and he would meet them tomorrow at the intended destination. He then told Colly the boatman to call the minibus back to take them to the nearest hospital. The rest of the crew would have to spend the night in a hotel that had already been booked for them all two months ahead.

Of course everyone was concerned, and they were all agreed that the second boat should turn back and the first boat should go on across the wide expanse of the river. Jago managed to manoeuvre the boat upstream and across the river, and they were now leaving the rapid water and entering into a quiet canal.

The water here was as calm as glass; as it slowly and silently moved away from the bow it looked thick, like black treacle. The canal was narrow with dense jungle greenery on either side, and the trees meeting overhead made a tunnel. They had lost the sunlight and the blue sky; it was now dim and shaded, with the occasional bright spark of sunlight coming through the branches and thick leaves, and it gave the impression of being on an enchanted ride in an amusement park, or sailing into the unknown. The rushing sound of the river seemed as if it had just been switched off; it was now eerily quiet, with hollow echoes of tropical bird calls that came from somewhere deep in the forest, and as the boat moved on very slowly with the low chugging of the engine a strong and pungent earthy smell rose from the inky black water and the jungle greenery. Nothing seemed real, except the ever-wafting smell of cigar smoke as Jago the boatman puffed away at the never-ending stub.

There was nothing to see but thick dense greenery, so entangled that hardly an insect could get through. The boatman broke the silence by saying that there were hundreds of miles of jungle in Guyana that had never been explored.

'How far are we going into the jungle?' Steve asked.

'Twenty-two miles.' Jago parted his grey and grizzled whiskers with a smile, the cigar butt still in place.

'Twenty-two miles?' gasped Louise, looking at Jonah. 'Is it all like this?'

'No.' Jago grinned. 'It gets better, mistress.'

They moved on slowly with only the monotonous heartbeat throbbing of the boat engine, and the intermittent echo of hollow bird calls that all sounded so unreal; the boat was then turning slowly into an identical canal, with the same thick and dense greenery on either side. No one had much to say, until a dragonfly skimmed the black treacle and they all turned to look and point and their voices echoed back at them as if through a megaphone. The dragonfly was unusually large and was the most excitement they'd had since Stacey had fallen in the water.

On and on they went, the time ticking by slowly. Suddenly the engine was cut, and they all looked at Jago thinking that something was wrong, but then the trees parted and they were under a blue sky. Hot sunlight poured down and everyone put on their sunglasses. With the engine cut the boat drifted slowly over to the left side, where dense greenery covered what had once been a jetty but was now just broken and rotting wood.

There was a signpost that said *Mission*, but it was almost impossible to read through the entanglement of twisting vines and leaves; it had probably been there for a hundred years. There was no sign of a mission; no doubt it was there somewhere, now dilapidated, in the dense undergrowth that was so impossible to penetrate that not even a fly could get through. At least it was a sign that a village must have been nearby many years ago, but now great spider webs hung from the branches of the trees like thick grey ragged curtains, so still and untouched it seemed they had been preserved for centuries. Seeing the spider webs made Amber shiver; the one thing that really made her afraid was a spider, no matter how small, and God knew what other creepy crawlies lurked in this entangled mass of enchanted forest.

The eerie hollow echoes of exotic bird calls were the only sound that disturbed the stillness; maybe even the birds were lost and they were cries for help. Nothing moved, not even a leaf, not even the air, and nothing seemed real. Great thick giant-sized leaves seemed to rise up from the depths of the black glass-like treacle water. Maybe the water was even deeper in this dense mass, maybe it was just a swamp, but no one would ever know. It was just like a film set; the greenery could have been plastic. It would have been no surprise to any of them if they had been attacked by painted warriors with feathered headdresses armed with spears and shields, and then found that it was all set up by Elliot to get some fearful reaction, but this couldn't happen; even a flea would find it hard to penetrate these tightly woven vines of thick jungle undergrowth.

'It's nice to see the blue sky and the sun,' Steve said to the boatman, 'but why did you stop here, after coming through all that shade?'

Jago's grey grizzled whiskers broke into a yellow grin, still holding the cigar stub. He offered them beer or water from a cold box that was much appreciated. 'It's the only safe place to stop, maaan, the snakes can't fall off the trees into the boat.'

'*Whaaat?*' both Steve and Jonah gasped together, looking up at the trees and then glancing at each other with frowns.

'*Snakes?*' It was a surprised whisper. Amber sat bolt upright. 'Snakes!' she said again, and she automatically looked up; they all did. Ed, who had been filming almost every leaf, turned the camera upwards. He saw nothing, but hoped he might have caught a glimpse of a snake hidden somewhere in the tightly woven branches.

'Yes, mistress.' Jago grinned. 'Very dangerous, snakes, under de trees and when dey in de boat, maaan, it hard to get dem out, so best to keep movin'.'

'But we've come all this way under the trees.' Amber sounded amazed.

'Yes, mistress, dat why we keep moving, we not stop.'

They all looked wide-eyed at each other. And then, while the boat was now still, something disturbed the black treacle. There was a slight ripple and then it was like looking down onto a sheet of shiny black glass; whatever it was did not surface.

Amber had thoughts of turning back, but now they had come too far; turning back would be impossible. It might also be impossible to turn the boat around in a narrow canal, and of course they would have to go through the tunnel of trees again, where now they knew the snakes lurked above. She looked at the bottle of water in her hand. It wasn't her style swigging out of a bottle, and was it clean? She wiped her fingers around the top, and twitched her nose, then, thinking that she had no choice, cringed, putting the bottle to her red-painted lips. She put the cap back on and put the bottle on the floor, and then flicked her red fingernails as if they were sticky.

Jago's brown eyes had a slight flicker. The white lady was used to fine living, he thought; she wasn't going to like the jungle. He silently raised his thick grey eyebrows at her and grinned inwardly, and she lowered her long false eyelashes.

For just a split second Amber caught the look in his eye, and she looked away quickly. She knew her finicky ways irritated people but she couldn't help the way she was now, and the look on the boatman's face made her feel embarrassed. She'd come from an ordinary background to stardom; she'd gone from bottled Coca-Cola to now sipping fine wines and champagne from delicate glasses; she was queen of the screen, and so she had altered her ways to suit her lifestyle. There were times when she knew she overdid it, but she had created this image and she now couldn't just let it drop; there was no turning back.

'Well, are we here, then? Is this *it*?' Jonah frowned, wondering just how they were to leave the boat. He had been sitting too long, and his wet clothing was drying but was still damp and uncomfortable. He would be glad to get out and stretch his legs, but where could they go?

'No, sir, we not there yet.' Jago grinned. ''Bout one, one an' a half hours, thereabouts, den we be twenty-two miles into de jungle.'

Twenty-two miles went through all their minds as they looked at each other; another hour or more to go yet.

The engine came to life and the whole boat shuddered; they were on the move again and the monotonous low throbbing of the engine beat in their ears. In five minutes the water swirled into thick treacle ripples again without a sound as the boat turned into another canal, but the scenery was exactly the same. Ed had nothing to film. It was like being in a maze.

They were once again under the cover of the trees, and now from time to time Amber glanced up, having that scared feeling in the stomach, wondering what would happen if a snake suddenly fell into the boat. No one would want to be the first over the side into the inky black treacle. She turned quickly to her right as the water surged in thick ripples again and the tail of a crocodile was slithering from the bank, no doubt disturbed by the movement of the boat. They all glanced at each other anxiously, wide-eyed; no one spoke.

They moved slowly on and on and then suddenly they were out of the dimness of the overhanging trees and the sun shone hot from a clear blue sky, just for a moment. The movement of the boat disturbed crocodiles that slithered from the bank into the water, which in the brilliant sunlight had lost its treacle blackness and could now only be described as reddish brown, and just like Coca-Cola. Ed found it fascinating as he turned the camera on the crocodiles, but they were a shade too quick for him; it was scary as they could now see the dark shapes below the surface of the red-brown Coca-Cola water. Amber and Louise looked wide-eyed at each other, their thoughts obviously the same; they both sat dead still, afraid to even move their eyes, and then they were again under the trees and in inky black water with the threat of snakes overhead.

On and on the boat made slow progress and then out into the sunshine again, where the Coca-Cola water was still and calm; they were approaching a clearing. The grass by the river looked long and green; further up the bank it was brown, scorched dry and parched by the hot sun. Set back from the river there were two wooden huts on stilts. The boat floated straight ahead, the bow ploughing into a V shape cut out in the grassy bank. The boat stopped, held secure and steady; there was nowhere to tie up.

Jonah was the first out onto the bank, which was quite steep, and the boat wobbled dangerously at his movement; he was glad to stretch his legs, and then he gave every one of them a hand. The boatman lifted their bags with ease and threw them out onto the grassy bank. Amber thought him quite agile, but then perhaps he wasn't as old as she'd first thought. The boat was then backing out and pulling away, the boatman raising a hand in farewell. They waved goodbye, as Ed filmed the boat leaving.

An odd bird call made it sound as if there was life somewhere, but as the sound of the chugging motor died away, the river became glassy again and the atmosphere deathly quiet. Standing now in a group on the lonely grassy bank the five looked around them, their thoughts all the same. They were here in a clearing, in the middle of the jungle, alone, and now with the boat gone they were trapped; there was no way out.

The men picked up the bags and as they were about to walk towards the wooden huts, two young black men dressed in safari shorts and shirts came running down towards them. They were both of medium height, but the taller of the two apologised for not being there on the riverbank when the boat arrived, and introduced himself as Henry and his companion as Rani. They were young and strong and all smiles, taking the luggage between them as the five followed them through the brown and parched grass to one of the wooden huts.

There were eight to ten steps up and they entered into a spacious living room; there were window frames on either side, open, which was a bit pointless as there was no glass. The furnishing was sparse; a thin and well-worn carpet covered just the centre of the wooden floor, on which stood a wooden coffee table and two armchairs with green-grey cushions. To their left a small two-seater sofa with wooden arms, thinly padded and covered in a thin beige cotton-like material, stood against the wall under one of the glassless open window frames; at the far end of the room and facing them, a wooden staircase led up to a loft.

There were two doors to the left of the stairs and Henry showed them two bedrooms. Rani put Louise and Jonah's bags in the first one, and Amber was shown into the second one. She stood in the doorway, twisting her lips, and took a breath. The furnishings were poor. She wondered if Elliot had known. She'd had thoughts of a proper house, or a small hotel, but *this? Well!*

The room was empty but for a four-poster bed, with a large snow-white mosquito net. She had a quick flashback to her pink satin sheets at home, but this was not home, and thank goodness it was only for a day or so. There was a wicker laundry basket, she supposed for storage, and two nails above it hammered into the wooden wall for hanging things. The far wall behind the headboard of the bed was no more than a three-foot-high fence and looked out onto a wooden walkway over the clearing surrounded by jungle trees and bushes. The full-sized wall to her right had a door with six glass panels that led out onto the narrow walkway facing more trees and bushes beyond the clearing; this was the back of the hut. In fact there was nothing but trees and bushes all round except for the river at the front of the hut where they had first come in.

On the narrow walkway was a small wooden hut, no more than a small garden shed, with a rush roof; this was fitted out as a bathroom with a white porcelain toilet and basin. The shower had a plain rough concrete floor with a one-brick-high surround to keep the water in; there was a wooden rack with white towels. She had to admit it all looked nice and clean.

She turned on the tap. At least there was running water, but it was brown like Coca-Cola, straight from the river. She grimaced; it was all very primitive. And was she expected to wash her face, her body and her silver-blonde hair in *river water*?

The grimace still there, she turned and went back into the bedroom. She looked down at her expensive Louis Vuitton bag where it had been left inside the door on the floor, containing her fine silk dresses; she had also added extra, and had even packed an evening gown just in case it was needed, and fancy high-heeled shoes, and small beaded bags, but she hadn't needed any of it in Barbados, and she certainly wasn't going to need any of it here. She frowned hard. The only makeup she had was some small free samples of face and night cream, about enough for one application only, and a small sample lipstick that was so pale and not her colour, and even that was melting. She always kept these small samples in her bag just for air travel. They were easy to carry and she rarely used them anyway; they were just for emergencies. She didn't often take all her makeup when on location as Louise carried a full range of makeup needed, including suntan lotion and nail varnish.

She glanced at her long red fingernails; the polish would need to be renewed in a day or so, but now all was lost and there was nothing, so the free samples would really fill the emergency situation. She would not need dresses or shoes here, *or* the diamonds that were in her silver tote bag. Elliot had said it would only be two days, so she would have to manage; he had also said that it was jungle, and she had expected jungle and trees, that was the whole idea, but she could not believe that he would have brought her to *this*. She'd had thoughts on jungle scenes, but they would not be expected to work all day, and she had expected a restaurant in the evenings... but *this*...

Taking a deep breath she stormed out of the bedroom; the others were all in the living room. 'I can't stay *here*! What*ever* is Elliot thinking, bringing us *here*? I want to go back!' She shrugged her shoulders and lifted her chin indignantly, almost stamping her foot like a child being told that they can't have an ice cream.

'You can't go back.' Ed Bennett grimaced and inclined his head. 'We're twenty-two miles into the jungle, and there's no way out now until the bloody boat comes back.'

'Well, Elliot said it would only be a couple of days, but how long are we supposed to stay now? There is nothing to do here.' Amber sounded amazed, her voice raised in her high-handed manner.

'Well,' Steve said, arching his eyebrows and splaying his hands nonchalantly, 'I guess until Elliot and the rest of the crew get here.'

Jonah inclined his head; he was equally amazed. 'Well, that might take days now, seeing that he's gone to the hospital with Stacey.'

'Yeah!' Ed nodded, flicking his eyebrows.

'Well, can't one of you phone Elliot and tell him what it's *like*?' Amber tossed her silver-blonde head and lifted her chin.

Jonah took out his cell phone and pressed a few buttons. 'It's dead; there's no signal.'

'No, there's no signal out here' said Henry as he was just coming through the living room. 'The only way you have contact now is back in Georgetown.'

'Well, how do we contact Georgetown?' asked Jonah.

Henry looked a bit surprised, as if Jonah should have known. 'Well, when the boat comes back on Thursday. You could send a note.'

'*Thursday?*' Amber's blue eyes sparked fire, and her mouth stayed open. 'Well, can't you contact the *boatman*?'

'No, ma'am.'

She took a deep breath and looked wide-eyed at them all, then turned away, shaking her head and feeling deflated. 'This can't be happening!' Then she realised that no amount of moaning and complaining would help.

'We're *stuck*!' said Ed.

She was speechless, but only for an instant. 'I'll certainly give Elliot a piece of my mind when he gets here!' She suddenly looked at Steve. 'Well! When they get here, where are they all going to stay?'

Steve looked at Jonah, and then at Ed; they all had hopeless grins, splaying hands, hunching their shoulders and shaking their heads.

'Indeed,' Jonah said, widening his deep brown eyes, 'where *are* they all going to stay? And the boat won't come back until Thursday; that's another three days.' He flipped his hands again. 'So Elliot won't be here tomorrow, then?'

'And then,' said Steve, '*then* we'll have to start filming, and I guess that will take another couple of days, so it will be almost a week.'

Amber stood with her hand clamped over her mouth, her eyes still wide.

'What's your room like, Amber?' Louise asked.

'Hmph!' Her head went up and then down. 'It's a room? If you can call it a room, it's got a bed!' She raised her eyebrows in mock-amazement, with a slight smile. '*And* a low fence.'

'Yes, like ours.' Louise nodded.

'Well, you're bloody lucky.' Ed rolled his eyes. 'Steve and I have a choice of the armchair or the sofa.'

'What? You mean there are no more rooms?' Amber was amazed. 'What if we had all arrived together, then, if there are only two bedrooms?'

'Indeed.' Jonah nodded, scratching the back of his neck with raised eyebrows.

'Dunno.' Steve inclined his head and splayed his hands, turning as Henry came in with glasses and a bottle on a tray. Henry set the tray on the coffee table and then poured them red wine; they each took a glass.

'Henry, what about the other hut? Can't the two of us stay in there?' Steve was referring to himself and Ed.

Henry shook his head. 'Not furnished.'

Steve and Ed looked at each other; there was no answer to that.

'But surely both huts were booked,' said Jonah.

'No, sir.' Henry shook his head again in surprise, about to walk away.

'Wait a minute, Henry! Are you sure?' Jonah had a puzzled frown.

'Yes, sir.' Henry looked at the five of them. 'Yes, sir! We are only booked for four people.'

'Fourteen?' Jonah corrected him. 'But two had to go back. So there will be twelve when the others arrive.'

Henry shook his head. 'No, sir, only four people, for three days.'

They all looked at each other, shaking their heads, but there was no point in arguing there had obviously been a misunderstanding.

They sat down, with their wine; they agreed it was good quality. They were all a bit bewildered. Jonah and Steve took the armchairs by the coffee table which was in about the centre of the room. Ed, still standing, looked around for somewhere to sit. There was a small stool in the corner; he got it and joined the men. Louise and Amber sat on the thin sofa under the wide-open window frame, with just enough room for the two of them. As they sat down the thin cushion puffed up and clouds of dust rose around them and they quickly waved their hands in front of their faces.

The dusk was coming on and Henry came in with a hurricane lamp and put it on the coffee table. Until then, they had not really given a thought to the evening, and there being no electricity.

'Cheers.' Ed raised his glass with a slight chuckle, but it was more like a sarcastic gesture than a happy one.

They all raised their glasses. 'Cheers?' Their voices were sullen.

The dusk came on very quickly and the hurricane lamp sent eerie shadows around the spacious, sparsely furnished wooden hut. It was eerily quiet, apart from the sounds outside as the jungle came alive with the tropical night that seemed so still and silent, and yet was buzzing with the sound of insects. They were used to the sound of traffic. There were no lights, no people, no music, and the river, now in the darkness that had come on so quickly, was black and still as death. It was a wilderness, and yet all around it was alive with a noisy sizzling sound like water hissing from a leaking pipe.

The lighted hurricane lamp on the coffee table attracted a giant moth that fluttered around the lamp, so big it made the girls gasp in alarm. Jonah hit out at it and it disappeared somewhere up into the rafters, as swarms of gnats clung closely together above the lamp like a tangled mass of thin golden wire. With the door wide open to the now deep darkness of the early evening they could see the flashing green lights of fireflies dancing around the trees. The night was hot and very still, the humidity high, and there was no fan to cool the air.

Amber was about to rest her back on the thin and not very comfortable sofa when Louise stopped her, pointing out the inch-long ants marching up and down the window frame as ants do, in one long line going up and one long line coming down, far too close to their heads. The girls looked at each other in horror and sat bolt upright, away from the window frame.

Henry came back with a bottle of red wine to replenish their glasses, and asked if they would like red or white with their dinner; he said they were to have a barbecue. They all said red, knowing that the white wine would not be cold, and judging by the surroundings, they all had thoughts on what the food would be like. Ed had decided to drown his sorrows in booze.

No one spoke and an eerily quiet atmosphere hung heavily in the room, except for the very loud sound of one tiny whistling frog that was very close, and may have even been in the room. They had heard the whistling frogs in Barbados, and had thought that they were birds, until someone had explained that they were never seen or heard in the daytime but as soon as it was dusk the frogs joined the buzzing chorus and the clicking of crickets. And now there was the whine of mosquitos that were attracted by the lamp, which buzzed around their heads and whined in their ears, and they got plenty of exercise frantically brushing them away.

Jonah had thoughts of termites, which he was sure would be quietly gnawing away at the wooden hut, and the hundreds of other unknown jungle creatures that lurked out there. There was no doubt the night was alive. Trees creaked and swayed and leaves rustled, but there was no breeze; it was small rodents unseen that scaled the branches in search of food, and although there was a stillness their ears were pricked for the slightest sound. It was like being in an eerie no-man's-land cut off from the outside world.

Henry broke into the uneasy silence by saying that the dinner was ready, and they followed him past the bedrooms and out of the back door onto the wooden walkway, which apparently went right around the hut. A flight of wooden steps led down into the clearing; the sound of the night creatures was even louder here, and seemed like one continuous buzz. Bats, silhouetted against the dark night sky, swooped from tree to tree; Rani was cooking and smoke rose high above the trees, and the aroma of sizzling steak and jacket potatoes filled the night air, arousing their taste buds.

They took their places at the table that was laid, much to their surprise, with a snow-white cloth, sparkling cut glass and silver. Henry poured the red wine from a glass decanter. The food was delicious. They started with a shrimp cocktail; this cheered them up and they chatted happily, enjoying more wine as they sat under a midnight-blue, star-studded sky with a pale moon that turned the trees to a soft shade of pale grey. The humidity was high and the night so still that nothing seemed real; it could have been a film set, magically romantic with one haunting hollow bird call, possibly the last of the night as the birds settled cosily in their nests until the dawn broke again. They'd had a lot of travelling, they were tired and, for the first time that day, they all felt relaxed.

Ed was taking a few night-vision shots. 'Do you ever go into the jungle?' he asked Henry.

'No, sir.' Henry grinned, very assured and shaking his head firmly. 'There are parts of the jungle that have never been explored. It's too dangerous; just behind these trees there are jaguars and cheetahs.'

'*What?*' Amber jerked upright in her chair, remembering Elliot saying there would be no wild animals. This brought them all back to reality.

'Do you ever see them?' Steve sounded disbelieving, although he seemed afraid now to take his eyes off the trees.

'Yes, sometimes.' Henry nodded.

'But aren't you scared having a barbecue, with all this smoke and the smell of food cooking?' Louise looked amazed.

Henry looked at Rani and shook his head, a bit bewildered, as if he didn't understand the question. 'No.'

Amber thought that he and Rani had never given it a thought that animals might be attracted by the smell of food. She stared into the trees, watching for the slightest movement and hoping that someone had a gun.

They finished their drinks; the conversation had almost died, and all eyes were on the trees, and the tropical evening was not so magical or romantic any more.

It was about nine o'clock, and they made their way up the stairs and back into the hut, thanking both Henry and Rani for a delicious meal, and wondering and discussing amongst themselves where all the food came from. They sat in the open sitting room; the hurricane lamp was not bright enough for them to read, and so they all decided the best thing would be to go to bed.

Jonah and Louise said goodnight, and Amber also followed them to her room that was just next door, saying goodnight to Steve and Ed. Pillows and blankets had been left folded on the armchair and the sofa. They tossed for the sofa; Ed lost.

Ed was putting two armchairs together when they were surprised by an old man coming in through the front door; he said that he was taking the hurricane lamps and leaving them each a torch. He walked through the living room and tapped on Jonah's door and gave them a torch and asked for the hurricane lamp, and then moved on to Amber's door, leaving her with a torch. Saying goodnight, he left quietly with the lamps by the back walkway, down past the barbecue. No one knew where he had come from; they had not seen him during the day. Amber looked over the three-foot fence in her room and saw him disappearing into the night.

Steve and Ed didn't undress; still in their shorts and T-shirts, they switched off the torches. Steve closed the front door. Ed, in a half-lying-down and half-sitting-up position, couldn't get comfortable; Steve was now lying down, his long legs still resting on the floor, the sofa so small and thin, the seating hard. The pale moon sent shadows through the open window frames, and apart from the noise of the insects outside and the whining of a mosquito that Steve brushed several times from his ear, all was still. Although he couldn't see them above him, the ants walked on. Then suddenly there was a bloodcurdling scream that had both men on their feet in an instant and Jonah rushed out of the bedroom door. All three men looked at each other in the shadowed torch beams as Amber came flying out of her bedroom, wearing a pink satin and lace negligee, her hair tied up with a pink satin ribbon, and bumped into all three of them with some force.

'There's a, er, er,' – breathless whisper – 'a spider!' It was a fearful cry, her breath puffing as if she had run a mile.

Ed and Steve exchanged glances, with a twitch of their lips and matching *Oh, my God* expressions. Ed went back to the armchairs, giving Steve a *you deal with it* sort of look, and Jonah went into his bedroom and closed the door, leaving Steve standing there and Amber pale with fear. Her mouth was still open and her hands tightly clasped up under her chin as she stood aside and Steve went into her room.

'Where is it?' he asked.

Amber, close behind him, gestured very nervously at the six glass panels on the door. 'There!' She was pointing to the bottom glass panel near the door handle.

Steve shone his torch, and there, filling the whole of one glass panel, was an enormous spider. It was greyish in colour, its body as big as the palm of a man's hand and its legs as thick as fingers; even Steve took a step backwards. Not knowing quite what to do, he took off one of his trainers and lashed out at it, and it jumped across the room, flying through the air at them both. Steve gave a loud gasp and Amber squealed in fright as the spider hit the floor at Steve's feet and ran away across the room at great speed. It shot under the bed, and it was so big they could hear its eight legs tapping on the floor.

Amber's eyes were wide with fear, and she wrapped her arms around herself, trying to stop herself from shaking and falling apart. 'Where did it go?' It was a terrified breathless squeal.

'Dunno.' Steve had a queasy feeling in his stomach; he wasn't afraid of spiders, but this was something else. He was shining the torch around the floor and under the bed, but they saw nothing, 'It probably went out and over that fence.' He nodded in the darkness. 'You'll be all right now.'

He knew she was frightened, but turned saying, 'Good night. Get some sleep. We've all had a long day.' He inclined his head. 'And tuck that mosquito net in tight; you...' He was about to say, *You don't want it crawling in beside you*, and then thought better of it. 'Good night,' and he left, closing the door quietly.

Amber stood holding the torch, frozen to the spot.

'She all right?' Ed's voice came out of the shadows as Steve's torch beam flashed around the living room.

'Yeah! It was certainly big, though.' Steve grinned. 'Biggest I've ever seen, legs thick as your fingers.'

'Yeah.' Ed grinned and chuckled silently in the darkness, not believing a word of it. And just at that moment Amber opened the bedroom door again.

'Steve,' she squealed anxiously, a nervous tremor in her voice, 'come quick, there's another one!'

Steve, just about to sit down on the sofa and slip out of his trainers, started back, and Ed got up and followed him. And there on another glass panel was another huge spider; this time it was black and very hairy. Ed saw it in the torchlight. He didn't like spiders anyway, but agreed with Steve: this was something else, an animal, and something that he would rather not deal with. He walked away, leaving Steve to deal with it again.

Steve was a bit more cautious this time; he didn't want it to fly at him again. He went as close as he dared and cautiously opened the door, and then banged the torch on the panels, hoping the huge spider would run up the door and outside, but it didn't; it ran up the door and up the wall and up into the rafters. Amber, standing back, froze, knowing that Steve could not reach it.

'You'll have to leave it,' he said. 'It won't hurt you.' Although he was a bit uneasy and hoped he was right.

He was about to go, shining the torch once more around the room and up onto the rafters. It was still there. The light made it run a few steps and then it stopped right over the top of the bed.

'Oh, don't go, Steve, please, please don't go! I'm scared!'

'It'll be OK. Get to bed; it can't get under the mosquito net.' Then he wished he hadn't said that.

'Steve!' She was breathless and tearful. 'Please don't go.' She had a hand on his arm, begging him; her face in the torchlight was pained and really scared.

'Well, what do you want me to do, stay the night?' After all the animosity and bitterness towards him that there had been during the last year, the last thing he ever thought she would ask *him* to do was stay the night!

'Y-y-yes! Yes! Please, Steve. Well, not really, it's not really what I want, but I'm dead scared. *Pleeease*, Steve.' It was a tearful cry.

He felt like saying, *Get on with it*, but knowing she was dead scared, perhaps he should stay. He felt a bit uneasy himself, but he poked his head out of the door. 'Good night, Ed.'

Ed sat up again as the torchlight flashed across the room and hearing the bedroom door close, he grinned. *Some guys get all the luck.* Then he reached for his torch and moved over onto the sofa. He was tall; the sofa was short. He put a pillow under his legs and his knees hung out over the arm of the sofa. It was most uncomfortable, but still, it was better than sleeping in there with the big spiders; he didn't fancy that.

Amber stood in the shadows holding her pink satin nightdress up above her ankles and taking deep breaths, her heart racing. The last thing she ever wanted was to have Steve Salvettini again in her bed, but it would be better than staying alone in this room with an enormous spider overhead. What would she do if it dropped? *But spiders don't usually drop, do they?* She shone the torch up. 'It's gone! But where's it gone?'

Steve grimaced, looking around; it had gone! He flipped his hand out haphazardly and the torch flashed around the walls. 'OK, OK! Do you want me to go or stay?'

'Erm, er, I, I don't know, I...' She shrugged her shoulders. 'I don't know. Yes!'

'Yes *what*?' he said with irritation.

'No!' She sniffed back fearful tears. 'Where's it gone?'

They both shone the torches, but saw nothing. Amber was frozen to the spot; afraid to even move, she stood there, torch in one hand and the other holding the pink satin nightdress clamped tightly above her knees. One enormous spider was enough, but now there were two...

'Get into bed,' said Steve irritably. 'You'll be OK. And I'll tuck the mosquito net in tight.'

She walked cautiously across the floor, shining the torch and watching her every step, shivering in the humidity from head to toe, then quickly slipped out of her sandals and under the net, glad to get her feet off the floor. He tucked the net in tightly. She lay very still with her eyes wide, shining the torch through the net up onto the ceiling; she could see nothing through the net but knew there were many

101

wooden strutted beams, and it could be hiding in any crevice anywhere.

'Close your eyes, and get some sleep! *Good night!*' He walked out, closing the bedroom door with a firm click.

The flashlight came across the living room, and Ed sat up. 'Christ! What *now*? We ever gonna get any sleep? He moved over to the two armchairs again, settling himself down. 'We have enough trouble with *her* during the day; we can do without it all night! Did you catch the ruddy thing?'

'No!' Steve sat and started to slip out of his trainers.

The bedroom door opened again and a splash of torchlight went around the living room and Amber's voice came out of the shadows. 'Steve.'

He stood up, with a quick and annoyed intake of breath though his teeth, seething. 'Yeah? What *now*?' He went back to the bedroom. 'You want me to *stay*?'

It was a tearful breathless, 'Yes! Yes, *pleeease*, please,' a desperate whisper.

Steve slammed the bedroom door, and she reluctantly got back into bed, and he tucked the mosquito net in tight again. 'Turn the light out, and get some sleep; it won't hurt you.'

She switched off the torch, and in the shadow of pale moonlight coming in over the low fence and through the mosquito net she saw him take off his shorts and hang them on the nail on the wall, and then the mosquito net was being lifted and, although it was dark, she felt his strong and bronzed body slip in beside her. She automatically moved away from him. 'Don't you dare touch me!'

'Lady! *All* I want is to sleep! I'm *exhausted*!' It went quiet. 'But what do you want me to do, if a spider is already in here?'

'*What?* It isn't, is it?' She sat bolt upright; her eyes were wide and scared. 'Oh, don't, Steve! *Don't!* You don't know how scared I am! You said it can't get in.'

'Well, how do you know it didn't creep in while you were calling me? How do you know one didn't get tucked in during the day when someone must have made this bed up? How do you know there's not a small gap in this net? Perhaps it's in here now, and it can't get out. It's probably frightened of *you*. I know I am.' He twitched his lips.

'Oh! Don't! Don't!' she squealed, switching on the torch again.

'Better to turn off the light; it might attract them. Better to not know. It'll go away in the dark.'

She hoped he was right. She switched off the light and slid down onto the pillow, away from him, and lay with her eyes wide staring into the semi-darkness.

Steve put his hands up behind his head, his elbows spread wide across the pillow, and grinned into the darkness. He didn't relish the thought that one of those hairy beasts might be in the bed, but what could they expect here in the jungle? As long as it was just a spider. What if a cheetah should jump up over that fence? It didn't bear thinking about; he tried to dismiss it from his mind... but at least the bed was more comfortable than the small sofa. 'You OK?'

'I don't like this!' Her normal disgruntled tone came back.

'Oh, come on, it's like old times.'

'*Not! Quite!* Don't you dare touch me!'

'Well,' he said, raising his eyebrows, 'you'll probably touch me if there's a spider in here. You can sleep with them alone if you like.' He felt her shiver; he grinned. 'I know it's scary; would you like me to put my arm around you?'

'*No! No!* Don't you dare touch me!' She turned her back on him, wishing he would ignore what she said and put his arm around her anyway... she waited but he didn't.

All went quiet and he lay listening to the sounds of the night. Since their break-up, she had hated him, and their bedroom scenes had now been with technicians and close-up camera shots all around them. He smiled at the thought. On film it all looked very convincing, but when he'd kissed her, she *had* kissed him back, and it had made him wonder.

Well... he'd really had a heck of a year with her and her fussy and fastidious ways, but he had to admit it did add a bit of spice to life. He supposed it *had* been enjoyable, and much better than her hating him for something that was not his fault. They'd had a lot of publicity over the break-up; he supposed that any publicity was good, but...

Anyway, together, the quiet time out of the limelight had been fun, but whether he would want to go through it all again he didn't know. He wasn't even sure if it was love; they liked each other a lot, and they had got along happily, but, had they got married, he wondered just how it would have worked out. The press were still hoping and waiting for the big day, which of course would never come, but he was sure it wouldn't have lasted long. Who could really live with *Amber* anyway?

The break-up had not been his fault, and nothing had actually happed with the young actress Dulcie Shand; he had been quick to realise just what was going on, but the photographer had been quicker, getting his best and most convincing shots, and it had all happened in a second. Trying to explain it to an irate Amber was impossible. He'd admitted to having had a few drinks, and he shouldn't have been so easily led, and he shouldn't have been in her bedroom anyway.

It had all happened when the girl, Dulcie Shand, could not get home from a party and he had offered her a lift. He had not intended to go to her room, but she was drunk and could hardly stand and he felt he couldn't just leave her. He had carried her into her apartment and was putting her on the bed when she suddenly put her arms around his neck, pulling him down onto the bed, and kissed him. He also was a little unsteady on his feet from the party wine and had toppled on top of her, and the photographer that she had hired was there flashing the camera. Realising he'd been duped, Steve had jumped up and walked out, calling her a few well-chosen words; the girl and the photographer's laughter could be heard down the hall. She was obviously not as drunk as she had pretended to be.

The next day it was splashed over the papers, and Amber was in a fury. But what had happened in a matter of seconds, he had to admit, did look like a tryst; the girl, wearing a strapless evening gown, had looked from the angle of the photograph as if she were naked. He didn't want a break-up with Amber and tried to explain, but he couldn't blame her for thinking the worst. It had just happened. He should have been wise to the unforeseen deception. And the young actress never got the publicity that *she* was hoping for anyway.

His thoughts came back to the mosquito net and hoping that there was not a very small gap where some creepy crawly could get in; a mosquito was obviously more dangerous than a giant spider. He eventually dozed off.

It was in the early hours of the morning he was awoken by Amber shaking him. 'I want to go to the bathroom,' she said, 'and you will have to come with me; I'm not going out of that door alone.'

Steve good-naturedly sat up, blinking his eyes in the pale shadowed moonlight that streamed in over the low fence, then taking the torch from under his pillow. He pulled at the mosquito net that was tucked well in under the mattress and swung his long legs out, reaching with his toes for his trainers, then went round and pulled the mosquito net out from Amber's side of the bed. She got up, quickly grabbing her satin dressing gown from the nail on the wall. Steve froze, waiting for the scream that would wake the whole household on seeing the huge spider run up the wall, away from the movement of the pink satin; it made him cringe. Luckily she didn't see it. He kept the torchlight down as she slipped into her flat sandals.

He flashed the torchlight around the door with the six glass panels; there was no sign of spiders, and they both stepped out onto the wooden walkway. The pale moon gave little light across the clearing, but the trees loomed up like great monstrous grey shadows against the dark night sky that was studded with a million stars; the setting could have been quite romantic under different circumstances. He held the torch low and glanced at his watch; it was three fifteen.

Even though there was no one else to hear or wake – they were here in the jungle clearing on their own – Amber whispered, giving him very precise instructions in her demanding manner to shine the light around the toilet, and then to keep it low, and discreet, as she did not intend to fully close the door. He stood waiting, keeping the light down, with the door just ajar. And then, sensing a movement, he turned, quickly shining the light and seeing the tail end of a snake going around the corner of the walkway; it made his heart beat fast, just as Amber screamed out, 'Keep the light on here; it's pitch dark!'

Amber came out of the bathroom all of a flutter, and he apologised but said nothing about the snake.

He decided that while he was up and out here he would also use the toilet, and she took over his role, keeping the torchlight low, with the door just ajar. It was deathly quiet, too quiet, except for the buzz of insects, and even that had calmed down a bit. She peered hard into the darkness of the trees, wondering if those cheetahs and jaguars might quietly be lurking in the undergrowth; did she detect a movement or was it imagination?

Suddenly leaves on a nearby tree rustled; she jumped and shivered in the humidity, but then realised it was probably a bird. Or maybe the light had disturbed a rat. That also made her shiver.

Every sense of her being was alert and on edge; her eyes were wide, staring into the darkness. She slowly turned the torch just as Steve was coming out and suddenly a great *pang* went through her head, as an enormous black hairy spider was caught in the torch beam; it was on the door and far too close to her head. She jerked back with a loud gasp and a silent scream in her throat as Steve pushed the door open almost in her face. '*Oh!* Did you see it? Did you see it?'

He thought she was referring to the snake. 'Yes, but it's gone now.'

'No, *no*! It's there on the door. Oh, it's gone again! It's *gone*!'

Realising she had seen another spider and she was again in panic, he took her by the arm, encouraging her back into the bedroom. He then had thoughts that the snake could have slithered in here as they had left the door open. He flashed the light discreetly around the floor and into the dark corners; nothing moved, all was quiet, but then snakes didn't make a noise, did they? He had seen it disappear around the corner of the walkway; it wouldn't have come back. But then it might, or could it have slithered over the low fence? He dismissed the thought.

Amber stood in the shadows, holding her pink satin nightdress up above her knees again in fear; he wasn't exactly happy about the situation himself. She kicked off her sandals and got quickly back into bed, and he tucked in the mosquito net, which they had left loose while going outside. Then another thought struck him, and he quickly and discreetly flashed the torch around the inside of the mosquito net. He saw nothing, but a shiver went through his body; could a spider have got into the bed? They certainly were giants. He dismissed that thought again very quickly; the more he thought about it, the more creepy everything became. He got back into bed beside Amber, feeling uneasy and shining the torch around the inside of the net again. Spiders didn't make a noise either, did they?

'I'm scared.' Her voice came out of the dimness. 'Say one of them got in here while we were outside?'

'No, impossible, I tucked the net in. And they are more scared of *you*. Even I'm scared of you!' He smiled. 'They won't hurt you, anyway.' Hoping that he was right, he shone the torch around the inside of the net once more. 'No, there's nothing!'

He switched off the torch. The moon gave a pale silvery glow across the rafters that were not clear through the net, but apart from the buzz of the insects outside all was quiet.

Then came a loud scratching and crunching noise. Amber sat up quickly. 'What's *that*?'

'Dunno, something outside.'

'No, no, it's in here.' Her eyes were wide and she scanned the dimness of the room through the net.

He switched on the torch; the crunching stopped. 'It's outside.'

'Is it?' She lay down again, and the scratching crunching started again; it kept on. It seemed as if it was coming from under the bed. Amber's eyes were wide, staring into the darkness; she lay dead still, but he could feel the tension coming from her. It made him feel uneasy too; it sounded so close. But they both eventually drifted off to sleep.

Steve was up early, showered and shaved. As he opened the six-panelled glass door Amber stirred, in her usual sleepy manner, opening her eyes to bright sunlight and closing them again; Bessie was not there... and then she suddenly realised where she was. She scanned the mosquito net; she missed her pink satin sheets, and Delilah was not there either with her breakfast tray. She sat up with a start as Steve smiled and said, 'Good morning.'

She could see through the mosquito net that he was dressed in a clean white T-shirt that clung tightly to his wide and powerful shoulders and broad robust chest. He looked very virile, his handsome face clean-shaven, his jaw square; the strong muscled arms were suntanned and dark against the white shorts, as were his long, strong and sturdy muscled thighs. She felt her heart leap. How could she have turned so bitterly from this handsome brute? She loved him. How could she treat this man with such contempt? All men had a fling. She could try to make it up to him, but would he want it now? She knew for the last year she had been a pain...

She yawned, daintily patting her mouth with her long red fingernails – it was right out of some film that she had made in the past – and asked sleepily and sexily, 'What's the time?'

He, as handsome as he was, was a no-nonsense guy; he looked at his watch. 'Six fifteen. Gonna be a nice hot and sunny day!'

He left the room. Through the net she watched him go, and sighed, 'Oh, so handsome.'

Steve found Ed in the living room, sitting on the sofa, and raised his eyebrows. 'Morning. Get a good night's sleep?'

'Morning.' Ed nodded wearily, sitting with his elbows on his knees and rubbing his hands through his thick brown curly hair as if he'd been on a boozy binge. 'What a bloody night. Didn't sleep a wink. There's a snake in here somewhere.'

110

'Snake?' Steve looked around quickly, surprised to see it curled up in the far corner. 'It's over there.' He stood very still. The snake didn't move, and then Steve edged very slowly to the door and opened it wide. The warm sunshine streamed in and the snake must have felt the warm air, and they stood now shoulder to shoulder and holding their breath, watching as it slowly uncurled and slithered around the far side of the room, quite oblivious to them, and then went out and slithered down the steps and was gone.

They both let out a breath. 'Probably couldn't get out,' said Steve.

'Thanks.' Ed sounded most grateful. 'I wanted to open the door but I was afraid to move. I heard it slithering around in the night; don't know how it got in. I shone the torch, and it reared its head. I just stayed dead still, I was afraid to bloody move, but I did get a couple of shots of it.' He smiled.

'Well, I'd rear my head if you flashed the camera at me in the middle of the night.' Steve had a comical smirk. 'Probably came through the window.'

'But it couldn't have slithered up the wall?'

'Who knows? We had one slithering around the walkway about three o'clock this morning.'

'How d'you know?'

'We've been awake all night with the bloody spiders. I hope Elliot gets here today, and we can get this damn film finished and over.'

Ed nodded; his thoughts were that if the snake had come through the window, it must have slithered right over him. He felt a cold shiver run down his back.

Amber pulled out the mosquito net and stuck her legs out of the bed, scanning the whole room before putting her feet down on the floor, and then pulled her sandals nearer with his toes and stuck her feet in them quickly. She stood up and took the pink satin dressing gown off the nail on the wall, turning it and inspecting it before putting it on. Then before opening the six-panelled glass door she checked every square, the wall and the rafters; no spiders, *but where were they?*

All was quiet except for the distant hollow bird calls, and the sun was very hot as she made her way across the wooden walkway to the bathroom hut. She opened the door very cautiously, checking it for spiders after last night, and then peered in. The hut, or more like garden shed, was darkish; there were no windows, but thin shafts of sunlight shone in through gaps in the rush roof and ill-fitting wooden walls. She went in, a bit reluctant to close the door, but of course she had to. Still, she didn't lock it; there was no reason for anyone to come in.

Luckily yesterday after breakfast, before leaving the house in Barbados, she had cleaned her teeth, and popped the toothbrush and paste into her silver tote bag. She cleaned her teeth again now, not daring to swallow any of the brown water, and pulled a face at the dry iron taste. Last night with the spiders, the last thing she had thought about was her teeth.

Then she ran the shower; it poured out like black coffee. There was no shower curtain; it was just open with a rough concrete floor and a one-brick-high surround to keep the water in. The water pressure was low but it was hot, warmed by the sun. There was no shower gel and she used the bar of soap instead. She had to admit that she did feel better for a shower.

There were two white towels hanging on a rail; Steve had used one. She took the other one and wrapped it around her; it was a medium size, not a bath towel like she was used to, but it was clean.

She was about to step out of the shower, over the brick surround onto the wooden boarded floor, when she saw long black hairy legs coming from a crack in the wooden post at the top left-hand side of the door frame. She froze! Holding her breath and gripping the towel tightly around her and standing dead still, every nerve in her body tense. She had to get out of here, but how? The door was shut, and she had to pass the spider, and there was no one to come to her aid.

She moved very, very slowly towards the door, keeping well to the right, which was still too close, and still holding her breath, trying to pluck up the courage to pass it. Then, as if sensing her movement, two of the black hairy legs lifted up as if waving good morning and then retreated back to bed in the narrow crevice. She stepped forward cautiously, pushing the door open very carefully with no jerky movements, hoping that it wouldn't jump at her like the spider had done at Steve last night; she then pushed the door wider and stepped outside very gingerly and very quickly, gripping the towel tightly around her as if it could protect her from this savage beast. She stood dead still as if waiting for the attack; a cold shiver ran right through her body but nothing happened. Then she took a deep breath, and even though she was petrified she just couldn't resist taking a peek through the narrow gap where it had gone.

'*No!*' She gasped out loud, stepping back as a pang went through her heart and she shivered, seeing two of the brightest eyes like mini torch beams shining out at her. She ran across the walkway and back into the bedroom, closing the door as if being chased. She stood like a statue staring at the door, every nerve in her body tight and tense, waiting any minute for the door to burst open. She gripped the towel tightly around her, her heart pounding in panic, until she very gradually began to relax, then remembered that she had left her pink satin nightdress and dressing gown in there hanging on a nail.

She peeped out of one of the glass panels, hoping that no one had seen her dash across the walkway with the small towel that didn't cover much, but there was nothing out there but jungle. She would get Steve to get her things later; there was no way she was going back in there to get them...

Makeup! she thought. She would have to go back into the bathroom to use the mirror, but she had nothing. *No!* She'd put some cream on her face from the small sample tube in her bag which she kept for air travel, enough for one application only, and she had a small hand mirror to just put a little shadow on her eyes from another small sample that wouldn't last more than another day. She couldn't replace the false eyelashes, and she had no mascara either. Even the lipstick was just an emergency sample that she'd never used, and even that was melting, and it would only possibly last a couple of days if she used it very sparingly.

And then she got into her shocking pink shorts again, and a clean skimpy white T-shirt which she took from her bag. There were several dresses and white trousers and high-heeled shoes that she knew she would never wear while she was here in the jungle. She wondered now why she had packed so much, but she *had* thought that there would be a restaurant nearby for the evenings; she'd never given a thought to real raw jungle.

She closed her bag tightly and zipped it up against any crawling things, and made her way out to the living room. There was no one there, but she could hear their voices and the laughter. She opened a door that was on the other side of the living room and there they all were, sitting at the table on a small open deck. Everyone looked up; the laughter died away at seeing Amber, without her heavy makeup and looking very plain.

'Morning!' It was a shy and sharp, feeble 'good morning'. She half-smiled, as everyone came out of the stunned silence, and there was a sort of jumbled, 'Good morning, Amber.'

They glanced at each other and got on with the meal. She felt uncomfortable; she felt naked. She took a seat at the far end of the table. Henry and Rani were there, and black coffee was poured and eggs and bacon put before her, a thing she would never dream of eating, but she said nothing and just got on with it, even to taking a slice of fresh white bread.

On the low fence that surrounded the small kitchen-dining room that was really only just big enough for the five of them to sit, two large blue parrots with bright yellow-orange chests waited for the slightest crumb, their mighty black and shiny claws rising and impatiently gripping the woodwork. Then they were joined by a toucan that fluttered down and landed on the fence beside them with a flapping of its heavy black wings, snapping its large bright orange curved beak open and shut with a loud hollow clapping sound. It was the first time that any of them had ever been so close to such birds in the wild, their sharp black and beady eyes watching their every move.

'I hear you didn't have a very good night,' said Jonah, glancing at Amber. 'Steve was just telling us about it.'

'Yes, what a night. We did hear you moving about.' Louise raised her eyebrows, the slightest grin just catching the corner of her mouth. She also was without her usual perfect makeup, but her black skin shone and looked perfectly natural. Again, looking at Louise, Amber felt inferior.

'Oh!' Amber's eyebrows rose, with the superior high-handedness again. 'I suppose that is what you were all laughing about? Well, yes, it was the spiders. I'm afraid of them and don't mind admitting it.' She didn't mention the little episode in the bathroom a few minutes ago. She lifted her chin with the same haughty arrogance as usual. 'And I'm so glad that Steve was there; they are enormous, aren't they, Steve?'

He bunched his lips with an intake of breath and nodded. 'Yeah!'

She went on, 'And then there was this terrible scratching and scraping under the bed.'

Jonah, Louise and Ed looked at each other with a kind of silent titter.

But Steve was serious. 'Well, I must say it was pretty scary and these things are big.'

Henry, who was about to pour more coffee for Louise, smiled at Amber. 'They are only house spiders; they won't hurt you, and the scratching that you describe was most probably a spider eating a cockroach.'

Amber snapped down her knife, her mouth open with an intake of breath, her eyes wide with alarm as she looked around the table at them all. At the sudden clatter of the knife one of the parrots jumped up and down, flapping its large blue wings, and squawked as if laughing. Amber looked wide-eyed at Steve; he also felt a jolt at the thought of a spider eating a cockroach. And it had also stopped the others in their tracks. They looked at each other with alarm, and the parrot jumped up and down again and squawked as if in fits of laughter. They all turned to look at it, and smiled; it broke the tension.

'They certainly are enormous.' Steve inclined his head.

'Also,' Henry added, 'I should warn you not to get up in the night and put on your shoes. Spiders and scorpions like to sleep in them.'

Amber looked quickly at Steve; again, he drew in a quick breath, thinking how he had stuffed his feet into his trainers, and Louise scrunched up her toes under the table.

'Oh' Henry added, 'and don't clean teeth in the tap water; use a bottle.'

This time they all looked at each other.

'*Well*,' said Ed, 'I wouldn't mind just having a shower.' He raised his eyebrows. 'In fact, I wouldn't mind a *bed* either.'

'I'm sorry, I'll arrange it this morning. I'll bring a bed up from the village,' said Henry. 'Tonight, you sleep upstairs, but you will have to share a bathroom with someone.' He lifted his dark eyes. 'I'm sorry, we were only expecting four people.'

'But there should have been fourteen of us,' said Ed. 'Two had to go back. What about the other hut?'

Henry was shaking his head and looking a little sheepish. 'Not furnished.'

Louise and Amber exchanged glances, and Amber blew air down her nose, her lips bunched in anger, thinking that she would give Elliot a piece of her mind when he got here. 'Well, *when* Mr Stirling gets here, he'll come with the crew of twelve, so the other hut will be needed.'

'OK.' Henry scratched his head, looking a little puzzled and wondering now where he was going to get twelve beds in just a day or two.

Louise knew how Amber felt; it wasn't easy being here in the jungle, the glamour gone. She knew how Amber felt without her makeup. She herself liked to use makeup every morning; she felt naked without it. She also liked to wear nice clothes, but she wasn't so flamboyant with her style as Amber. Showering in Coca-Cola water was enough to make any woman cringe, and with the insects buzzing and biting, and snakes slithering around, it wasn't a very happy situation, but a spider scratching on the floor and eating a cockroach was something else; it made her shiver inside. She would get Jonah to take a closer look around their bedroom tonight.

After breakfast, they spent two hours reading the script and rehearsing their lines. They had hoped that Elliot would come, but Henry had assured them that there would be no boat today. There was nothing much to do and so they settled down to just read; there were a few out-of-date magazines on a small table in the corner of the living room. All was quiet for a while, and then Louise stood up, lifting long dark hair from the back of her neck and saying how hot it was; she needed some air. She walked to the front door and went down the steps.

Soon after, Amber went to the front door; she couldn't believe her eyes, seeing Louise swimming in the river. She turned to Jonah. 'Louise is *swimming*? In that *dirty brown water*!'

Henry, who was sweeping the floor, looked up. 'Oh, it's not dirty, mistress, it's very clear. It gets its colour from the leaves on the river bed.'

'But swimming! In *there*?' Amber was aghast, frowning at him.

He smiled. 'It's safe.'

Jonah said nothing; satisfied with Henry's assurance, he went back to the script he was reading through. Amber stood for a minute and then went back to the bedroom for her sunglasses; the bed had been neatly made up and the mosquito net tucked in. Her eyes swept around the walls, the floor, the rafters. Rani was sweeping the floor in the hallway. She had to admit that although primitive, it was clean, *but* it could have been better if the birds had not messed on the backs of the chairs in the living room, and the inch-long ants would not crawl up the walls, and cockroaches would not scamper across the floor, and the *spiders*! Well, there was no answer to *that*!

She glanced around at the bare woodiness of the room, just the bed and a laundry basket, no furniture. Even with the sunlight flooding in over the three-foot fence the thought of the spiders in the night made her shiver, knowing that they were hiding somewhere there. She felt that this was an animal kingdom and humans were not welcome, but there was nothing that they could do.

She put on her sunglasses and came back through the living room, the men all quietly reading, Ed with an outdated magazine and a cigarette. She went to the front door; the scorching heat of the sun hit her. She sauntered down the wooden steps. A pathway had been cut through the long brown parched grass down to the river; halfway down the pathway to her right the grass swayed with a hissing sound, as a snake unseen slithered through the grass. She stopped dead, afraid to move, holding her breath and waiting any minute for it to strike; she hoped that it was slithering away and not towards her. All seemed quiet. She moved on very cautiously a few more steps, and then to her left the same thing happened, and she stopped dead again, her heart still racing. She swallowed hard, not daring to move, waiting again until all seemed quiet, then moved on down cautiously, taking one slow step at a time to the river's edge.

Louise was in the middle of the river, splashing about and calling to her, 'Come in, it's lovely!'

She would have loved to have gone in, feeling the hot sun blazing down on her fair skin, and wished that they had some suntan cream, but it had all been lost in Louise's stage makeup bag. Even a hat would have protected her fair skin.

Although cool, the water was red-brown in colour. There was not a ripple apart from Louise splashing, but who knew what lurked deep down beneath it? Her thoughts were that Louise was either brave or stupid.

'Come in, it's really cool.' Louise's voice echoed back as if she were in a tunnel.

Amber shook her head; the Coca-Cola water didn't look inviting, and the thought of what might be lurking deep down made her cringe. Yesterday they had seen a crocodile. Yes! What *was* lurking in those deep brown depths?

She stood for a while watching Louise, the sun hot on her shoulders. There were large logs at the river's edge, and after looking for anything crawling, she decided to sit down, dabbling her feet in the cool water. It was great, but she felt nervous.

Louise was still trying to coax her to come in, but Amber shook her head, then, feeling an itch on her legs, found the log was now crawling with ants. She stood up quickly, frantically brushing down her shorts and her legs, and then turned, hearing a shushing sound, and saw the body of a huge snake slithering across the pathway. She froze. Only its middle section was visible, its head in the long dry grass as it moved to the right, the back end of its body hidden in the long grass on the other side of the path; it seemed to take some long minutes and gradually disappeared, and she breathed again.

She then turned back to the river and Louise, and as she turned, she saw a large snake, just a few yards from her, lying flat out on top of the water close to the bank. It must have been about twelve feet long; she didn't measure it. It stayed very still, but her thoughts were that with Louise splashing about it might move.

She turned, calling excitedly to Louise to come out and pointing towards the snake. Louise called back, 'No, it's great; you come in.'

Amber felt in a frozen state; what if the snake suddenly dived and Louise was attacked? What could she do?

She was relieved to see that Louise was now swimming towards her, but the danger was still there. Amber was holding her breath until Louise finally reached the logs and came out onto the bank, grabbing her wrap and brushing off ants. Amber was pointing to the snake; it hadn't moved. As they walked back up the pathway, more snakes slithered away into the grass; they froze wide-eyed before moving on, and were glad to reach the steps of the hut, Amber telling Louise about the one that had crossed the path.

When they mentioned the snakes to Henry and asked whether it was safe to swim, he grimaced. 'Well, *we* swim there,' he said. 'Snakes love to lie in the sun. I guess it's cooler in the water.' It didn't answer the question of whether it was safe to swim, but Louise said she would not go swimming again.

In the afternoon after lunch, arrangements were made to take them up the river by canoe; they were to visit a village where Henry and Rani lived.

The canoe came into the V-shape in the bank, where they had first arrived. The young boatman, whose name was Cappy, steadied it as it rocked a bit dangerously as they all clambered in one after the other, Ed being the last as he was busy filming.

With the weight of them all seated, the canoe was very low in the water, and with Rani and Cappy at either end paddling they set off down the calm river. They turned into a tree-covered canal that was quiet until the canoe disturbed the water, and then crocodiles were seen lying in wait with just their eyes peeping above the surface of the very still, inky black water. Louise and Amber exchanged anxious glances, and then one on the bank came in with a slithering splash. Louise cringed and glanced quickly at Amber again with fearful eyes, thinking that just a few hours ago she had been swimming not far away.

Ed, of course, was camera-happy as usual as one of the crocodiles opened its great jaws wide, and he got good shots of the colourful pink mouth and the vice-like teeth that shut with a snap. He also got some good shots of tropical birds, all so colourful, yellow and green, black birds with red heads and flashes of green. A bright blue parrot with a yellow breast, sitting on a branch, squawked and flapped giant wings; they didn't know if it was a pleasant greeting or angry because they were invading its space. And then a monkey jumped from a tree, and Ed got a quick shot before it disappeared under the greenery. Suddenly something moved in the undergrowth, and they all said, '*Ooooh*,' together. Cappy said it was a big animal, but none of them actually saw it clearly.

The trees above cleared and they were open to the sky again, and then pulled into a wider part of the canal with the red-brown Coca-Cola water. Moving on to a grassy clearing, they were surprised to see Henry there to greet them. The canoe was held steady as they stepped out into ankle-deep water and thick soft squelching mud. This of course was not to anyone's liking, but worse for Amber with her finicky ways, ruining her delicate rhinestone sandals. Still, there was no other way and of course she had to get over it.

Henry explained the excitement of the small Guyanese group that had now joined him; they were eager to greet the travellers as they rarely saw visitors. He then introduced them to his sister and some of his family and a group of excited children; they were ready with smiles and happy greetings and handshakes there on the riverside. The Guyanese all spoke English, so it was easy to understand their excitement, as they were all trying to say hello at once.

Although Henry's family had been to the capital, Georgetown, some of the villagers had never left the clearing. Others came running and were ready to join in with handshakes and welcome smiles, and Amber soon forgot about her muddy feet and the expensive flat sandals.

The whole group was now following them as they followed Rani, who was to show them around the village. Ed still followed with the video camera; this for him was a real treat and he didn't want to miss anything. Not that there was much to see; the village was just a grassy clearing with wooden huts dotted about and built up on stilts.

Rani led them up a wooden staircase and into one of the huts. They were very surprised to find a woman cooking with a flame about two feet high, and in a wooden hut; they couldn't believe their eyes. The woman turned, leaving the flame, and with a smile offered them mango juice in coconut shells. Amber twitched her lips and pulled a face, refusing and shying away, but Steve nudged her in the back and whispered, 'Take it.' She gave him a disdainful look, but then took the generous offer with a reluctant smile.

'It's good?' The woman nodded with a beaming smile.

Amber smiled – 'Yes, it's good' – but twitched her lips again. It wasn't the juice; it was the shell she didn't like.

The woman then gladly showed them around the small hut. Six of them lived here, her husband and four grandchildren; she pointed them out, three boys and a girl.

They were all kicking a football in the clearing with other children.

'Do they go to school?' asked Louise.

'Yes.' The woman smiled. 'My daughter is the schoolteacher. The school is over there.' She pointed.

'You only have the one room here?' Jonah looked around in surprise; it was a small house and was hardly big enough for six people. There were a few cushions on the rough flooring and a blanket of sorts, and a small board on four legs; he supposed it was a table.

The woman nodded and smiled, pleased to see Ed aiming the camera around her home and at the flames, about two feet high, still licking around the large black iron cooking pot; she seemed oblivious to the danger. 'Yes, just the one room,' she answered. 'We all sleep here.' She pointed to trunks of trees, the rough bark still on. With being used every night, they had now taken the curved shape of the bodies.

'Why do you only have fence-like walls?' Amber looked around her.

'It lets the air filter through,' said Rani. 'The wood draws the heat and there is no electricity for fans.'

'Well, aren't you afraid that wild animals might jump in at night?' Amber was thinking now of her own bedroom with the fence-like wall.

'Not really,' Rani answered. 'It does happen on very rare occasions but it doesn't really worry us, does it, Mamma? Oh, this is my mother.' He glanced around at them all. They all smiled as the woman turned from the flames again, still seeming quite unaware of the danger.

Ed was still filming as they all trooped back down the wooden stairs, thanking Rani's mother. And then they were following Rani, who took them to another hut up on stilts; this was the schoolroom, a small hut with about ten chairs around a wooden table. There were a few pictures pinned to the wooden posts, and there was a small blackboard on an easel. No books, no pencils, nothing.

'We have fourteen children in here every day,' said Henry's sister, whom they had met on the riverside; she had now joined them on their tour. 'But this morning, I gave them a day off because you were all arriving.'

'Oh, are you the schoolteacher, then?' Steve smiled.

'Yes.' She smiled back.

They came back down the stairs and moved on to another wooden hut on the ground level and just up five wooden steps. Rani explained that this was the local shop. It had a rush roof like all the houses and a fenced wall all around, a doorway but no door. There was a counter with shelves behind it; they were bare. He explained everything was locked away in cupboards.

The shop sold almost everything, they were told. There was plenty of food, but it all had to be kept in metal containers away from insects and wild animals; tins were displayed on the shelves only when the shopkeeper was there because the monkeys came in and stole the tins, and they had learned to slam the tins on sharp rocks or tree branches to get them open. Adam the shopkeeper was there every day, but not this morning.

Steve frowned. 'But where does all the food come from?'

'From the main town, Georgetown,' Rani said, 'across the river. Old Jago brings it up the canal twice a week; he's the boatman that brought you here.' They all nodded. And then Rani added that Adam the shopkeeper was there with him now, bringing in more supplies.

'And these villagers have *never* been across the river?' Jonah's voice rose enquiringly with a look of utmost surprise.

'No.' Rani inclined his head, a little sadly. 'Maybe only one or two. My mother, of course, studied in England, but rarely goes over to Georgetown; she's quite happy here, and so is my sister.'

'What about you?' asked Steve.

'Oh, Henry and I live in Georgetown; we teach in the school. We were both educated in England.'

'Oh, so the two of you met in England?' Steve raised his eyebrows knowingly.

Rani chuckled. 'We are brothers; there are four of us, three brothers and our sister Annette, who you have just met. We are all teachers. Our father sent us off to England to be educated. Both Father and Mother were educated in England.'

They all smiled; they had learned something. Rani then led them to the chapel, where they met Father Handley, a tall and kindly grey-haired man with medium-light skin. He had a gaunt long face and unusual green eyes, and with a brilliant smile he welcomed them warmly with handshakes all round. He showed them the chapel, which was lit with candles, another fire hazard. The chapel was quiet and peaceful in a grassy glade surrounded by palm trees, set back from the river, and just a short walk from the village. It was then that Rani explained that this was his father, and then the story came out that their grandmother had been English, and had met their Guyanese grandfather at university in Cambridge, and so the children and the grandchildren had all been sent to England to be educated.

'And you don't miss being in England?' said Louise, very surprised.

'No.' Father Handley smiled. 'We are very happy here; it's peaceful, without the worries of the world. The villagers need us, but we can leave any time we want to. We do leave the village on occasion, but we are not gone long and very pleased to get back.'

'But what do people do here?' Ed frowned. 'Do they work?'

'Oh, yes. We have quite an industry, in a small way, of course.' Father Handley smiled again. 'We have carpenters, metal workers, farmers that grow most of our vegetables; we have a few cows and goats and pigs. The women sew and embroider things like tablecloths and table napkins, pillow cases; we also have hand-woven carpets, and our products are sold in Georgetown. Some of our needlework and carpets are exported to the United States of America,' he said very proudly. 'Not much, of course, but everyone here is busy.'

They came away amazed, having now seen all there was to be seen, and made their way back down to the water's edge. This part of the river flowed gently, lapping at the grassy bank to become thick and muddy, and the river had a strong smell of damp greenery. Henry was already in the canoe. They paddled into the water, squelching through the soft thick mud again, Amber cringing with mud up over her ankles, and splashed into the canoe to take a seat. Rani then climbed in at the rear, and they set off.

The whole village and Cappy came to the water's edge, waving them goodbye with big smiles and calls of, 'Come back again soon!' The holy man Father Handley was there with an open prayer book and wishing them a safe journey, although it was only about half an hour's paddle away, but Amber thought they would need more than prayers, should the canoe capsize among the snakes and crocodiles along the way. She hadn't said anything, but being on the river and the canals did nothing for her nerves; it scared her each time and she held her breath, waiting any minute for something to happen. They were in the middle of the river; here the Coca-Cola water was calm, and as the canoe moved further away the villagers still waved. They knew that their visit had really made the village's day.

A mile or so up the river and they were back in the canal again with the overhanging trees shading them from the blazing sun; the canoe was low in the water with seven of them in it and there was no space for the snakes to fall in. Amber glanced up and shivered at the thought.

There was another canoe racing towards them; the black water seemed to ripple heavily away from the bow, as the four burly men were paddling fast. They were each naked apart from a loincloth; they all had straight black and shiny hair, cut short to their earlobes, and a square fringe. Ed, filming, said it reminded him of the start of *Hawaii Five-0*, which made them all laugh. The sharp pointed bow of their canoe parted the black treacle like a knife; the men waved an arm in greeting and without a smile as they swiftly went by, and they all waved back and smiled, then the inky black water seemed to close over and was once again still.

'They're fishermen,' said Henry.

'What?' Ed frowned heavily. 'In *this* water?'

'Yes,' Rani said, smiling, 'and they fish with spears like ancient warriors. But they fish mostly in the fast-running Demerara River, with nets to get the shrimp. Most of the Caribbean shrimp comes from the Demerara.'

'Really?' Amber grimaced with a frown, thinking that she wouldn't eat shrimp again. Suddenly there was another splash, as a crocodile slithered into the canal just a few yards from the canoe. Amber's mind went back to Father Handley's prayers, and all thoughts of the shrimp disappeared from her mind.

'It probably sounds strange to you, but some men even still use bows and arrows in the forest.' Henry smiled at the surprised look on all their faces.

Ed looked up. 'What do they hunt?'

'Wild boar; it feeds the whole village. Birds, monkey.' Henry sounded quite matter-of-fact, as if it was an everyday occurrence. And it most probably was; it was survival.

'I thought people didn't go into the jungle,' said Louise.

Henry smiled. 'Oh, they don't go in too deep.'

It was deathly quiet as they moved on slowly with just the soft sound of the paddles pushing the water away, then there was another splash and they all looked to the right.

'Do they come very near the boat?' Louise sounded nervous, not taking her eyes off the tail end of the crocodile.

'Oh, yes,' Henry answered, 'but they rarely attack. One did get into the village once, and took a boy.'

'Oh! How awful,' exclaimed Amber. 'I suppose there was nowhere to run to get away from it.'

'Oh, no.' Rani shook his head. 'It took him in the night. It crawled up the steps into a house.'

'Oh, my God!' Amber gasped, remembering Father Handley's prayers again. 'How old was he?'

Henry grimaced. 'Um, about fourteen, wasn't he, Rani?'

Rani nodded. 'Yeah, I think so. About that.'

Amber held her breath; she was not alone, and Louise also gasped, thinking with the animals here they were not safe, including the ever-moving ants, not to mention the mosquitoes.

The days dragged by slowly; they sat in the living room rehearsing the script on most days, and then read the old magazines over and over again. It was too hot to sunbathe, and too dangerous to swim, or even walk in the grass. The phones didn't work, so they were completely cut off, and life was becoming a bore.

CHAPTER SEVEN

It was three days before they had any word from Elliot. He had sent an email to the hotel in Georgetown where they had originally been booked to stay overnight after filming the jungle scenes and before returning to Miami. The email had been brought by Jago with the supplies. Steve read it out.

'Can't make it to the clearing, stay to end of week, leave Sunday, proceed to Riverside House, upstream. Will meet you there. Elliot.'

Steve and Jonah frowned at each other; of course they wanted to know where Riverside House was. Steve showed the email to Henry, who nodded and said that it was about forty-five minutes upriver and they would need Jago with the motorised boat; he would arrange it.

That evening they were to have another barbecue. The table was laid out the back in the clearing again with the snow-white cloth, the cut glass and the silver, as it was on their very first night.

They sat around the table, enjoying glasses of red wine and the delicious smell of steak grilling, the smoke rising high into the trees. It was all very romantic, sitting out under a velvet starlit sky. The food was good and the wine really kept their spirits up.

After Elliot's message they were eager to leave, but not knowing what to expect and having a few more days to endure the jungle living had made them all a bit subdued. They had discussed it several times, saying that it had been an experience, very different from what they had expected, and something they hoped they would never have to do again. They now knew the script back to front but had not put it to any action, and they were all ready to get back to work and civilisation, but, as Jonah reminded them, they had not yet done the jungle scenes, and that was why he was here. Perhaps Elliot had found another location for them.

'Or perhaps Elliot has cancelled them?' Steve flicked up his eyes. 'Perhaps you'll get paid for just being here on vacation.' He chuckled.

'Vacation?' Jonah laughed. 'Hmm, perhaps we'll all have to come back?' He raised his thick eyebrows, and twisted his lips comically.

'Hmph! I hope not! Some vacation,' Amber said, rolling her eyes, 'having to share a bed with *you!*'

Steve inclined his head. 'You can share it with the spiders alone if you like.'

There was a long pause, while Amber pressed her lips hard together, conjuring up pictures in her mind of her luxurious house and the beautiful pink satin sheets, the bathroom with her creams and sprays. Her face now felt tight and was red with the heat of the sun, and she had run out of small sample-sized tubes of face cream and night cream. The light was so bad in that shed she could hardly see to put on lipstick anyway, and sharing it with a giant spider who watched her every move was not at all comfortable; she also watched *its* every move, as it crept from its hideaway in the crevice of the door and spied on her with its bright shining eyes. It was nerve-racking, but she guessed they were getting used to each other; well, maybe the spider, whether he or she, was getting used to *her*, but she would never get used to *it*! The very thought made her cringe and sent a shiver down her spine. Steve was also invading her space, although she had to admit she *was* glad he was there. He didn't actually do anything, but at least she was not alone.

She glanced at her long red-painted fingernails, now chipped and one broken; it brought tears to her eyes after all the papering she'd had. She had always tried to be so perfect, not a hair out of place, but now her hair was lank; drained by the heat of the sun and having used soap and not shampoo, it was dull and sticky. She didn't know how she had survived without her creams, perfumes and sprays. She wondered if life would ever get back to normal; well, what she termed normal, anyway. She had not realised just what a luxurious life she'd had with Bessie there to organise everything and the staff fussing around her. She knew she had led them a merry dance, and vowed inwardly that when she got back – *if I ever get back, that is* – to what she termed *normal*, she would try to calm her ways.

If they could only see her now, slopping around in the same pair of shorts and T-shirt for the last three days, her delicate and expensive flat sandals caked in mud. She had no use for the beautiful designer dresses that Bessie had so carefully packed in tissue paper, and the shoes in soft shoe bags, all still packed in her zip-up hand luggage bag; she was even afraid to open it, in case any of those crawling creatures could get inside. She felt so miserable, tears welled in her eyes; she had gone from rags to riches, and now back to rags. Even Kitty Hawksenburge would never have looked like this. And she missed Bessie, and their beer and hamburgers, and the fun they used to have after the shows. She sniffed back the tears, and swallowed hard, turning her head away from the others, not wanting them to see her crying.

She would certainly give Elliot a piece of her mind! She knew it was not really Elliot's fault and she hoped that Stacey was all right. But Elliot had said the jungle scenes would only take about two days, and she had thought that at least there would have been somewhere she could dress for dinner; she certainly had not expected raw *jungle* like *this*! Well, none of them had, and they were all miserable anyway. None of them had expected to be here more than overnight. And now they were living like Tarzan and Jane, and *she* was sharing a bed with this, *this*... she couldn't think of a word to describe how she felt about Steve Salvettini.

Her lips still tight, she turned to him. 'I don't want to be with the spiders alone, but I certainly am *not* enjoying this situation!'

'Well, do you think I'm enjoying it? You're not the most desirable bed partner.'

Amber's mouth opened to say something.

Ed pursed his lips and butted in, with raised eyebrows. 'Why not take a turn on the couch? When I was down here I only saw a snake go round the room once – that was on the first night – but I haven't seen a spider. In the night I'm peeing over the walkway; I haven't even got a john. Plenty of mosquitoes, though.' He rubbed the angry red spots on his arms.

Amber bunched her lips tight together and took a deep breath, giving him a disdainful look. 'It is certainly *not funny*!'

Ed raised his eyebrows again, crinkling his forehead. 'It certainly ain't, *lady*; you're bloody right there. You weren't sleeping with the snake! And living with you two bloody bickering all the time is as much as any of us can take!'

She was lost for words, which was most unusual for her. Tears welled in her eyes again. She was hot and uncomfortable, she felt dirty, her skin was burning and when she got back, *if* she ever got back, makeup would have to do a really special job. She cringed at the sight of her nails, but how they had been chipped she didn't know; she'd done nothing since she had arrived, and she always took such care of them. It really upset her to break one, but what could she do, stuck here in the jungle? What could any of them do?

She wondered if Jane had had all these problems; she wondered now if the Tarzan stories had been inspired by something like this. And then wondered how they would be playing these scenes when Elliot got here, with no makeup and no lighting. She guessed that was what the jungle was all about anyway.

'Oh, when will we get out of this *hell*?' she suddenly blurted out.

Steve leaned across the chair, putting an arm around her shoulders. 'Oh, come on, Amber, it's only been a few days. It can't be helped. We are all in it together, none of us like it, but we have just got to wait now, just until Sunday when the boat comes in. Come on now, take it easy.' He squeezed her shoulder, trying to jolly her along.

She nodded, tight-lipped, and took a deep breath, knowing he was right, but she felt that inside she would burst with the tension. It was like being in an open prison; there was no way out. Now they had to wait until Sunday for the boat, not knowing where they would end up; it might even be just as bad. Tears welled in her eyes again and rolled down her cheeks; luckily no one could see them in the flickering candlelight.

It was just then that the old man who had come in every evening to take the hurricane lamps came running across the clearing with a shotgun in hand, shouting, 'Jaguar! Jaguar! Inside! *Inside!*'

Nobody moved; of course they were all startled and confused, not knowing what he was saying, and then it struck them: *jaguar?* They stood up from the table quickly, knocking chairs over and looking in all directions but seeing nothing in the darkness beyond the candlelight. And suddenly there was the glint of a shotgun in Henry's hand, and he was waving it at them to go up the steps, which they did with a rush. Ed had stood up with the others and moved from the table and then dashed back for his precious camera, which was under the table near his chair.

They were now all standing on the upper walkway alongside Amber's room, anxiously staring into the darkness; Henry and Rani, on the stairs, both had shotguns at the ready, the old man somewhere unseen. So far no one had seen anything. Then there was a movement in the trees, and in the shadows of the flickering candles, they saw a large dark shape appear, unclear against the darkness of the night. Then it stopped! Looked around to see if it was safe.

They held their breath. Jonah put an arm around Louise; he could feel her beside him shaking.

The great animal became a little clearer as it prowled into the light of the hurricane lamp that shone out from the barbecue. Its head was down and as it slinked cautiously across the clearing, coming nearer to the table, they heard a hushed growl. The eyes in the candlelight looked red.

A shot rang out; they heard a yelp. The sound echoed and whined through the trees, shattering the silence that seemed dense but for the massed hum of insects, and it made them all jump and their hearts pound, and then the silence fell again.

They watched with intense apprehension as the great animal sprang up onto the table and staggered a bit, obviously hurt; blood dribbled from its hind leg, but its great strong muscles rippled under a black and shiny coat. Its huge paws padded about on the table, shattering the glasses and the crockery. The cutlery and the lighted candles in glass hurricane shades fell onto the grass, the shades breaking, and the portable trestle table wobbled under its great weight, but it found no food. They saw a flash of white teeth and heard a hushed snarl and then in one fast movement it darted down, off the table, and grabbed a plastic bag near the barbecue with the leftover food in it, as another shot rang out. It ran off, limping and dragging the plastic bag back across the clearing into the trees.

They held their breath; even the noisy jungle seemed silent, as a shell whined away through the trees again...

The old man, unseen, was somewhere under the wooden stairs, then he emerged, shotgun still raised and ready.

There was a great sigh, as everyone let out their breath at the same time and relaxed their shoulders, but they still stared hard into the darkness. No one dared to move, and then the guns were lowered and the tension eased.

'*Wow*, that was a close call.' Ed grimaced, inclining his head. 'I think they winged it.'

'Yeah, it was the old man, I think,' said Steve. They were now making their way back to the living room.

Ed glanced around before he sat down, checking for snakes in the corners, but said nothing to the others. 'I think I got a bit of it on the video, but it was a bit too dark out there.'

No one answered him.

In his mind Jonah was thinking of his part, wondering if Elliot, when they finally got around to filming the jungle scenes, would have him hiding and coming out of those trees. He didn't say anything, but the thought worried him, and he was hoping if so that the scene wouldn't take too long and that the old man would be there watching and ready with the shotgun.

Both Amber and Louise were feeling sick inside, Amber worrying in case an animal came up the steps into the hut. The only ones that didn't seem worried were the inch-long ants; they just continued walking in their line up and down the window frame.

Henry came into the living room with fresh glasses, and Rani opened a bottle of red wine. 'I guess you will want a drink after that?' He smiled.

They all sort of half-grinned, taking a glass from the tray. 'Glad you've got some glasses left.' Steve flicked up his eyebrows.

'This is all we've got.' Henry also raised his eyebrows.

'I'll never sleep tonight.' Louise looked at Henry. 'Could it come up the steps?'

'Just what I was thinking,' said Amber.

He didn't say no. 'Well, we've never known one to come up the steps, and don't worry, old Jiggy sits out there all night on watch, and he's a pretty good shot. He winged it; it won't come back tonight.'

'Well, it could do; he didn't kill it,' said Louise.

'Oh, no, we are not allowed to kill,' said Rani. 'Animal conservation and all that. And it doesn't happen very often.' He smiled and wrinkled his nose. 'We just put on the show for visitors.' He grinned broadly. 'Don't worry, jaguars rarely attack humans. We know they are out there, but seeing one probably only happens once in three years.'

'Well, maybe the three years are up.' Jonah raised his eyebrows. They all grinned.

'Couldn't you barricade the steps with something?' asked Amber.

Henry nodded. 'We do, but a thing that big *could* just jump over the top. We've never known one to do it, though.' He glanced at Rani, who was shaking his head.

But Amber remembered. 'What about the fourteen-year-old boy?'

'Oh, that was years ago,' said Henry, 'and that was a crocodile, and before we had the tin cans.' He saw the look on her face. 'Jiggy fixes them up on the steps at night. If anything moves out there, they go down with a hell of a crash and it frightens the animal away. You don't really need a shotgun. Everyone does it, and nothing gets by old Jiggy anyway; he's out there all night watching.' He raised his eyebrows at Amber. 'He had a good laugh the other night with you and the spider.' He grinned again.

Amber, embarrassed, took a breath, then glanced at Steve. She wondered if old Jiggy was out there somewhere in the mornings when she was nipping in and out in just a towel.

No one slept that night.

CHAPTER EIGHT

The next day they had nothing much to do, and Henry asked if they would like a boat trip up the river again. They decided yes. Sitting around, they were just getting more bored; they were used to being very active. And they all still had last night's scare on their minds.

Cappy brought the canoe down and slotted it into the V-shape in the riverbank, and snakes slithered away unseen as the travellers made their way through the long dried grass to the water's edge. Clambering into the canoe wasn't easy; it wobbled and dipped dangerously as they all took their places once again. Jonah's great bulk alone had the girls squealing and hanging on to the side of the canoe. Louise and Amber, both being small, sat side by side; Steve sat behind them and Ed then took the back seat, with the video camera as usual. Amber wondered if he slept with the camera; he never seemed to put it down.

Cappy stayed on the bank and Rani and Henry took up the paddles at either end. They soon entered the canal, disturbing the calm water that gleamed like polished black mirrored glass in a thin shaft of sunlight that escaped through the treetops.

Having travelled the canal before, there was not much to interest them. Jonah pointed out an exotic bird with the brightest of colours, but it fluttered away too quickly. Amber got into one of her sulky moods because she hadn't seen it, but she soon squealed when a huge crocodile came close to the canoe that, with all their weight, was very low in the water. The crocodile opened its mouth wide. Ed was just not quick enough to get a shot as Henry hit out at it with the paddle, and it closed its huge mouth again with a loud snap and dived.

Amber crossed her fingers and held her breath. They all waited in terrified anticipation for it to retaliate by coming up under the canoe, but luckily it didn't, and they floated on. The girls, still holding their breath, glanced at each other fearfully and then clasped hands, feeling the support of each other.

The canoe moved slowly with just the quiet and gentle splash of the paddles; the only other sound was an eerie, hollow distant bird call. They moved on for about half an hour without incident; they saw a monkey taking a long leap into a tree and disappearing into the shade of the leaves, the weather being too hot even for the animals.

The river trip had passed the time, even though now they had seen it all before, and it was now lunchtime, and they were back at the wooden hut, enjoying cold shrimp and salad. Amber had vowed after being told that they came from the Demerara River never to eat shrimp again, but she did it anyway; they were fresh and she enjoyed them.

That night, after having dinner in the small dining area, they went to bed. It was windy, and there was a rain shower that hammered noisily on the roof; the wind blew in over the low fence, shaking the mosquito net and so strong the wooden hut shuddered. Outside the trees swayed and shook, their leaves angrily rustling and shivering. The noise increased to a crescendo as thunder crashed loud overhead and fork lightning lit up the whole sky, flashing through the hut then leaving them in darkness.

The thunder rumbled again and the lightning flashed and the rain was hammering so hard on the roof that Amber thought the whole hut would collapse or the roof would cave in, or even lift and blow right off. She put her hands over her ears as another terrific crash of thunder shook the hut and fork lightning flashed again, crackling through the trees, and then a crash as they fell. She turned with a squeal, clinging tightly to Steve, who put an arm around her and grinned to himself in the darkness; then, realising just what she was doing, she struggled out of his arm and quickly turned her back on him and stuck her head under the pillow, wondering where the spiders went for shelter.

The next day the hut was still standing. A few trees had fallen, but now everything was dry, and the sky was blue and the sun bright and the humidity was just as high as before.

Breakfast was quiet; no one had slept through the night, and the day was going to be a boring one. They sat around reading the script to each other, learning their lines, but it only lasted an hour; they found it too hot and too tiring. There was nowhere to walk; well, they could have walked around the hut, but there was the danger of the snakes and maybe that jaguar could be lurking somewhere in the undergrowth, so it wasn't a happy situation, and now, after the storm, there were branches strewn all over the pathway down to the water's edge and all around the hut. The old man Jiggy was clearing some of it and hacking away at a large fallen tree with a machete.

Henry had managed to get some newspapers from somewhere. They were three days old, but at least it was news; they knew nothing of the outside world. Amber got to wondering just what the village people would do all day if they were not working, and that was probably why they were excited to see visitors; it was the highlight of their whole week, possibly their whole year.

The day went on and they had a light lunch, and soon it was dusk and the darkness of the early evening was once again upon them. They had another barbecue, but now they were a little apprehensive, all eyes scanning the clearing after the incident with the jaguar. All turned out well, but they took their after-dinner drinks back into the living room, where the dim light of the hurricane lamp attracted a golden tangle of gnats, and through the open door the loud sound of buzzing insects was just like one continuous whistle. The ants at the window frame were still hard at work.

They sat quietly with not much to say. The hot and humid air made them tired, and soon after the normal torchlight search for spiders Amber was once again under the mosquito net with Steve and hoping that it would be the last time. In the morning after breakfast they were to move on to meet Elliot, and they would be getting back to work. The cameras would be rolling and lighting all set up, and they would be back to some sort of civilisation.

'Our last night together,' Steve sighed dreamily, turning his head on the pillow towards her; she saw his comical grin in the semi-darkness. 'I'm gonna miss my nights with you,' he said mockingly, eyebrows raised and waiting.

Amber sniffed. 'Well, I won't miss *my* nights with *you!*'

He grinned. 'I knew you'd say that!' He put on a frown. 'But you needed me last night.' His brown eyes opened wide and an amused smile twisted his handsome face.

She sniffed, irritated as usual. 'This is an absolute disgrace, the whole thing is an outrage and I can't wait to tell Elliot just what I think.'

'*Ooohwooh.*' Steve's voice wobbled in a sort of sing-song mode as he fluttered his eyelids. 'I'm sure Elliot will be waiting and expecting your views on the jungle.' Steve flicked up his eyebrows, with a chuckle. He could just see the scene now, she raving as usual, and Elliot shouting back. The two of them never really did get along... well, no one really did get along with Amber anyway. And what a mess she looked these days, although it couldn't be helped, living here like Tarzan and Jane. Even when they had been together she had never let her image go; he had rarely seen her without her makeup, and he admired her for taking pride in herself. Knowing how she must be feeling now, he grinned again in the semi-darkness; he couldn't resist poking a little fun. 'If the public could only see you now.'

She turned her head towards him. 'Well, it can't be helped here in this God-forsaken place. But you're not going to tell anyone that I look terrible without makeup, I *hope*? *Or* that you *had* to *sleep* with *me*? *And*' – she sort of shrugged her shoulders – '*just sleep!* You would be the laughing stock of the whole studio; there are men that would give their right arm to sleep with me.'

'Not when Ed shows them the before-and-after photos.'

'Oh, he wouldn't!' She sat up.

'Wouldn't he?' Steve chuckled. 'You want to take a bet? He could get a fortune for shots like that.' He was joking.

146

Amber eyes were wide and scared in the darkness; her mind went to planning that tomorrow she would somehow get Ed's camera and throw it in the river, and then thought again, *No, not after all the work he's put in; it wouldn't be fair and we might have to do this all again.* Perhaps he wouldn't think about it anyway, and surely Steve wouldn't egg him on? Or would he? It could be revenge for the way she had treated him this year. Maybe she could bribe Ed not to show the photos, but then again, that might give him ideas. She closed her eyes, but sleep didn't come easy.

CHAPTER NINE

Sunday came. They were all packed and anxious to be off, saying their goodbyes to Henry and Rani, tipping them well and thanking them for the week; the boys had really looked after them well. They were just about to go down the steps, when a messenger came in a small canoe from the village saying that Jago had a problem with the boat and couldn't get there today.

'What about the other boat?' Jonah raised his eyebrows hopefully.

'It's already out,' Henry told him, 'and won't be available for at least a week.'

They sat down again in the living room, all feeling very jaded. Amber was most disgruntled. 'This film has a jinx on it. What else can go wrong with this damned filming?'

'It's no good you getting all upset.' Steve looked at her. 'It can't be helped.' He flipped his hands. 'We'll just have to wait; there's nothing we can do.'

'So how are we going to let Elliot know?' said Louise.

'Oh, *Elliot*! He'll just have to wait! Just you wait until I see him! Putting us through all this! And for a whole week! And now the damned boat has broken down! How much longer are we expected to stay here?' Amber's voice rose with her usual angry aggression.

'Just calm down,' Ed shouted back angrily. 'It's not Elliot's fault. We will probably have to stay just another night, that's all; the boat will be here tomorrow.'

Amber breathed heavily and looked away in disgust, wringing her hands hard with annoyance, but what else was there to say? He was right.

The day had been long and tiring again with nothing much to do, and now they sat as usual having drinks in the living room, too hot to go outside. They were all feeling a bit in despair, and tonight it was going to be another barbecue as the gas cylinder in the kitchen had run out. Henry had said that he'd have to go and get more supplies. He would also have to get more bed linen as he had thought that they were leaving and he had sent it all to the village for washing.

Amber's thoughts were disgruntled again at having to spend another night with Steve. The spiders were still there; there were probably more than just the two, but she had managed to calm her nerves; she'd had to, as there was no way of chasing them away. Still, she certainly didn't want to be in that room on her own. She then began wondering about the next move and whether it would be like this; it surely couldn't be worse, or could it?

Sharing a bed with... She shook her head. *With HIM...*

She had to admit that she felt grateful for his nearness, and in her heart she felt that she had softened towards him. But again, she had to keep up this image that she had created, and although she now felt warmed towards him she didn't want to give in. It wasn't really in her nature to be aggressive, but she *had* created this image of self-importance, and it *had* got her noticed. How would little Kitty Hawksenburge have got noticed?

Her thoughts came back to the giant spiders, and she cringed.

They were up early; the morning was again bright and sunny, and as Amber came out of the shower she looked into the crevice. Seeing the bright shining eyes of the giant spider staring at her, she said, 'Goodbye. Let's hope we can both live in peace again.' She shivered.

On making the breakfast table, she found the boat hadn't arrived yet. Was it going to be another boring day? She hoped not. But it was...

They had not long finished a light lunch, no one was very talkative and the heat was unbearable, when suddenly in the middle of the afternoon the boat turned up, and it was a quick scramble now to collect all the belongings that they had taken from their luggage such as toiletries. They had thought they would have some warning that the boat was on its way, but no, it was just suddenly there and ready to go, much to their relief.

Saying goodbye to Henry and Rani, once again they all clambered into the boat, eager to get away. The luggage was piled in. Of course Amber's was the biggest, but it had all been a waste of time; she had spent the entire week in her shocking pink shorts and one clean T-shirt. At least she was thankful to have been free of mosquito bites. Poor Ed had suffered the most with bites all up his legs and arms, but he hadn't complained, and Rani had got him some repellent and relief from aloe vera plants that grew wild.

Amber turned her nose up again at the grime of the old fishing boat, but she guessed that this time her appearance was suited to the boat. This was the worst nightmare she could ever have imagined, and her thoughts now were on Ed's camera, but she didn't have the heart to destroy it. She was hoping, wherever they were going, there would be a shop and some sign of civilisation. They were told that they would be going up the wild and rushing Demerara River again, and Steve had thoughts on whether the boat could stand up to another hard battering from the water pressure.

The boatman was a young guy, very smiley and chatty, asking if they had enjoyed their stay and whether they had found the food good and whether Henry and Rani had looked after them well. They all said that Henry and Rani had been wonderful, but it wasn't really a holiday, they were supposed to have been working, and of course they said that they were actors.

The boatman already knew this. He said that his name was Raymond and that he was Henry and Rani's younger brother; he had just come from the University of Cambridge for a holiday, and he was staying in the village with his parents. Of course, they all said that they had met his parents; this, again, he already knew. He said he was most interested as he had seen many of Amber De Carla and Steve Salvettini's movies. Amber secretly cringed at this, knowing the way she must look now, as Raymond smiled at her. 'You look so different, Miss De Carla, but you can play any part; you look just right for the jungle scenes.'

Amber sort of perked up. 'Do I?' She guessed that she did look right for the part; there could be no glamour in the jungle. Then she said, 'Oh, don't talk about it, it's been a nightmare.' They all chuckled.

'Yes,' Jonah said, 'it's a bit too primitive here for us, coming from America.'

Raymond smiled and nodded in agreement.

There was nothing to see on this journey but river as the old boat chugged slowly through another canal and then out into the rushing Demerara River, slowing even more through rough and rushing sandy brown water, and with it splashing over the side they were getting quite wet. The river was as wide as the sea from the shore to the horizon and a long way off on either side they could see nothing but the dense jungle trees. After some time the chugging of the boat slowed and they were approaching a grassy clearing, and a long wooden jetty appeared in front of them, then Raymond was tying up.

Jonah was the first out; it was quite high, and he helped the girls first and then Steve and Ed, who was still busy shooting film. There wasn't anything so far that they had done that Ed had not captured on film.

The men carried the luggage along the long boardwalk; ahead of them there was a wide and well-cared-for lawn with trees and flowering shrubs. Suddenly Elliot appeared, coming towards them down the sandy garden path; he was all smiles, his arms out wide. 'Welcome, you made it.' He sounded happy. 'How are you all?'

For a moment, no one answered.

'Better away from the jungle,' Amber snapped, bitterly.

Elliot grimaced at her bedraggled appearance, obviously knowing something was wrong. He glanced at Steve, as if to say, *Nothing's changed.* Steve rolled his eyes and took a breath with a knowing nod.

'How is Stacey?' Louise was concerned.

'Not so good.' Elliot inclined his head and rolled his eyes. 'She spent a day in the hospital here in Guyana, but she still wasn't well. I contacted Tappener and he sent an air ambulance to take us to LA, and she went back into hospital again. She has completely lost her nerve. They say it could take a long time; some bug in the stomach from the water, they think? They were sending specimens for analysing to the clinic of tropical diseases. I don't think they know what it is yet.'

They walked on up to the house. It was a large white stone building with a yellow painted front and a polished brass doorknocker; there were bay windows either side.

'Come in.' Elliot smiled as he pushed open the door. Inside the dark wooden floors were highly polished and it was well-furnished, with comfortable beige armchairs and a small coffee table that held ashtrays and magazines. Long flowered drapes hung from deep pelmets at the windows, and landscape paintings decorated the walls.

A woman came into the spacious hallway, and Elliot introduced her as Helen Francs, the housekeeper. She was tall and well-built, aged between fifty and sixty, with greying short hair and square silver-rimmed specs. She shook hands with a pleasant smile, greeting them warmly. Ed recognised the Swiss-German accent. They then followed her into the lounge, a spacious room furnished with a beige carpet and cherry-red armchairs, and a maid in a grey uniform brought them coffee.

'Are we on an island?' Amber glanced around the well-furnished room and then out through the window with a view of the jungle trees again.

'No,' Helen said, smiling, 'we are on the mainland. I expect you saw the island opposite when you came in. There's just one house on there; it's privately owned, and it does give the impression that this is an island too, but we are just on the other side of the river, and we have miles of jungle here behind the house.'

'Oh, don't say that,' said Amber. 'We've just had a week in the jungle, and I've had enough! Well, we all have.' She glanced at Elliot. 'Do you know there were giant spiders and inch-long ants and we nearly got attacked by a jaguar?'

'Yes, we occasionally get a wild animal here in the garden,' said Helen. 'I would advise you not to walk in the garden at night or very early in the morning. We really don't get any trouble, but it's good to be cautious.'

Amber turned, aggressively, to Elliot. '*Fancy* leaving us in that terrible place for a whole week.' Her voice rose to almost a squeal.

He shrugged his shoulders. 'Well, we should have only been there a day or two, if it hadn't been for Stacey's accident.'

'Well, even a day or two would have been too long. At least *you* didn't have to endure it! Why didn't you send a boat and get us out of there? And, *besides*, there wouldn't have been enough accommodation for us all. And *you* don't know what we have been through!'

'Oh, well,' Elliot said, 'the boys would have had to make do. They wouldn't have minded sleeping rough under the stars, just for a couple of nights.' He shrugged, wrinkling his nose with a smile.

'*What?*' Jonah and Ed said together, their faces wrinkled with frowns of amazement.

'Is that what you had in mind in the first place?' Jonah's frown deepened.

'You've got to be joking,' Ed snapped, his voice rising.

They all looked at each other, in bewilderment, knowing that Elliot had not got the foggiest idea what he was talking about; he hadn't experienced it.

'You *are* joking, right?' said Steve. 'This is jungle, man, not Central Park.'

Elliot nodded and glanced out of the window, seeing the manicured lawn and the river beyond. 'Yes, it might be jungle, but it was well-organised.'

'*Organised!*' they all blurted out loudly together.

Elliot physically jerked back.

'Organised, maybe,' said Jonah, 'as far as food et cetera is concerned, and I must say the men did look after us well, but a whole week? Two days would have been more than enough for anyone. It really isn't good enough, Elliot. You don't know what the girls have had to endure this last week, snakes and crocodiles and a jaguar, ants, giant spiders and mosquitoes. It was awful. None of us are used to that kind of living, and there was no communication; we were just stuck there. It's been a damned rough week and we have all had enough!'

Elliot was taken aback; he said nothing. Jonah was always so placid, so amiable; he'd never seen this side of him before.

'Well, where are the crew anyway?' said Ed.

155

'Oh, I came alone,' said Elliot. 'After we flew back to the States to get Stacey into a hospital I wasn't sure what we were to do, and the crew couldn't be out of work, so they got another assignment.'

They all looked at each other in bewilderment. They had spent a whole week in the jungle roughing it, and now the crew were on another *job*?

'Well, so you knew it was going to be more than a day or two, then? And I haven't even had a chance to act out my part yet.' Jonah sounded quite indignant. 'And I hope you're not thinking of going back there into the jungle, *are you*? Because I'm *not* taking Louise back there!'

'No.' Elliot shook his head, thoughtfully. 'No, I'm making other arrangements for the jungle scenes.' Although he didn't really have anything in mind yet.

'Bit late now.' Steve grimaced. 'Hope the arrangements are a bit better than the ones you made coming out here. *Surely* you weren't expecting the guys to sleep rough outside in the jungle? Do you know, *man*, we couldn't even walk around the hut for the snakes?'

Elliot shrugged his shoulders, and clenched his fists. He was feeling a bit uncomfortable; they were digging at him from all sides.

'Hmph.' Amber took a deep breath; her eyes flashed fire, giving Elliot a venomous look, seeing the shrug and his nonchalant attitude. *'Don't!* You *ever!* Send me on a location like *this* again!'

Elliot was about to answer, but Helen Francs came in to show them to their rooms, which they found were very comfortable and civilised.

Dinner was very nice, around a long polished dining table with nice linen and silverware. They drank good wine, and the girls were pleased to have had a shower with shower gel and shampoo and then to have been able to get dressed for dinner. But the conversation was now very strained. Elliot knew he was in the doghouse. When he asked if they'd had a chance to look at the script, they all chimed in saying they'd had nothing else to do.

'*Look* at it? We know it *backwards*!' Amber snapped angrily, bunching her lips, her blue eyes ablaze. 'To be honest, I'm sick of it!' She looked away from Elliot in disgust.

Steve raised his eyebrows, nodding in agreement, and took a deep breath. He glanced at Jonah, who nodded; they were both of the same mind.

Elliot bit his lip and lowered his eyes and thought it better to say nothing. They continued to eat in silence.

After dinner, most of the group retired to the lounge. Elliot left the table and walked through glass dining-room doors onto the low veranda for a smoke. He was glad to get away from the silent aggravation that he could feel building up against him. The night air was clammy, the humidity was high and in minutes his shirt was wet with perspiration, but it was quiet and peaceful. He took a deep breath, and then turned as Ed followed him out.

'Hot night,' said Ed.

'Yeah.'

They sat in the white-painted wooden garden chairs and Elliot offered Ed a cigar, which he took gratefully, having run out of cigarettes earlier in the week. Elliot struck a match, and gave the box to Ed. It was quiet as they drew on their cigars, and a pleasant aroma rose into the night with the smoke.

'I hope you're gonna let me work some of this videoing that I've done this week into the scenes.' Ed glanced sideways into the dimness.

'Yeah! Yeah! I guess we can use some of it.' Elliot nodded, casually.

'It's really been a tough week for us all, you know. We're not going back, are we? We can't go back, as you will be able to see from the video. Everyone's on edge.'

'Hmm, so it seems.' Elliot grimaced in the darkness. There was just a chink of light coming from the hurricane lamp that was still on the dinner table, filtering through a tiny gap Ed had left in the heavy drapes that closed over the glass doors.

Elliot took a deep breath; the night was filled with the fragrant scent of frangipani and jasmine, but there seemed no air. Looking up, he saw the black velvet sky was filled with a million stars, and the sound of buzzing insects competed with the mixed sound of the continuous rushing of the river; these sounds were all strange and very tropical to Elliot, who had only spent one night in comfort here at Riverside House. 'I hope you captured this tropical buzzing sound on the video.' He turned, but all Ed saw in the darkness was the red glow of the cigar.

'Oh, sure, I didn't miss a thing; just hope you can use most of it. Wait until you see it; I caught snakes and crocodiles. And the jaguar? Well,' he said, raising his eyebrows with a nod, 'that certainly was *a night*.'

Elliot nodded, with a nonchalant grimace. 'Yeah, well, I guess if you're looking for these things.'

'*Looking* for it?' Ed frowned; his voice rose in amazement. 'I didn't have to go looking; I was living with it. It was all around me every day.' He shook his head and raised his eyebrows again. 'I don't think you realise just what the jungle really *is*. We were completely cut off from the world! We couldn't even walk outside the hut, even in the daytime, without the snakes slithering away from our feet. It was a wonder no one got bitten. It was bloody scary, I tell you.'

Elliot raised his eyebrows, again nodded and grimaced, thinking they were all making too much of having to rough it a little. He drew heavily on the cigar for a moment, then took it from his lips. Pungent blue smoke rose above his head, as he looked at the fiery red glow on the end until it turned into a blob of white-grey ash.

A pale moon suddenly peeped from behind a cloud, turning the lawn and the trees to a silvery grey, and for just a few minutes the fast-running river glinted like black diamonds, then the moon disappeared as suddenly as it had appeared, and they were left in darkness once again.

Suddenly, there was a dark shadow under the trees; it was crossing the lawn. Ed felt a pang stab at his heart, having a flashback of the jaguar; he was almost out of the chair and turned to Elliot quickly, as the animal was coming towards them. It was black and big, and its eyes glinted in the dim semi-night light, and then it barked, and just at that moment a man came from behind the trees and called out, 'Charlie, come here!'

Ed breathed again, feeling his stomach settle, his heart pounding hard. '*Wow!*' he gasped, letting out his breath, as if he'd been running. He said nothing, not wanting to alarm

Elliot. A few minutes passed as they contentedly drew on their cigars.

'He's coming back again, look!' Elliot chuckled.

They saw the dark shadow slowly slinking across the lawn again; it came closer, but it was all too late. It leaped with lightning speed at the wooden balustrade and there was a cracking of wood and the balustrade collapsed under its great weight, the open mouth showing huge white teeth; they both shouted in alarm and Elliot fell sideways off the chair as Ed jumped up and reared back and then almost in the same movement lunged forward, pushing the great animal away from Elliot and accidentally stabbing it on the head with the cigar. It was then he realised that it was not the dog but a black jaguar. It gave a screeching cry of pain, twisted and turned and ran away into the darkness. It was a moment of sheer terror and it all happened so quickly that everything seemed to stop.

Ed was still standing panic-stricken, his legs shaking, his heart pounding hard, his chest heaving. Seeing the half-cigar near his foot on the wooden boards he stamped it out, and then he bent, trying to help Elliot up with shaking hands, but his strength was completely gone.

Elliot was also shaking, and cried out in pain, 'I've been bitten. I've been *bitten*!'

Ed was a bit confused; although the animal had been fierce and so close and had scared the life out of them both, as far as he knew it hadn't actually touched Elliot. But Elliot was sitting on the floor holding his ankle. 'Oh! Oh! I've been bitten, I've been bitten.'

It was dark but Ed could see that Elliot was in a lot of pain, and he himself felt quite helpless. He shouted through the open door for help, and they all came quickly. Ed, still shaking, his legs weak, tried to explain what had happened.

Jonah got Elliot up and inside, and looked at the ankle. He could see two small marks, and supposed that it was a snake bite, but he wasn't sure. Ed was still trying to explain that it wasn't a snake, it was a jaguar that had jumped the fence, and they had thought it was a dog.

Then, hearing all the commotion, Helen came in. Looking at Elliot's ankle, she said it was a snake bite. She went out again quickly and came back with some disinfectant and a bandage, but Elliot's head was rolling; he seemed delirious, and she quickly twisted the bandage into a tourniquet, telling Steve to hold it tight while she called the doctor. The doctor said that he would be there in a few minutes; he lived on the island just opposite and he was coming across by canoe.

They were all worried, and crowded around Elliot, all talking excitedly at once and confused as to what had happened. Ed was still severely shaken, and still trying to tell them. 'It jumped the fence, it's all broken,' he said in despair, but no one was actually listening to him.

'What? The snake?' Steve turned to him in amazement.

'No, jaguar. Never saw a snake. I thought it was a dog.'

'*Jaguar?*' Steve frowned. 'What jaguar? Where did it go?'

'I dunno. I stabbed it on the head with the cigar and it ran away.'

'*Cigar?*' Amber turned in astonishment. 'You stabbed a *snake* on the head with a *cigar*?'

'*No! Jaguar!*' Ed shouted.

'*What?*' Everyone stopped and looked at him.

'A *jaguar*!' Ed almost screamed again. 'I keep trying to tell you, it jumped on the goddamned fence, and the fence collapsed under it. Elliot fell off the chair and I jumped up and pushed it away. I thought it was a big dog and I caught it on the head with the cigar, and the snake must have been right there on the patio with us but neither of us saw it in the dark. We thought it was that dog coming back.'

'What dog?' Jonah frowned.

Ed took a deep breath, still shaking, trying to calm himself, but getting more irate with their silly questions. 'There was *this big dog*!' he said, slowly and very precisely and very loudly. 'It had only been there a few minutes before, and it was coming towards us, in *the dark*! And a man had called it away. It's a wonder the thing didn't attack *him* or the dog; it must have been so close. And I didn't really have time to think, it all happened so fast.' Ed was shaking his head vigorously; it was just an automatic reaction. 'I just lashed out at it in the dark to push it away – I thought it was the dog, attacking Elliot – the cigar still in my hand, and I accidentally stabbed it on the head, and it ran away. I was shocked when I realised that it was a wild animal. I really thought it was the dog.'

Doctor Santanga arrived. He was a tall and hefty middle-aged black man with a heavy black and greying beard, and greying tight curls at his temples. He came quickly through the door, black bag in hand. 'Where's the patient?'

They all stood aside watching, while the doctor gave Elliot a shot and cleaned and bound the wound. Elliot was beginning to sag; he still seemed delirious, but now with the shot he was recovering, and saying the pain was a little easier.

'You need a drink?' Ed nodded to Elliot and smiled. 'So do I. Is it all right?' He raised his eyes to the doctor, who had said very little and who was now by the door, just leaving.

The doctor turned with a twisted smile that said neither yes nor no, and then said, 'If there's a problem, give me a call.' He nodded to Helen and left.

They all sat in the lounge with a drink; Helen had brought a bottle of red wine. Just half a glass of wine made Elliot feel sleepy, and he went to bed.

'I'll be glad when we get out of this place.' Amber was rubbing her hands, with her normal agitated annoyance. 'It's been nothing but a nightmare since the day we arrived! And we've done nothing except look at the script.'

They were all in agreement.

CHAPTER TEN

The next morning the table was laid for breakfast on the veranda and they all took note of the broken fence before sitting down. The maid came to pour them coffee.

Elliot had told them last night that after breakfast a boat had been arranged to take them on to the gold mines, where they knew from the script there was to have been more shooting of the film; the Harrisons would have been followed there by the drug pushers. Of course so far there had been no action at all, and they could do nothing without Stacey in her police role and the crew, even if Ed still videoed it. And so Elliot had said that, as it had all been organised months ago, it would be interesting to go and just have a look around. They were all in agreement, and hoping that Ed would capture something on camera and his technicians would be able to piece it together, as they didn't want to have to come back to Guyana again.

A black man with greying hair came ambling through the garden with a huge Rottweiler at his side. 'Good morning.' He smiled pleasantly, his lips lost under a heavy grey moustache. He stopped the other side of the broken fence. 'What happened here? Oh, I'm Kenny; I'm the gardener. Sorry if Charlie worried you last night.' He looked down at the dog and patted his head. 'There's really no harm in him, even though he looks fierce; he loves people. He heard you talking and he was curious, wanted to investigate, ha, ha.' He patted the dog's head again. 'But he soon changed his mind when I called him. He thought he was going to get a treat, ha, ha, but I took him back and locked him up so he wouldn't come back again.'

'Yeah, he did give us a bit of a fright,' Ed said, smiling, 'and we thought it was him coming back, but it was a jaguar!'

'*Jaguar!*' Kenny blurted out, his brown eyes showing white with surprised fear. 'Is that what broke the fence?' He put his hand on the sharp spikes of the broken wood.

'Yeah!' Ed nodded. 'It's a wonder your dog didn't bark; it almost followed you, as you called the dog. We thought it was the dog coming back until it pounced on us.'

Kenny let out a breath through his teeth. 'Pounced! On you? Hmm, it's rare, never heard of that happening before, but best not to come out here at night.'

'Our friend got bitten by a snake too,' said Amber.

'*Did* he? What, last night? Is he all right?' Kenny's large brown eyes showed white again.

'We had the doctor see to him,' said Steve, 'but he's not up yet.'

'Well, hope he'll be all right.' Kenny grimaced. 'Don't get too much of that here either, but then, we don't have too many visitors.' He inclined his head. 'I live over there in the cottage,' – he nodded to the right; they all looked, but it was all trees – 'and we don't come out much at night, and I usually keep Charlie in, but we had just come across from the boathouse last night. I usually go there in the daylight; not wise to be out here at night! Well, hope your friend will be better; have a good day. Come on, Charlie.' The dog

165

followed him. 'We'll have to get that fence mended.' He was walking away and nodding and talking to the dog.

Elliot had not come down for breakfast, so Jonah went to wake him up; he shook him hard but couldn't wake him. The doctor was called again, and a decision was made to take Elliot off to the hospital.

Then there was a lot of arguing as to who should go with him, and they were all agreed *not* Amber.

In the end, when the stretcher-bearers arrived, Helen Francs volunteered to go, saying she was more used to going on the river and knew her way around. She told them the boat would be coming to pick them up and wished them a good stay at the gold mines and said not to worry; Elliot was in good hands.

The fast motorised fishing boat took Elliot and Helen with the doctor; an ambulance had been arranged to meet them on the other side of the river to take them to the hospital the other side of Georgetown.

The group sat around until mid-morning, when the maid came to say that the boat had arrived to take them to the gold-mining town.

At the jetty, Raymond was there, greeting them with a happy smile. The jetty was quite high, and so Steve, being tall, went down first. With Jonah holding them at the top the girls were helped safely on board, and then Jonah clambered down, and Ed handed him the video camera before he jumped in. All aboard, they set off once again up the fast-running Demerara River, the sandy water splashing up over the bow as the boat chugged along against the current, and

Amber shivered as water spots splashed on her skimpy pink shorts.

By the time they arrived, they were all wet, but it would soon dry in the heat of the morning sun. They waved goodbye to Raymond, who called after them that he would be there when they came back. He had already arranged that the minibus driver, Fabien, would phone him when they were on the way.

They walked to the end of the jetty. The minibus was not there; the place was deserted and deathly quiet. They started to walk along the wide dirt road. Although it was a bright sunny morning, everything here appeared dull and desolate like a western shanty town, although it could hardly be called a town; to their right there were just a few small wooden buildings, which looked derelict, and to their left, along the side of the river from where they had just come, green hills went up high. They could see dark holes in the hillside, which they assumed were the gold mines. They saw a mule walking among the trees. 'If that's where we are going, there must be a roadway up there,' said Jonah.

Then ahead of them they saw two solitary miners sauntering slowly along the road carrying shovels over their shoulders, but they were too far ahead to call.

Walking on a little further they saw a donkey tethered to a post, outside one of the wooden buildings; it looked like a shop, probably where the miners got their supplies. There were two wooden steps up onto a wooden walkway; the fencing around it was broken. There was a small window, and as they came nearer they could see that the glass was broken and what little glass remained was thick with grime and dust. There was an old cart standing in a gap between this and the next building; apart from that there was nothing.

Then suddenly a minibus was hurtling towards them at speed, a build-up of black dust behind it, and then it stopped short with a slight skid, both Amber and Louise waving their hands in front of their faces as a cloud of dust flew up covering them. The driver jumped out and asked if they were the film people. He had been sent by a Mr Stirling to collect them and take them into the town.

'Town?' Steve frowned. 'I thought we were supposed to visit the gold mines.'

The driver grimaced and slid the door back, shaking his head. 'I was told to take you to the town. You can't drive up there.' He nodded towards the hillside. 'You have to go by mule.'

They boarded the minibus; the driver got in behind the wheel and turned them around. The engine roared into life and the whole thing shuddered and shook, and they were off at speed on another scary bumpy ride; maybe it was the same driver, or maybe all drivers were like this in Guyana?

The countryside was all trees and fields, but they eventually entered a town, where there was a busy market and hundreds of people walking, buying and selling. The driver slowed right down, hooting the horn every minute and shouting to get people to clear the way, and then a cow lazily crossed the road.

From then driving on the road was clearer, and there were open fields again on either side; they were on the outskirts of the town. They then came to a busy building, where people were milling around, and some sitting about on the steps. The minibus stopped and the driver got out and slid the door back; they got out, not knowing where they were. He said this was the gold exchange, where the miners came to stake their claims and sell their gold, and the big and busy building next door was the gold market, and this was where he had been told to bring them.

'Well, will you wait for us?' asked Jonah.

'Yes, sir, I'll be right here.'

They walked a little cautiously into the gold market; it was daunting, especially for Amber, Steve and Ed, the only white people there, and the faces around them looked grim as they saw strangers making their way through the crowds of mostly men. The building was huge, half rounded corrugated iron like an aircraft hangar; it was crowded and noisy with traders and buyers. There were hundreds of stalls, selling nothing but gold: gold dust, gold nuggets, gold bars, gold plates and statuettes, ornaments, trinkets and gold jewellery. Every single thing for sale here was gold, mined and fashioned here in the town, so Helen Francs had said.

Steve thought there must have been hundreds of tons of gold there. He also recalled the script had said that this was where the Harrisons were accosted by the drug dealers, but of course there were no cameras and no action, and so they just wandered around looking.

Both Amber and Louise made for the jewellery to try on bracelets and earrings and necklaces. Amber tried on a gold ring with a big blue stone, showing off her red chipped fingernails. Louise admired the ring with a smile, showing Amber the gold charm bracelet that she had on her wrist.

Ed of course had the camera rolling, until he was accosted by a very efficient and burly police officer saying that he was not allowed to film in here. Being white people, they of course attracted a lot of attention. The officer wanted to confiscate the camera. Ed protested, saying he was working for a Hollywood film company and making a film with Amber De Carla and he could not afford to let the camera go after months of work, but promised he would shut it down.

A man in the crowd called out, 'Do you know Amber De Carla? I've seen all her films.'

'Really?' Amber stepped forward. 'I'm Amber De Carla.'

The man looked her up and down and laughed at her appearance. '*You?*' It was a sarcastic sneer.

'Yes.' Steve butted in, expecting some trouble. Jonah was close to Amber's elbow.

'I know *you*,' said the man, pointing a finger. 'You're Steve Salvettini. I've seen all your films with Amber De Carla.' He turned to the watching crowd with excitement in his voice. 'They're film stars; it's Steve Salvettini.' The crowd were getting more interested and gathering around.

At this Amber was quite put out, and in her haughty fashion, she stepped forward again. 'I *am* Amber De Carla! Maybe I look a little different, but we have been filming in the jungle for a week, *and* we are still filming. I must say it's not very glamorous working in the jungle. You don't expect me to have glittering evening wear, *do you*?'

'The man stepped a little closer. 'Yeah! Yeah! You *are* Amber De Carla!' He turned to the crowd excitedly. 'Yeah! It *is* her!'

Someone nodded with a wide smile. 'Yeah, it's Amber.'

Some smiled, glancing round and looking at others; some had never even heard of Hollywood, let alone film stars.

'Big stars!' The man's voice rose, and the crowd closed in, getting more interested with his enthusiasm. Then others joined in, some saying that they had seen their films, and there were a lot of smiles as notebooks, cards and odd scraps of paper were pushed onto them with requests for autographs.

Another police officer had pushed his way through the crowd; he also recognised them as film stars. After showing the police officers their passports and other identification, Ed was allowed to keep his camera, which was a relief, but was told there was to be no more filming in here. Then one of the officers turned to the crowd, saying that the excitement was over and they were to go back to their business and let the guests enjoy the gold market.

After the crowd had dispersed, the stars spent some time at different stalls. Both Amber and Louise bought pieces of jewellery – bracelets, necklaces, earrings – and while they tried them on, Ed casually flicked his phone, secretly getting a few video shots of Amber and Steve and Jonah.

They then were making their way back through the crowd. The girls walked between Steve and Jonah for protection, not that they needed protection – there was no trouble – but the crowd parted, standing aside, and there were suspicious eyes watching the rich white Americans leaving with their pockets full of gold. For once in her life Amber kept her head down; it was a very uncomfortable feeling. The man who had first recognised Steve followed them out to the minibus with a few of his friends, some still asking for autographs, which they gave gladly, but they were pleased to get back in the minibus with the door shut, and soon to be on their way back to the river.

The minibus transported them back to the jetty where Raymond was waiting with the boat to take them back to Riverside House, just for one night, before going on to Georgetown the next morning.

That evening they sat having drinks before dinner, and Helen came into the room asking if they had had a nice day. Of course they all said yes, and Amber and Louise showed her the pieces of jewellery that they had bought, saying what a fascinating place it was.

'How is Elliot?' Jonah asked.

Helen told them that Elliot was comfortable in the hospital; he had been unconscious all the way, but he had been awake when she had left. Doctor Santanga had stayed with him; they had given him some anti-venom as a temporary measure, and were waiting for the right anti-venom to be flown in in the afternoon. Doctor Santanga was confident that with the right treatment he would recover almost at once.

At dinner they all felt relieved knowing that Elliot would recover, and they enjoyed their last evening in Riverside House, the girls again being able to dress.

The next morning after breakfast it was Jago who came with the boat, and they all said their goodbyes to the staff. Helen had walked down to the jetty with them, the luggage had been pushed down on a trolley by Kenny the gardener, and Charlie the Rottweiler was close by his side.

Jago had stowed the luggage on board and the engine throbbed into life and they were on their way down the Demerara River, the tide now behind them and rushing them quicker away from the jetty. They waved goodbye to Helen and Kenny.

After a while they were turning into one of the canals, losing the sun and in the inky black treacle under cover of the trees again with the strong smell of greenery. This time they weren't so long in the canal, and they were soon crossing the fast-running river again; Riverside House was now far away upstream.

Jago stopped by the riverbank, and passed their luggage up to the men. He waved them goodbye with a grey-whiskered smile and went on his way.

Once again they were on the riverbank a few miles upriver from where they had started and in the middle of nowhere, half-surrounded by dense jungle greenery; it was deathly quiet but for the sound of the rushing river. They waited for the minibus that would transport them to Georgetown and the thrilling thought of a hotel, but just for one night. Elliot had had it all arranged months ago and they were hoping that the driver had not forgotten to come and pick them up.

The wait was long and it was hot in the midday sun with very little shade from the trees, and a lot of grumbling from Amber that they could really have done without. They watched the odd boat go by, the only movement apart from the rushing river, and then they saw a canoe piled high with a pyramid of pineapples; how the man kept the canoe steady was a mystery. Then their attention was taken by something rustling in the dense trees, and they all turned with feelings of alarm, expecting a wild animal to come tearing though the bushes at any moment, but luckily it didn't happen. They saw nothing, but it certainly kept them on their toes scanning the area; animals would possibly come to the river to drink.

The minibus arrived after two hours, much to the frustration of Amber, but to all their relief; they were weary and tired of sitting in the sun. It was the same driver, so they were now prepared for another hair-raising ride. They held their breath as he backed the minibus to the main road that was once again busy with people walking everywhere and the sacred cows lazing without a care in the world in the middle of the busy traffic, and full of the honking of horns and drivers shouting to people to get out of the way.

They were delayed for an hour in the boiling heat again as there was a traffic accident up ahead, which came as no surprise. Waiting for the police to clear the road took ages, and the heat was unbearable with no air conditioning. Eventually they took off again with a jerk, glad of the warm air that rushed through the opened windows. The roads were chaotic, and they were glad when the minibus slowed down and the driver informed them that they were entering Georgetown.

'This is it?' Ed stretched his neck, looking out of the window.

It all looked poor, not the big metropolis they had expected. The main road seemed to be the only road and it was deserted, the surface uneven from lack of maintenance. Tall dry grass grew on either side of the road, and road signs were worn, dirty and almost not readable. A few small shops stood on one side of the road, badly in need of repair, the brown paint peeling under a relentless sun, and the signs hanging and swinging by a nail. The wooden fences that surrounded a few houses and shops were broken, and the greenery that was now brown and scorched by the sun still grew wild. It was a ghost town, just like in a western movie; it was Dodge City, even to the bundles of dried tumbleweed that came rolling down the road towards them on the warm breeze. It could have been a film set, and they would not have been surprised to see the stagecoach come racing through the town and cowboys in a drunken fight being thrown out of the saloon. Except that it was quiet; there was no gunfire. No men. No horses. No mules. No nothing! It *was* a ghost town!

The minibus drove on slowly right to the end of the street, where a grubby sign waved in the breeze on a torn, frayed and faded red canvas canopy; it said *HOTEL*.

They left the minibus and walked into the hotel. The driver said that the charge for the minibus had already been settled by a Mr Stirling, and handed out all the luggage to Ed, who again was to be the last to leave. Ed gave the man a good tip, which he took gratefully. Just then a porter came out with a trolley to take the bags.

Inside the hotel, it could have been a hundred years old, and the small reception hall had a depressing feeling. Everything was dark brown wood, even to the low ceiling, and there was a strong smell of polish mixed with the smell of the musty old wood. It was dismal with shafts of yellow sunlight the only light, coming through a small open window to the right-hand side and playing on the top of the highly polished but well-worn and ancient reception desk.

On top of this was a modern fan that swivelled and cooled the air, a good sign that they did have electricity.

Behind the desk sat an elderly black man; he could have been an old fixture of the hotel. He had a shiny balding head and what little hair he did have was greying and curly; he also had a heavy grey moustache that covered most of his wrinkled face. He got lazily off a high stool and stiffly onto his feet, looking weary and overworked as if their arrival had disturbed his afternoon nap, and with slow movement he turned the register so that Steve could sign.

It was so quiet that even the scratching of the pen seemed to fill the reception room. There was no other sign of life anywhere, and Amber wondered if they were the only guests that the old man had seen for weeks; he was most probably bored. But his dark eyes brightened a little when he realised that they had reservations and that they were the film people from Hollywood. He seemed a little surprised but said that he had been expecting them, and eyed them critically. They were all looking a bit bedraggled with the heat; maybe he was expecting glamour. Amber, feeling ashamed, melted into the background.

He then welcomed them with a wide white smile and called the bellboy, who came from a back room. He was young, black and handsome with high cheekbones, smiling dark brown eyes and a white even smile, probably in his mid-twenties, wearing a faded blue uniform with bright and shiny brass buttons. He gave them a broad smile and was eager to have them follow him to the small lift. The lift could only barely take three people at a time, so Amber and Steve squeezed in. The lift rattled and jerked and Amber held her breath; it didn't feel safe. The young man showed them to separate rooms down a narrow, dark and dismal brown and woody hallway, and said that he would send up their luggage.

Amber closed the bedroom door and looked around the small room, dark like the rest of the hotel, and poorly furnished, with an ancient dressing table, the mirror pitted. There was a well-worn and sagging armchair with dark green upholstery, dark red curtains now faded to pink from the sun blazing through the small window that looked out over the pointed rooftops of small wooden chattel houses; the double bed had a dark red counterpane and snow-white pillow cases. The room looked neat, clean and tidy, but gave the impression that it had been well-occupied. There were a couple of pictures on the brownish-golden walls.

She opened a door expecting a bathroom, but it was just a small cupboard with a few coat hangers. She twitched her nose at the strong smell of old wood. The jungle hut had been more modern compared to this, but still it was only for one night, she *hoped*. Even her friend the spider wouldn't have felt at home here.

There was a tap on the door, and an older man in a faded blue uniform brought in her luggage. She tipped him well and he smiled, more than pleased, bowing his head gratefully, and thanked her.

'Where is the bathroom?' Amber asked.

'Down the hall, mistress, second door on the left.'

'Thank you.' Obviously a communal bathroom; she wondered how many she would have to share it with. At least it would surely be free of spiders. It ran through her head again: *thank God this is only for one night.*

There was a phone on the bedside table; it rang loudly with an old-fashioned ringing, the bell piercing her ears and startling her and making her heart beat fast. She hesitated before picking up the receiver. It was Jonah, saying that they were meeting in the bar downstairs before dinner, at seven thirty.

Amber found the bathroom; it was anything but luxurious, just as she had expected. The shower was a handset in the bath, the white porcelain badly stained brown under the taps where the water had dripped for so long, but at least the water was clear, and there were several small tubes of shower gel and shampoo, and a pile of snow-white baths towels on a rack.

After going back to her room and finding a hairdryer in a drawer, much to her relief, she then put on her very limited makeup, which consisted only of a very thin scraping of blue eyeshadow and a touch of melting lipstick: the very last of her samples, which she'd managed to hold back for emergencies. She took a dress out of her zip-up Louis Vuitton bag; even for all of Bessie's careful packing in tissue paper it was now very creased, but it would have to do. It was nice just to get dressed again.

She made her way down to find the bar. Steve was there alone; he smiled and said she looked nice. She nodded a thank-you; she appreciated it, but wondered what he really thought.

He had ordered a bottle of champagne. The barman poured it and they clinked glasses; Steve said it was to celebrate their survival from last week, God knew they needed it, and they chuckled together, sharing a pleasant few moments before the others joined them. It was the first time that she felt she had relaxed with him. He had been such a comfort to her and she wanted to say so, but she wouldn't dare to let him know how she was feeling.

The barman, who said his name was Jamie, was chatty and asked whether they were the actors, and where they had come from. He was surprised when they said that they had been in the jungle for a week; he said he would never dare to go there. He was even more intrigued when they said that they had come from Hollywood, and then asked for their autographs and was thrilled as he had seen videos with Amber De Carla and Steve Salvettini. She saw him looking closely into her face, really not believing it, and it made her feel embarrassed, but he seemed happy enough.

Louise, Jonah and Ed arrived together, and Steve ordered another bottle of champagne.

The dining room was again of dark wood, with candlelight and a small bowl of flowers on each table, but it could hardly be called cosy. There were several other people dining, although they were not full. The food was reasonably good, at least, and after a few more bottles of wine, they retired, both Amber and Steve glad to have a room to themselves...

They slept well and all met early in the dining room for breakfast. After breakfast Steve asked the slow man on the reception desk for the phone number of the hospital; they were planning for the minibus that was to collect them and take them to the airport to drop them off at the hospital first to see Elliot. But when Steve got through the nurse told him that Mr Stirling had left yesterday afternoon.

CHAPTER ELEVEN

Back now in Hollywood, California, three weeks had gone by. Elliot had recovered and was back in the office, and they had all settled down again. It was good to be home, and since their return there had been two cocktail parties, which they had all attended. Both Amber and Louise felt relieved now to have makeup and their hair styled, and to be mixing with civilisation and back to normal. But the jungle had tamed Amber, and Bessie had noticed a big difference in her manner.

Ronald Tappener was hosting a cocktail party at his luxurious home. The setting was beautiful; they were on the high-up patio that overlooked the beach and the sea. The night was warm and a pale moon shone across the water. Elliot's wife Elaine was standing, glass of champagne in hand, talking to Amber, asking, 'Just what was it like in the jungle? It must have been awful for you. Elliot told me snippets. He said it was terrible; he said you were all upset, and seeing crocodiles and snakes and a jaguar; he said it was really scary.'

'Yes.' Amber smiled and then frowned, then went on to tell Elaine about the spiders, the crocodiles, the snakes.

'Oh, how awful.' Elaine was shaking her head. 'Well, Elliot has not been the same since he's been back. He's changed; he's certainly not himself.' She smiled and chuckled. 'I said it must be jungle fever.'

'I expect it was the snake bite,' said Amber quite seriously.

'Snake bite?' Elaine looked most surprised. 'Who got bitten?'

She didn't wait for an answer, as at that moment a young woman pushed past her through the crowd, saying, 'Hello, Elaine,' and then moved on.

Elaine smiled, and then turned back to Amber and went on about Elliot, 'And as for those gold mines, he said he'd never seen so much gold; maybe that's what's changed him.' She chuckled again. 'I think it must have gone to his head, ha ha.'

Amber frowned, thinking Elaine didn't know; she hadn't heard about the snake bite? So he obviously hadn't gone straight home from the hospital in Guyana?

Then Amber went on to tell her more about the trip into the jungle and about the gold market, which of course Elliot had not seen, owing to the snake bite.

'Yes, Elliot said it was wonderful. He brought me this bracelet.' She held up her wrist. Amber admired the bracelet, a little puzzled. 'The first time he had ever been to a gold mine; well, I expect it was the first time for you all. It must have been a great experience.' Elaine smiled.

'Yes.' Amber was a little bewildered. 'Well, it wasn't really a gold mine; it was the gold market.'

'Yes, Elliot said that was fabulous too.'

Elliot had obviously lied to his wife. He had been at Riverside House when they had arrived there, but where had he been before that? And where had he been since leaving the hospital in Guyana?

Steve came up, and the conversation changed, and a waiter was pouring more champagne. And, as at all cocktail parties, people moved on and intermixed and Elaine was now lost somewhere in the crowds.

A week had gone by and arrangements had been made to continue the shooting of *The Tiger's Eye* in Miami, Florida, where they had first staged the plane crash scene. This meant that they were once again to be on location, and they were to leave in the morning. Elliot had discussed this with Ronald Tappener; a coach was to pick them up at the studio and a private jet had been arranged for the flight to Miami.

There were twenty of them, the same crew as before, camera, sound and lighting, and Ed Bennett once again was in charge. Elliot had agreed to let Stacey Devlin come along and just watch, now that Diana Whitlock was to take over her part. Elliot had rented luxury trailers for the stars, and the technicians could find their own accommodation.

Stacey Devlin seemed and looked quite well, although she was still suffering from nerves and her complexion was pale, but apparently she had got a bug in the stomach from the Demerara River water and was still on antibiotics, and the hospital's department of tropical diseases was still trying to find an actual cause. Amber had seen a change in her. Stacey seemed far more confident than she had been at first; she seemed more bold in her outlook, no more the frightened mouse that she had been at the night of the awards dinner. That was the first night that Amber had really spoken to her socially; she'd had a supporting part in the film *Love to Kill* and they had worked together, but all they had really said to each other on the set was, 'Good morning.'

But now Amber noticed that Stacey seemed to stay very close to Elliot. She was at the studio every day, and there was no reason why she shouldn't be there, but it just seemed strange. It was either that she *couldn't* work or that she didn't want to. Maybe Elliot had promised her stardom in another production, and she wanted to stay close in case she was forgotten; it seemed that she was always around. But Amber had never got close to her; they were just two different people. Even when there was a coffee break and they all sat around discussing the filming, the lighting or the way a scene should be played, Stacey seemed to sit close to Elliot, and rarely commented.

Now, with Diana Whitlock, things were different. She and Amber got along well, but now the takes had to be retaken right from the beginning, since she had now taken on the role that Stacey had intended to play.

After coming back from Guyana, Amber had calmed down a lot in her day-to-day life. The shock of the whole week had taken its toll. Everyone had remarked on the change in her, but now, going on location again and having to do retakes, she was in one of her old moods, and bubbling over with annoyance as usual. 'Why didn't we do these jungle scenes in Miami in the first place, Elliot? Fancy sending us off to some God-forsaken place like the jungle. I'm fed up with this film, and I wish I'd never agreed to do it!' She fumed nearly every day, and, although the others were in agreement with her, no one really voiced their opinion.

The shooting was going well, the retakes with Diana Whitlock had gone well, and Jonah got to play his part at last, coming out of the jungle-like trees and looking like a wild man, his huge black and muscled body glistening with oil. Louise and her team had done a good job with the makeup, his face slashed with red and black and yellow paint; he looked very fierce.

After reading so much in the jungle they were so well-rehearsed that nobody fluffed their lines; they were word-perfect and everything went smoothly, and there was no doubt that Elliot was a brilliant director.

Ronald Tappener had come down to see how things were progressing. Amber had thanked him for putting on the private jets, and then of course she had told him about the jungle, and he had apologised but said that it was really up to Elliot to set the scenes. Tappener had only stayed the one night on location, owing to business meetings the next day, and they had all been out for a very pleasant dinner together.

The next day, Amber and Diana had enjoyed coffee together before the shooting began. Since Diana had taken over the part of supporting actress, they were retaking the scene where the Harrisons and Gloria Stoneham were staggering away from the air crash, the pilot and the co-pilot just dummies slumped in the cockpit and covered in blood. The Harrisons would be seen staggering from the plane and hacking their way through the jungle greenery, when they were to be attacked by a life-size mechanical tiger that was supposedly stalking them, but Elliot had now substituted it for a life-size mechanical black jaguar that was glimpsed in the trees from which they had run, the animal operated by

Al Martin with a remote control. They were trying to beat it off with long sticks; it jumped at them and snarled.

At the end of the day, it all looked very impressive as they watched the retakes. Ed had intercut the Guyana shots of the real jaguar with the scene, the red eyes and the huge black paws and the jump onto the table, but it now looked as if the jump was at Donald Harrison. At that moment 'Donald' fell flat on his face, then there was a flash of teeth and the growl, this from where it had jumped up onto the barbecue table; it all looked so very real.

Then the scene changed and Jonah was seen coming through the trees with a real live tiger walking beside him like a big dog; the tiger's handler Bart Wilson was standing close by, but of course out of sight of the cameras. Jonah raised his arm and pointed, telling the tiger to 'Go attack!'; Bart Wilson, in the background, ordered the tiger, whose real name was Major, to 'Go get the toy.'

Major then bounded forward and there was a fight scene as Al Martin stood the jaguar up on its hind legs, and Major's big teeth were seen to grab the jaguar by the neck and shake it, of course in play, but tearing the fake fur to show snippets of red like blood. The tiger mauled and pawed it and growled at the jaguar like a dog playing with a favourite toy. It was then called off by the wild man, but of course the tiger obeyed the call of his master Bart Wilson to '*Leave*, Major, bring here!' And then he came away dragging the toy like a successful kill with him and gave it to Bart, off camera.

In the next scene Jonah was patting the tiger and praising him. All this time Steve had been lying face-down on the ground; he was fine, but had received a few bruises on his back and his thighs where the tiger's big paws had accidentally pounced on him. Of course this had all been rehearsed weeks before, three jaguars having been made and now well-used and patched up.

Major was well-trained; he would shake hands, putting out a great paw, but on the screen the great talons looked like an attack, clawing at Donald Harrison's arm and leaving blood pouring out. There was then a scene where Donald Harrison was lying flat-out and covered in blood, Amber kneeling at his side in floods of tears. Elliot had said, 'Cut!'

The trainer, Bart Wilson, was an ex-policeman. He'd had Major since he was a six-week-old cub, when Major's mother had died in the circus; it was thought to be foul play. Bart was the policeman on duty at the time, and he had asked to take the cub, and had given him police dog training.

Major, on request, could give out a huge snarl, showing great white fangs, and it looked so aggressive on screen, making them all shudder. For the fight scene with the jaguar, there had been flashes of teeth and it had looked so fierce, but it was all play. He had been given the mechanical jaguar weeks before so that it was not strange to him, and he had just mauled the toy quite happily while Al Martin kept it moving with the remote control, until, of course, Major's teeth went right through and the mechanism was broken, and then he was given an identical new toy.

Major was now three years old and was a beautiful animal; he loved people and could be fully trusted, although he spent most of his time while on set in a cage. To keep him active through the year, Bart Wilson was engaged with the Barnham and Bailey Circus and they travelled the country performing.

The crew had all petted him and he loved it, and Jonah said he was enjoying working with him. Now he had got used to Jonah and would obey Jonah's commands, and Jonah said it seemed as if he was smiling. Amber was the only one who would not go near. Elliot thought she was afraid to get her hands grubby.

In the pawing scene, the tiger had come a bit too close and Amber had shied away quickly and caught her shoe and had broken the strap, so in the break-time she left the set and went to the trailer used for wardrobe. Simon, the guy who was in charge, was not there; she guessed he'd gone for coffee. She sat down in the trailer and while waiting she thumbed through a magazine.

On hearing voices and thinking that it was Simon coming back, she looked out of the window and was surprised to see Elliot creeping through the trees with Stacey Devlin, their arms around each other. She had noticed on one or two occasions that Elliot had been attentive to Stacey, but she had thought that it was because she had not been well and, although Amber found him a hard man, she supposed that he did have a softer side when he wasn't directing. But *now* she frowned and wondered; he was old enough to be Stacey's grandfather.

The Harrisons were on their last leg of being chased across the Caribbean by the Miami drug squad. The shooting for *The Tiger's Eye* had taken another six weeks, and now it was closed. Diana Whitlock had played her part well, after taking on the role so late in the production, but it had made the stay longer on location, having to do the retakes.

The accommodation in the trailers had been comfortable, but of course they were now all pleased to be packing up and going home to LA.

CHAPTER TWELVE

The private jet touched down in LA. It was good to be home. John was there to meet Amber, and as Downs opened the front door, Bessie was there with open arms; in all, it had been four months since she had last been home.

Amber had settled back home again and she and Bessie were sitting in the garden on Bessie's little patio; it was a warm evening and very peaceful. Amber was telling Bessie all about Guyana. Bessie listened intently, thinking that a lot of it was just a story and a bit farfetched; Amber did tend to embroider a bit.

'Coo, fancy them giant spiders, as big as yer 'ands.' Her voice rose. 'You don't like spiders, do you, Kit?'

'No.' Amber shook her head with a slight smile; the very thought gave her the shivers. 'Well, how have things been going here?' she asked.

'Oh, everyfing's bin fine.' She grinned and raised her eyebrows. 'Got meself a man.' She dropped her eyes with a shy smile, and lifted them again, with a comical grin.

'Oh!' Amber nearly jumped up off the chair. '*Have* you? Who is he, what's his name? Where did you meet him?' Amber was all smiles and anxious to hear. 'Come on, tell us.'

Bessie thought she was just like the old Kitty, the pomp and show forgotten for a minute. She smiled. ''Is name is Ben Adams, 'e's divorced, an' I met 'im 'ere. 'E came to fix the telephones; we 'ad a problem while you were away. I walked around the 'ouse wiv 'im and then 'e 'ad to come back again, 'cause they still wasn't workin' proper, and we got talkin' an' 'e took me out fer dinner. Seen 'im several times since then...'

They smiled together; Amber's eyes sparkled with pleasure at seeing Bessie so happy. Then Bessie went on to say, ''Ad a letter from me ex-'usband Reggie. Don't know 'ow 'e knew I was 'ere. I 'spect 'e found out from Jenny. She's still sewing at the theatre, I 'ad a letter from 'er the other day, but she didn't mention that she'd seen Reggie. P'raps she didn't like to, eh?'

'He's kept out of jail, then?' Amber smiled and arched her eyebrows.

'Yeah! Don't know 'ow long for though, an' I don't know why 'e wrote to me.'

'Well, what did he have to say?'

'Nufin' much, askin' for money o' course, an' jest was I all right. Don't know why; 'e never bovvered before.'

'What's he doing?'

'Dunno. Workin', I s'pose; 'e is a worker. Trouble is 'e can't keep 'is 'ands to 'imself. Got a right temper, 'e 'as.'

They sat quietly for a while, then, seeing Amber deep in thought, Bessie said, 'What's up wiv you? I know there's somefin' wrong. Whatcher finkin' about?'

'Oh, it's so good to be home, Bessie.' Amber stretched her arms above her head, with a contented smile. 'I'm so glad to get away from that set; it's been nothing but trouble since the day we started.'

'What's up wiv yer? What's worryin' yer?'

'Nothing.' She shook her head. 'I'm just tired, that's all. Travelling.' She wrinkled her nose; she could see that Bessie wasn't about to give up. 'What?'

'Yeah! What?' Bessie folded her arms, a little piqued and still waiting. 'Well, aren't you gonna tell me?'

Amber thought for a moment. 'Oh, it's nothing! Phone Bella and make arrangements; we'll have dinner on the patio tonight, just the two of us.'

Bessie twisted her lips, and nodded; she knew Amber would tell her when she was ready. She went back into the room and phoned Bella.

A bit later they had grilled fish for dinner, accompanied by a bottle of white wine. It was delicious; Bella was a good cook.

'Well! Are you gonna tell me?' Bessie sat with her elbows on the table and her chin resting on clasped hands, eyebrows raised, waiting.

Amber didn't know if she should tell Bessie, but she knew Bessie wouldn't give up; she would keep asking anyway. 'Well...' she started slowly, 'I'm a bit worried... it's really none of my business, but... you know... I think Elliot's having an affair.'

'An affair?' Bessie's hands dropped and her chin rose as she jumped back in the chair and sort of mouthed the words again, frowning and wrinkling her nose. 'An *affair*? 'Oo wiv? What, *'im*? 'E's seventy-odd, ain't 'e?'

'Er, yes... he's over seventy.' Amber smiled at her friend's expression. 'Please don't say anything. I think it's Stacey Devlin... I *know* it's Stacey Devlin.' She nodded.

'Whaa'?' Bessie frowned heavily and scratched her head. 'She's about twenty, ain't she? 'E's old enough to be 'er bloody grandfather.'

Amber smiled again and took a deep breath, nodding. 'Yes, I know; guess you're never too old, but then Elliot always thinks he's attractive to young ladies. He tried it on with me, years ago, but I wasn't having any. She's been down on location with us for weeks, no need for her to be there. I thought she had just come to watch, seeing as Diana took over her part... and it was some weeks ago that Elaine asked me if there was something wrong with Elliot, she said he hadn't been the same. I said it was the snake bite, and she looked as if she didn't know what I was talking about; she even asked me *who* got bitten. And she was talking as if he'd been with us in the jungle, and at the gold mines, but then I wondered... you see, he hadn't really been to Guyana – well, not until the last couple of days. It was the way she said it, she implied that he'd been to Guyana with us, but of course he hadn't because he'd turned back when Stacey fell in the river. I didn't say anything, and then while on location in Miami I saw them – Elliot and Stacey, I mean – sneaking off into the trees. And they shared a trailer...'

'Better, then, is she?'

'Who?'

'Stacey Devlin? After falling in the river.'

'Well!' Amber inclined her head and grimaced. 'According to Elliot, she's still not very well. He said it's going to take a long time.'

'*What* is?' Bessie frowned with an open mouth. 'The affair or the illness?'

Amber chuckled. 'The illness, I suppose. Got some bug that tropical diseases is trying to find out, so *he* said. But she looked quite fit when he was patting her bum and she was kissing him in the trees.'

They chuckled together, seeing the funny side. 'Oh!' Bessie rolled her eyes, still smiling. 'Another one sellin' 'erself, I 'spect, tryin' to make 'er name and become a star.'

Amber looked at her open-mouthed. 'I didn't do that!'

'I didn't say you did! No, luv, *you* 'ad talent, and you've worked 'ard to get where you are, but these young bits o' stuff these days do nufin' but sleep around.'

CHAPTER THIRTEEN

Jerome had not been doing much. He'd phoned and taken Amber out to dinner, and was telling her how lovely she looked and how much he'd missed her. She gave him an affected sensual-lipped smile and half-closed her black lashes, like a girl on a glossy magazine. There was no warmth in it. She shrugged her shoulders, wondering in her mind why she had accepted his invitation to dinner.

He had selected a small exclusive restaurant because she was never free of the press. The food had been good and he had bought champagne, trying to impress her as usual, mainly for the sake of keeping in with her. She knew why he was trying to impress her, but she found him a bore. Why she had accepted his invitation she really didn't know.

Since she had come back from Guyana, and now had been on location again, she and Steve Salvettini had been more friendly. They'd had dinner evenings and he was exciting to be with, even though there was nothing intimate between them; they had just chatted about the film and everyday things, enjoying each other's company. They had laughed easily together about the spiders, now that it was all in the past. But Jerome did nothing but talk about himself, how he was now out of work and had been for almost three months; he was trying to get work, but even small parts had not come his way; he was getting a little older and the parts weren't available; he was a reasonably well-known star, but now it seemed the phone didn't ring any more; he was fed up and getting worried. She listened, waiting for him to come to the point, and then he did: could she put a word in the right direction for him, with Elliot or Tappener or someone?

She knew then, as she had known for many months, that Jerome stayed with her only for his own benefit, and that was why he had asked her out for dinner; he was hoping to be *seen*, knowing the press were waiting everywhere she went. In fact she guessed he had secretly informed the press that Amber De Carla would be at this little secluded restaurant tonight. It was all about *being seen*. He kept saying how much he had missed her. It wasn't because he'd missed her that much; it was that he had missed being *seen* with her, because without *her* he didn't get *seen* at all.

As for her, well, *she* just needed him as an escort; there was no fun in going to a restaurant alone. He had asked her out and she didn't really like to turn him down after being away so long, and she wasn't really doing very much, and so she had accepted. But now she was friendly with Steve again, there was no comparison.

He asked her how the shooting had gone.

'It's finished, and it has been much better since Steve and I get along a bit better now.' She noticed him wince; he didn't like it when she mentioned Steve.

'That young actress never made it, you know,' he said.

'What young actress?'

'Dulcie Shand, the one that caused all the trouble with Salvettini.'

'Why, do you know her then?'

'Yeah,' he boasted with a slight smile, hoping to make her a little jealous, 'I've taken her out a couple of times.'

'Oh, what, recently?' She sounded surprised.

'No, before all the fuss with Salvettini. She latched on to me, and I suppose I wasn't a big enough star for her. She was always asking how she could get to know Salvettini so she could get some publicity; she said she was game for a bit of scandal.'

Amber's eyes blazed. 'And *you told her how*?'

Jerome winced. 'No, no! Not exactly. I—'

He was shaking his head when Amber jumped up like a rocket and slapped him hard across the face. It was such a surprise that he rocked back, catching hold of the table, and the chair slid away. He lost his balance, going down with a crash and ending up flat on his back and then sitting on the floor, holding his face.

Other people in the restaurant stopped eating and turned at the sudden impact, as Amber stormed past the tables and out of the door. While Jerome sat startled, holding the side of his face as it came up red with the impression of her fingers, people began to grin and titter, and somebody whispered, 'That's Jerome Howard.'

He got quickly to his feet, he paid the bill, and was heard to comment as he rushed outside, 'I'll kill her!' But Amber had already got a cab and was gone.

The next morning, Bessie came in and swished back the curtains. Amber opened her eyes.

'Take a look at *this*!' Bessie flung the paper onto the bed, and Amber sat up in her pink satin sheets. The front page had a photograph of Jerome sitting and holding his face; the headline read *SLAPPED by AMBER! GUESS HOWARD WAS A NAUGHTY BOY!* She looked down to the column below.

People dining in Toni's Restaurant last night were very surprised when Amber De Carla shouted angry words and slapped her date full in the face, knocking him to the floor. Miss De Carla walked out of the restaurant, leaving Jerome Howard stunned and holding his face. Miss De Carla commented to reporters waiting outside the restaurant, 'He wanted some publicity! Give him some!'

Jerome had also seen the morning paper; it mentioned his remark, 'I'll kill her!' He felt very embarrassed, and now worried; he shouldn't have said that! He wondered how the photo and his remark had got into the papers.

He intended to phone Amber later, and sort it all out about Salvettini. He hadn't meant for Dulcie Shand to trick Steve Salvettini into bed, although he had sort of jokingly implied something like that. And yes, he had now got some recognition, but not the sort he wanted. It had been splashed all over the tabloids some months ago that Jerome Howard, being the greatest man, had conquered Amber, Queen of Hollywood, and now the queen had taken away his status.

The pink phone rang on the bedside table. Amber leaned out and answered it; it was Steve Salvettini.

'Hi,' he said. 'Have you seen the paper this morning?'

'Yes, just read it.' She chuckled into the receiver. 'I'll tell you all about it later.'

They rang off.

Bessie was still by the window, straightening the drapes. She raised her eyebrows. 'Looks as if you've dunnit agin, Kit.'

They grinned together.

'I never did like tha' bloke anyway. Wha' did yer slap 'im like tha' for?'

Amber grinned. 'I didn't know anyone took a photo; it must have been someone with a phone, because the press guys were outside when I hailed the cab. I don't think I'll ever be free of photographers.'

'Well, wha' made yer slap 'im?'

'Well, he almost confessed that he had egged that Dulcie Shand girl on into getting the bedroom scene with Steve. Even though Steve and I broke up, I never really did believe that it was his fault. He told me several times, but it made me feel so mad; I'd felt such a fool, the papers saying that I couldn't hold a man, or something like that, and he'd found a younger woman. I guess it will make headlines again if Steve and I are really seen together. And I do hope that we can get back together, Bessie. You know, I think I love him...'

Bessie flicked her eyes upwards.

'He was a great comfort to me while we were in the jungle. I really don't know what I would have done without him.'

'Well, whatever.' Bessie grinned. ''E's better than tha' creep 'oward. Slimy git, 'e only wanted yer for 'is own benefit. Now, tha' *Salvettini,* wha' an 'andsome bloke 'e is. You're better off wiv 'im, Kit.'

'Oh, Bessie, I really don't think it will ever be the same again.'

'It'll come right, Kit. You deserve the best, gel; you worked 'ard,' and she gave her a hug. For a moment Bessie thought it was like old times, but then she realised that it could never really be like the old times now that they had both come this far, and now she wouldn't want to go back.

CHAPTER FOURTEEN

Monday morning they were all in the cinema – Amber, Steve, Jonah, Diana Whitlock, Tom Fallen and Ed Bennett, Philip Croft the author, and of course Elliot and Ronald Tappener – to view the final cut of the film. Elliot had already talked over the few adjustments to the script some weeks ago with the author Philip Croft, before they had proceeded to Miami to shoot the jungle scenes at last.

Elliot had already viewed the finished film and was very pleased with the results. He apologised for sending them all to the jungle, knowing now that it had been really hard and very unpleasant for them all. He also said that he thought Ed had done a good job and he had never seen Amber so scruffy, and they all laughed. He was sorry for making them all dirty up again for the actual filming in Miami.

Jonah frowned. 'How were you planning to get that tiger to Guyana?'

'I wasn't.' Elliot grinned. 'I planned to shoot those jungle scenes in Miami.'

Amber was aghast. '*In Miami?* So why the *hell* did you send us all the way to *Guyana*, then?'

'I wanted to be authentic.'

'*Eoh!* Elliot! You make me *sick*!'

The Tiger's Eye was another great success, and everyone was extremely relieved it was over. Amber organised a party to celebrate the finish. It was the first big party that she'd had since moving into Sunny Hill. Mary Anne had sent out invitations to just about every one of today's stars, veteran stars, starlets, producers and directors, along with the crew of *The Tiger's Eye* and their partners. There were to be about two hundred guests with a red-carpet-like introduction.

Sunny Hill House had been transformed, with bright lights that lit up the garden. On a warm summer's night under a dark blue starry sky, the band was in full swing. People swarmed the garden around the pool, the men in black tie, the ladies in an array of designer evening gowns. Waiters had offered drinks and canapés, and there had been a huge buffet dinner from outside caterers; there had been seven chefs in white with tall hats, who had stood behind the magnificent feast and served.

The dinner was now finished and there was a loud buzz of conversation, as friends stood in groups around the bar or sat at tables chatting, some dancing as the band played on. Just about anyone who was anyone was there. Even Jerome, who had definitely *not* had an invitation, had wormed his way in by escorting Stacey Devlin. Amber had spotted him through the crowd earlier on in the evening, but it had been too late to cause a commotion and have him thrown out, and so she had dismissed it from her mind.

Amber noticed Stacey Devlin flashing her eyes at Elliot, but Elliot flicked his eyes away, lifted his chin and turned his back on her, notably not acknowledging her. Amber wondered if they had had a break-up. Elliot was talking to Elaine and Ronald Tappener and Tappener's daughter; he swayed a bit, having had too much to drink, and he reached out to the bar to steady himself. She also wondered if perhaps Elliot had at last come to his senses. Elaine obviously had not got a clue as to what was going on. But then, Elliot would have to sort out his troubles. Amber was happy to be some sort of reunited with Steve Salvettini.

Bessie was standing in the shadows of the bushes at the bottom of the steps, with a glass of champagne in her hands, just watching the beautiful people. She saw Amber mingling in the crowd and looking fantastic in a beautiful scarlet evening gown. She smiled to herself, recalling earlier in the evening when the two of them had come into the garden at seven o'clock, both wearing silken gowns of the brightest red. They had chuckled together and Amber had said, 'Snap!' and Downs had offered them a glass of champagne before the guests had arrived.

Bessie had felt very proud as Amber had complimented her on her choice of gown, and she had replied, 'Thanks, Kit, but it's all down to you. I could never 'ave done this on me own, and it's the first time I've ever worn a long dress.'

'*Gouwn*, dear! *Gouwn!*' Amber had mocked with a smile and with very rounded *ouwn*s. 'We don't wear *dresses* to parties; we wear *gouwns*.' They had giggled together, like old times; they had termed them 'the good old days', but were they? Bessie never wanted to be like that again. She sipped the champagne; this was the life.

She smiled to herself now and braced her shoulders, feeling quite proud, and secretly thinking that she had finally made it. She would never have done this in London, never would have even had the chance; she now felt as if she had some identity.

Kitty had told her to mingle, but she hadn't yet. There were a lot of celebrities that she recognised, but wouldn't dare to speak to.

It seemed to be a night for red dresses. Several ladies, some she couldn't even name, had chosen to wear red for this evening; it seemed to be the dominant colour, and she felt quite proud for choosing what seemed to be the 'in' thing. She ran her hand down the front of her red silk dress... *gown*. She smiled to herself. She had to remember to think *gown*, and not *dress*. Kitty had told her so many times about this. She smiled to herself again and then she saw Elaine Stirling had chosen red, and Louise wore red all the time; it was her favourite colour and against her dark skin it always looked beautiful.

Bessie sipped her champagne. How was she supposed to mingle? These were not her type of people, all too posh and la-di-dah for her; it was totally out of her league. She was happy to just watch quietly from the shadows, here at the bottom of the marble steps that led down from the wide-open patio doors of the library to the lawn and the pool.

Then Downs, who was off duty for tonight, joined her, saying what a magnificent party it was. He had a tray and a bottle of champagne in his hand, and topped up her glass.

'Thought *you* were off duty.' She smiled up at him and then said, 'Yeah, I've never bin to a party like this before, out 'ere under the stars, warm night. You can't do this in England; it's always too blo... ahem! Cold and rainin'.'

He smiled, used to her cockney slang by now, and they watched together as the beautiful people mingled easily in the fairy lights and the flickering light from the flaming torches, and the candlelight on the tables caught the sparkle of diamonds at throat, ears or wrist as the glamorous ladies moved. There was a high-pitched giggle and loud laughter and Bessie tried to catch snippets of conversation, but with the music playing it was one continuous babble.

As the evening wore on the electric lighting was turned down low; she felt it was all so romantic with just the flaming torches and candles. The night was warm and without a breath of air. Her mind wandered. She and Kitty had come a long way since the beer and hamburgers at the Three Whistles; she smiled at the thought. Whoever would have thought that *she* would end up like this?

The band played loudly and two girl singers were belting out a lively tune. A lot of people were dancing; Amber and Steve were among them. Bessie was thinking what a lovely handsome couple they made... and then she saw Jerome, who she had called slimy. He was with a girl wearing a red dress, a *gown*. Bessie twitched her lips and smiled to herself. As the girl turned she could see that it was Stacey Devlin. But how had *he* got in here? Surely Kit hadn't sent him an invitation?

A trumpet struck up a high note, and it brought her back to reality. Downs had moved on to replenish the staff's glasses; Bella and the maids were, like her, watching from the shadows at the other side of the steps. In her reverie she had forgotten Downs was there.

It was then the shrubbery was disturbed and she was suddenly aware of someone very close to her. She turned quickly and, looking up at the tall figure towering over her, she gasped. 'Reggie, wha' *you* doin' 'ere in America? *'Ere!* 'Ow'd you get in 'ere anyway?'

He smiled, bending down towards her and sticking his neck out. 'Surprised to see me, are you, luv?' He jerked back up. 'Got a job as a waiter, didn't I? Also got a dress suit.' He flicked the lapels, puffing out his chest with pride, his grey eyes sparkling in the dimness with amusement.

'Oh, very 'andsome, I'm sure.' She flicked her eyebrows up, her thoughts going back. Well, he had been handsome when she'd married him, tall and attractive, *when* he was dressed up; that was how she had first met him at a dance on a Saturday night. And then he had got into bad company, and then didn't work for a while, then had his violent moments. 'Wha' do you want 'ere, anyway?'

'Money, luv. You know. Wha' else? I told yer, I'm broke.'

'I told yer in a letter before, I ain't got none! Me wages go straight into the bank.'

'Well, give us wha' yer got, then.'

'*No*, Reggie.' She frowned, then braced herself and stood up tall. 'I told yer before, I ain't got no money! At least not to spare fer you!'

He gripped her arm tightly and stuck a gun in her ribs. 'Come on, gel, I need some dough!'

'*Ooh!*' She grimaced, with the corners of her mouth down and her eyebrows up. 'All very American, I'm sure, gun an' all... 'ow'd you get *that*? Or where did you steal it, more like? And 'ow'd you get in 'ere anyway?'

He didn't answer, but was guiding her along the garden path, close to the trees and away from the party lights, towards her room. He knew where to go; he had been watching her over the wall secretly for days with the binoculars that he had stolen from a yacht down at the port,

205

and she had no alternative but to go with him. They were now in the darkness and shadowed by the trees. She didn't think for one moment that he'd shoot her, but he could get violent and punch her around.

They came to the end of the house and turned the corner to her apartment. She slid the sliding door back, and he pushed her into the darkened room. She switched on a small table lamp that sent a pink glow around the room.

Waving the gun, he motioned her towards the sideboard, where he saw she had left her handbag. 'Come on, Bess, luv, give us some cash, then I won't bovver yer agin, honest!' He waved the gun at her again. 'I'm gettin' on a ship an' I won't be comin' back.'

'I'm not afraid of you, Reggie. You won't shoot me; you can't afford to shoot me. You need me! You need money!'

'Shut up and stop bloody well doodlin' abart! Get on wiv it!' He sounded very businesslike.

She swallowed hard; she was a bit worried, but she was sure he didn't intend to shoot her. Reggie wasn't the killer type.

'I know you got money in the safe over there.' He pointed the gun at the picture on the wall.

'*Whaa'?* 'Ow do you know tha'? 'Ere! You bin spyin' on me?'

'*Come on, 'urry up!* Open the bloody safe!'

She knew his ways, and could see that he was getting agitated. He was very handy with his fists; she'd experienced it before, and that time it had all been over money, when she had wanted some housekeeping and he had lost it all gambling. And now he was waving the gun.

'Alrigh', alrigh'!' She put up a hand. 'Wait a minute.' She turned her back on him and swung the picture open. 'But this 'as godda be the last time. I'm not a bloody millionaire, you know.'

'Come on, come *on*! I'll be missed; they're payin' me to serve drinks.'

'Well, they ain't payin' you enough! 'Ow did yer get a job, anyway, wivout any papers?' she asked over her shoulder.

He grimaced; he wasn't supposed to be there. 'Jest applied, didn't I? They were desperate for waiters. But I'm leavin' soon enough, I told yer I got a job on a boat. Give us five fousand dollars, an' I won't bovver yer agin.'

'Whaaa'?' Her voice rose in amazement as she turned to face him, frowning and screwing her eyes up. 'I ain't got five thousand dollars.'

'Well, give us wha' you got, then! Come on, mate.' He sounded in despair, wrinkling his nose. 'Come on, 'elp us out, luv. Yer don't wanna see me starve, do yer?'

'I don't wanna see you at all!'

''Ow long you bin livin' in a big 'ouse like this? Bet your boss 'as got a bit o' jewellery, ain't she?'

'*You* leave 'er out o' this! And don't you dare touch anyfin' in this 'ouse or I'll call the police.'

'No, you won't. Tha's not like you, Bess. Come on, luv.' He wrinkled his nose again with a half-smile. 'I ain't got much time.'

She tutted and turned her back on him in disgust, and punched in the code, then spun around to face him again. 'A thousand, tha's all I got. 'Ere, *take it* and get out o' 'ere!

And don't come back!' She stuck the notes out in front of her at arm's length.

The bullet hit Bessie right in the chest; she fell back flat on her back.

Reggie looked down at her in shocked surprise, then looked at the gun in his hand. He was about to kneel at her side when the door suddenly burst open, and Reggie turned and dashed out of the sliding window and was lost in the darkness.

As Downs stepped into the room, he saw the shadow of a man leaving and he rushed to the open glass door, but whoever it was was gone; he saw no one. He turned back into the room and then saw Bessie lying on the floor.

He went quickly to her and stood looking down at her, shocked for a moment to see blood staining the red dress and not knowing what to do. His heart racing, his mind in a whirl, he knelt beside her, and then with a shaking hand he took the phone from his pocket and dialled 911. And then he went quickly to look for Miss De Carla.

Downs spoke quietly and anxiously to Miss De Carla, and she and Steve discreetly left the party. When they were away from their guests, Downs told them what had happened.

Amber dashed down the hall and into Bessie's apartment and went down on her knees at Bessie's side, bursting into floods of tears. Bessie was dead! *Dead!* 'IT CAN'T BE, IT CAN'T BE!' she screamed, shaking her head, tears streaming down her cheeks.

Steve and Downs stood there, helpless and looking at the gaping hole in the red dress where the darker red of Bessie's blood oozed from her lifeless body. And Steve put a comforting hand on Amber's shoulder.

Sirens sounded in the drive. The party went on, guests thinking that someone had complained about the noise.

The medical examiner came into Bessie's apartment. Amber had to step outside for a moment; she already knew Bessie was dead, and she couldn't bear to hear it confirmed. But the confirmation came anyway when Bessie wasn't taken out to the ambulance, and a few minutes later the police arrived.

Detective Lieutenant Mike Collins introduced himself and his colleague, Detective Sergeant Baker. Collins then sent Baker to stop the music and detain the party guests.

Baker addressed everyone over the speakers, asking them to remain right where they were; no one was to leave and they would need a statement from every single person here. When he mentioned murder, everyone looked at everyone else, and a buzz went round; who had been murdered?

Detective Lieutenant Mike Collins and his homicide officers all wore latex gloves. There were officers everywhere. Some were dusting for fingerprints; everyone had their own special duty to perform. They inspected every single part of the room.

Steve was finding it almost impossible to console Amber, while Downs was telling Lieutenant Collins, 'I was passing the door and I heard the shot, and came straight in here; well, I did fumble a bit with the key, and just as I opened the door someone disappeared out of the sliding window, but I didn't see his face.'

'His face? It was a man, then, was it?'

Downs faltered. 'Well, I, I, er, I assumed it was a man, sir. I didn't really see anyone, just a quick shadow. I dashed straight across the room and out of the sliding window but there was no one, and of course it was dark. It was then as I turned to come back in that I saw Mrs Nichols on the floor.'

'No one else heard the shot?''

'Well, I don't think so, sir; no one else came. There was no one in this part of the house and I expect it was too noisy, and the staff were all at the other end of the house watching the party.'

'What were you doing in the house?'

'I came into the kitchen, sir, to get more wine. Miss De Carla had said that the staff could have wine or champagne. I hadn't long filled Bessie's glass, sir.'

'You came in here to fill her glass?' Collins frowned.

'Oh, no, sir, she had been standing at the bottom of the steps by the library watching the party.'

Collins nodded. 'She was alone?'

'Yes, sir. I stood with her for a little while, and we watched the party guests together, and then I moved on to fill the rest of the staff's glasses.'

'You said you fumbled with the key? You have a key to this apartment?'

'I have a master key, sir, it opens all doors.'

Collins looked at Baker. Why would she lock that door and leave the sliding windows open?

Baker shook his head, a little puzzled; he had just returned, after organising officers to check all the party guests. He was now on his knees, and reaching under an armchair. 'There's money under here, sir, a whole wad of it.' He got up off his knees and showed a handful of dollar

210

bills to Lieutenant Collins, and then counted them. 'A thousand, sir.' He lifted his eyebrows, then looked around him. The picture stuck out a little way from the wall. 'There's a safe behind this picture, sir, and it's open.' He opened the safe door wider. 'Bit of jewellery and a couple of letters.' He opened an envelope. 'One from Jenny, and one from Reggie. Boyfriend, you think?' He cocked an eyebrow at Collins, handing over the letter.

'Reggie Nichols.' Amber turned quickly from Steve and looked up, swallowing hard and sniffing back her tears. 'He was Bessie's ex-husband.' She was dabbing at her eyes with tissues, trying to stop the tears and compose herself. 'Why would she have letters from him? She hasn't heard from him in years.'

'He's asking for money?' Detective Collins turned over the page in his hand.

'Perhaps he was here to collect?' said Baker.

'Humm, maybe it wasn't enough?' murmured Collins thoughtfully. He raised his eyebrows, glancing at Baker.

'No.' Amber shook her head. 'That can't be him, she hasn't seen or heard from him for years... although, wait a minute, she did tell me that she had a letter from him while I was away on location.'

Lieutenant Collins slightly shook his head; he grimaced, and then shook his head again. 'Robbery, I'd say.'

'She came in and caught him at the safe, and she was threatened, you think?' Baker raised his eyebrows.

Lieutenant Collins twisted his lips thoughtfully, nodding. 'Hmmm.'

'It couldn't be Reggie Nichols,' said Amber. 'He's in England. He wouldn't be allowed here in America; he has a prison record.'

'Oh! He has?' Collins raised his voice in surprise.

'Yes, for violence.'

Collins and Baker exchanged glances.

The coroner was checking Bessie's face and hands; he stood up and shook his head. 'Doesn't look like a punch-up, but I'll know more later.'

It was then that the ambulance men came to take poor Bessie's body to the police morgue. Amber couldn't bear to look as they zipped her into a body bag and took her out on a gurney. She gripped her hands tightly together and leaned heavily on Steve.

'Come on,' he said, 'you need a drink. Leave the detectives to do their job.'

He guided her away down the hall and up the stairs to her own apartment, then, closing the door, he sat her in an armchair. She was dazed and almost in a state of collapse. He then picked up the phone and asked Downs to bring up a bottle of wine; he knew Amber wouldn't drink spirits.

A few minutes passed and a waiter arrived with a bottle of red wine and two glasses on a tray. Steve indicated that he should put them on the coffee table by the window, and asked him to open the bottle and pour the wine. 'Where's Downs?'

'Mr Downs is with the police, sir.'

Steve nodded. 'Yes, I'm sure he is. Sorry. Thank you.'

Steve nodded again, and the waiter left.

CHAPTER FIFTEEN

The police took statements from the two hundred guests, plus the household staff and the caterers who had been hired for the night, and also the musicians and the guards on the gate; they confirmed that no one had left. Everyone had been interviewed, even a few of the press that had been waiting about outside the gate.

Like many Americans a lot of the guests carried guns. The police checked these for recent firing, and for licences, and then confiscated and labelled them and said they could be picked up at a later date when there would be more inquiries at police headquarters. But no one had seen or heard anything, the shot being drowned out by the music and the party spirit, which of course had now quietened down. Gradually the party guests were dismissed and allowed to leave, although of course their cars were accosted at the front gate by members of the press eager to get a story.

All this time Reggie Nichols was still on duty with a drinks tray; he stood well back, hoping not to be interviewed by the police. He gave his name as John Smith, and said he had no identification on him; he claimed his wallet had been stolen earlier in the evening, then, asked if he had reported it, he said that he hadn't had time yet. He gave a false address. The gun, he'd hidden amongst the linen in the kitchen that was ready for the laundry; he planned to take it with him when he left.

The days went by. Amber was beside herself. Mary Anne had taken dozens of calls, and friends had called at the house at different times. Steve was there; he hadn't left the house since the party. Elliot and Elaine had come in all concerned, then Ed Bennett, and Louise and Jonah; they had all been very worried and anxious, knowing how close Amber and Bessie were. Diana Whitlock, who had only met Amber recently, had phoned with sympathy, and even Jerome had phoned apologising to Mary Anne for gatecrashing the party; he had met Bessie on several occasions, and would she convey his condolences to Miss De Carla? And after they all in their turn left, Amber and Steve were alone in the library. The atmosphere was strained but once again he was there supporting her, and she was grateful.

'What am I going to do without her, Steve?' She sniffed. 'I think I only worked to give her a good life; she was so poor when we first met. It was beyond her wildest dream to come here, but she loved it.' She wrung her hands tightly together, turning away from his gaze, not wanting him to see the tears welling in her eyes again, then she suddenly sat up straight. 'Oh, look! The rifle is missing from over the fireplace.'

Steve looked up at the imitation cobblestone wall above the fireplace. Between the two cream silk lightshades, the metal brackets that had held the rifle were sticking out of the wall. 'Perhaps someone has taken it down for cleaning?'

Steve didn't for one minute think that was the case, but he thought it might help Amber.

'No! No!' She shook her head. 'No one would touch it; call the police.'

'They are still here in the house,' said Steve.

The police were still looking for clues in Bessie's apartment, but they had found no signs of a struggle.

Steve phoned Bessie's apartment, and was surprised when Detective Lieutenant Collins came into the library. 'I've only just arrived,' he said. 'I brought a couple of the fingerprint boys. You said there was a rifle up there over the fireplace?'

'Yes,' said Amber. 'It's always been there; the house was fully furnished when I moved in. This is the library but apparently it used to be the gun room, so I was told.'

'Where is the gun room now?' asked Collins.

'There isn't one.' Amber shook her head. 'But there is a full box of bullets in the desk drawer.' She went to the desk and opened the drawer. 'Oh, someone's been at the box.'

Collins came over to the desk. 'How do you know?'

'Because the lid is half-off, and I've not touched them. I rarely sit at this desk; sometimes, maybe, but I have an office. I do most of my writing from there.'

'Well, why would you leave a box of bullets in here?'

She shook her head. 'I don't know, never really thought about it; guns don't interest me. I like this room, and if I have guests we have cocktails here or on the patio because it's nearer to the pool.'

Another two days had gone by, and Steve sat with Amber on the patio while Detective Collins told them that the bullet had been analysed and had come from a rifle, although of course he couldn't establish that it had been fired from the stolen rifle. It had been fired from some distance away, obviously from the garden, and he had his men searching the shrubbery for any evidence. So far they had not found anything, but he said every one of the guests had been interviewed again. He also said that Bessie's death could have been a case of mistaken identity, and that Amber should take extreme caution, and that he was putting two police officers on duty around the house.

'*Me?*' Amber flashed her long lashes at him in amazement, and then looked at Steve. 'Who would want to kill *me*?'

Steve's eyes twinkled; he almost laughed but kept it to a hidden grin.

Through more interviewing at the police department, the police had found that everyone who knew Amber De Carla would have been happy had it been her. All had admitted that she was a nightmare to work with: cameramen, the sound technicians, the lighting crew, and fellow actors. Even her house staff: Bella the cook had said Miss De Carla and Bessie had known each other a very long time, but even Bessie got upset with her, and Delilah, Miss De Carla's personal maid who had been run off her feet every single day, said she was demanding. Mary Anne, her PA, had said what a trial it was working for the great De Carla, but then she also said that since she had come back from the jungle location in Guyana, they had all seen a great change in Miss De Carla.

All fellow actors had said the same thing: she was impossible, *but* she had changed. Steve Salvettini, who had been her lover for over a year, had to admit nothing ever suited Amber, and she did aggravate everyone. But he also had seen a notable change in her. He grinned to himself, thinking back on Guyana.

In the library, the police had found many fingerprints; the party guests had wandered in and out. They found nothing on the wall brackets that had held the rifle, but there were a few prints on the white marble mantelpiece.

Jerome Howard, when interviewed by the police, had said that he'd had nothing to do with it. They could prove that he had not had an invitation, and had gatecrashed the party; he then admitted that he *had* gatecrashed the party by escorting a young actress, Stacey Devlin, who *did* have an invitation. He said he *had to be seen*; he was trying to get work, he needed work, and you couldn't afford to be forgotten and pushed aside in the acting world. While Amber had been on location in Guyana he had done nothing, and being seen with *her* had boosted his profile. He then related the tale of his short-lived affair with Amber, before she had gone on location.

The police showed him the paper with the photo of him holding his face in the restaurant; the incident had only happened a few weeks ago. He admitted saying, 'I'll kill her,' but it had just been a figure of speech, a fleeting fit of embarrassment, a burst of frustration, and of course it had really meant nothing.

'Well, isn't *that* enough publicity?' the detective remarked cynically, tapping his finger on the newspaper that he'd slapped on the table in front of Jerome.

'That's not the kind I want!' Jerome was aggressive. 'Look! She made a damned fool of me, and I guess I had evil thoughts; I felt I could have killed her at the time, but it was just a thought. Don't we all say and think these things from time to time? I was angry, and I was embarrassed, but I'm not the sort who goes around slapping women about. I know she saw me at the party, and I know I shouldn't have been there. And I guess I still hold a grudge; I'm still annoyed about the restaurant, and still embarrassed, but not enough to *kill*! Oh, no, man! Not enough to kill!'

'You still hold a *grudge*,' the policeman shouted in amazement, 'and you *admit* that? So you went there with the *intention* of killing Amber De Carla? And you made a *mistake*?' His voice rose accusingly, loud and clear.

'No! No!' Jerome stood up, and was told strongly to, '*Sit down, Mr Howard!*'

He sat down heavily in the chair. 'I didn't even take a gun to the party, and I wouldn't stoop to murdering anyone anyway! I never even spoke to Amber. I kept out of the way; I knew I shouldn't have been there.' Jerome put his elbows on the table and ran his hands through his fair hair in despair. 'I didn't do it!'

'It wasn't a handgun that killed Elizabeth Nichols,' said the detective. 'It was a rifle.'

Jerome jerked up. 'Well, where the hell would I have got a rifle at the party?'

'*That*, Mr Howard, is what we are here to find out! Where did you hide it before, and *where did you stash the gun afterwards*? Where is it? *Where did you hide it?*'

218

'*I didn't, I didn't!*' Jerome shook his head vigorously and jumped up again, knocking the chair over behind him. 'I didn't do it!'

The uniformed police officer standing near the door came forward quickly and, with a vice-like grip on Jerome's shoulder, he stood up the chair, then pushed him back down roughly into the seat.

When the coroner had made his examination and had taken the bullet from Bessie's body he had confirmed that it was definitely fired from a rifle. He assessed that it had been fired from a distance of about fifty yards and that it must have come through the open sliding window. The police had then combed Amber's garden and the shrubbery but had found nothing.

A few weeks had gone by and Ronald Tappener had approached Amber with a new script. She said that she was not ready. He sympathised with her loss, but asked her to read it, knowing that if he could get De Carla and Salvettini together again it was sure to be a success, and of course it would take her mind off the tragedy.

Elliot had called both Amber and Steve to his office a week later and had asked them about the new script; had they read it, and what did they think?

Steve was keen, but Amber was still very down after losing Bessie. She'd taken the script and looked at it, but she'd not found the enthusiasm that she normally had with a new script.

But now it was up to Elliot to try and persuade her. He had seen a change in her since the Guyana trip, knowing that it had really upset her, and now, having lost Bessie so soon after returning home, she seemed drained of all her energy. He said it would be good for her to get back to work, it would take her mind off things, and he was probably right.

Amber wasn't sure; she thought she would never get over the shock of losing Bessie. But Elliot, knowing that she was right for the part, pressed on. Like Tappener, he knew it would be another box office success, as always when she and Steve appeared together. Life was all about money, and he and Tappener were to make a few million to add to their millions.

Steve had come to Sunny Hill House for dinner; Downs let him in. The house was deathly quiet as he crossed the pink marble hallway and went into the lounge, where Amber got up quickly from a cosy armchair to greet him and he kissed her with friendly warmth on both cheeks. Downs brought him a martini and another one for Amber, and they sat quietly chatting about the script.

Soon Downs was calling them for dinner, and they moved to the magnificent dining room and sat at one end of the long polished table. Bella had cooked them a delicious fish meal and they drank glasses of white wine.

After dinner they moved out onto the patio; there was a bright full moon that lit up a light blue and starry sky, turning the green of the garden to a light shade of grey and the swimming pool to an even shade of blue. A slight warm breeze gently rippled the water and swayed the tall palms, their feathery branches silhouetted against the light night sky; it also rustled the leaves on the trees and the flowering shrubs that surrounded the whole garden. It was quiet and peaceful; the only sound now was the gentle fall of water from the two fountains.

Downs came with more white wine, filling their glasses, while they discussed and considered the new script; both Amber and Steve were so much in demand that they could take it or leave it, and the way she felt at the moment, she didn't want to work. The story was to be a murder mystery and, although it was to take place in Hollywood, it meant being away on location again.

Steve said he realised just how she was feeling with the loss of Bessie, but it might do her good to get back to work, and to get away from the house for a while.

She took a deep breath and nodded. 'Yes, you might be right; I have been mooning about for weeks, haven't I? And I just can't shake it off.' She put her elbow on the arm of the chair and a hand to her forehead, tears welling in her eyes. 'I'm sorry, I just can't stop crying.' She sniffed. 'But nothing is going to bring her back, is it? Oh, Steve, I do miss her, I really do. I see her standing in doorways, I hear her cockney voice.' She shook her head. 'I can't get it out of my mind.' And then she told him about the other night, when she had felt a presence in this room, and had felt that she was followed up the stairs. 'It was very scary... Steve, do you believe in ghosts?'

He grimaced. 'Dunno, never really thought about it.' He smoothed back his dark hair. 'But don't start thinking about silly things like that!'

'It's *not silly*. I can't help it!' Then she told him that Delilah had said that she had not hung up Amber's evening gown. 'It was the night that we went to the cocktail party.

I'd taken off the gown and threw it over the chair before going to bed – well, I'd had a few drinks, I know, but I also know that I never hung it up. But there it was the next day in the closet. And then, it was just last night, I took off my jeans and a T-shirt before going to bed and this morning they were hanging in the closet too...'

He had the slightest smile, and took her hand. 'Don't think like that, darling. It's all imagination. It's the drink; it fogs the mind. You hung the clothes up absentmindedly. Much better for you to get back to work; it will take your mind off things.'

She nodded, taking a breath and knowing that he was right; it would be better to get away from the house.

The next morning they were both in Elliot's office, and much to Elliot's relief they were saying that they would take the parts and work together again.

They started reading, and the shooting started a week later in the studio. They'd had just a quick run through, and preparations were being made to leave and go on location a few miles away. Elliot was talking of being away for at least three months, and with a laugh he promised it would be civilised and not like the jungle. Both Amber and Steve could laugh about it now, but it hadn't been funny at the time...

The film was to be a love story and a murder mystery. In the opening scene Camilla Carstairs would dash happily and excitedly into her apartment with good news, only to find her roommate Sarah dead on the floor. That of course brought real floods of tears to Amber's eyes, seeing Bessie in her mind's eye, and Elliot was thrilled with the performance and shouted, '*Cut!* That was perfect! Perfect, perfect, great!' And then of course everything stopped, because she had to get over the tears and then have her makeup touched up.

A few more days went by, and Amber was slowly going back to her normal self with the fuss and the arguments. Ed Bennett, in charge of a new camera team, was thinking, *Here we go again.* When Ed heard the camera team mumbling among themselves, he of course knew full well how they were feeling, and how it would be when they seriously started filming; this was only the beginning. At least Amber and Steve were now getting along all right.

But then the part of the boyfriend of the murdered girl was given to Jerome Howard. This of course didn't suit Amber at all, but there was nothing she could do about it; it was all up to Elliot. Jerome was pleased to be working, and thought that Amber had put in a good word for him, but then found that he was still being pursued by the police enquiries, and so was spending days at police headquarters when he was needed at the studio. Eventually Elliot put him off, saying that he couldn't put up with him coming and going and messing up the production. And so, much to Jerome's disappointment, he lost the job.

The police enquiries regarding Bessie's death were still going on and the police had at last tracked down Reginald Nichols. The boat that he had intended to join had left without him, a week or two before; the captain had heard that he was wanted by the police and didn't want to take any chances. Since then, Reggie had been sleeping rough in a disused warehouse on the dockside, which was where the police had found him. There had been a chase through the dockyard and he had been apprehended and handcuffed and then, at headquarters, fingerprinted.

On being interrogated at police headquarters, Reggie had said that he had not killed his ex-wife, and he had never owned a gun.

The interrogation went on; the detective presented him with a revolver. 'This is your gun?'

'No,' Reggie said again, 'I've never owned a gun.'

'It was found in the warehouse where you were living.'

'It's not mine.'

'It has your fingerprints on it.' Detective Baker was bluffing. 'Are you telling me that you have never handled this gun?'

'Yeah! Well, er...' Reggie screwed up his face and wobbled his head, hemming and hawing. 'Well, er... no! Y-yeah, *well*, I, er, er, well, yeah, I did 'andle a gun. I stole it from a drunken sailor, but I never fired it. And I didn't kill Bessie either!' he said very quickly.

'Tell me what happened! How did you get into the country in the first place?'

'Stowed away on a boat, from Souf'ampton. 'Ad a mate, worked on the *Lady Bee* − it's a cargo ship, an' it was comin' 'ere. 'Course, once we were at sea they couldn't chuck me out, could they?'

Detective Baker frowned; he'd have to look into this.

Reggie sat for a few minutes rubbing his hands and considering what he should say, and realised that he was going to jail anyway for just being here in the country illegally, so he decided to come clean and tell the truth. 'Well, er, well...' He winced, wrinkling his nose, then said he'd come to Bessie for help. He needed some cash. She'd helped him out before; she'd sent him money through the post. 'Well, o' course the few bob she gave me didn't last very long, did it? Mind you, I didn't come 'ere special like, it jest 'appened that the boat I got on was comin' 'ere. And so 'ere I am,' – he flipped his hand up – 'and I needed money!'

'Why did you stow away, if you weren't planning on coming here?' asked Detective Baker.

'Well, on this ship, the *Lady Bee*, I was bein' chased by the Old Bill, and I was 'idin' an' while I was 'idin' they upped the gangplank and it set sail. Couple o' days,' – he nodded – 'then I got caught! And as I said, they couldn't throw me overboard, could they? So I worked me passage, didn't I? Well, when the crew got off I sneaked out the cargo door and swam ashore.' He pulled a face. 'I'd 'ad a bit of a rough-up with some work mates, and one 'ad died. I didn't do it, mind!' he said very quickly. 'But the Old Bill was chasin' me and I was plannin' to get out of the country fast, and it just 'appened, I was sailin' an' on me way. I didn't plan it like tha'.' He looked at the man sitting across from him and raised his eyebrows with a slight shrug of his shoulders.

'And the *gun*?' Detective Baker questioned.

'Oh, that, I found it, and took it wiv me, just in case, like. I guessed she'd say no, I guessed she weren't keen to 'elp me, when I wrote to 'er last... but she did...' He nodded with a slight smile. 'She was a good sort, my Bess. I'll miss 'er!' He wriggled a bit in his chair, and bunched his lips. 'I fought... well, I fought p'raps we might get togever agin...' He nodded and went on, 'But she didn't wanna know, did she? Working in tha' fancy 'ouse. An' so I freatened 'er wiv the gun! Well, I weren't gonna use it, mind, just wavin' it abart a bit, like.'

Baker frowned; he was having a bit of a problem understanding the cockney lingo. 'You *found* the gun? You said that you took it off a drunken sailor.'

'Well, yeah! I did, sorta. We'd 'ad a few drinks, like, and a bit of a punch-up, an' then when 'e'd gorn, I found it!'

'He's *dead*?'

'Bloody 'ell, no! I give 'im a bit o' a black eye, but blimey! No, I ain't a killer. I don't know where 'e is.' And then he said again, 'It ain't my gun, honest. I never owned a gun, honest.' He was shaking his head. 'I found it in the ware'ouse and I don't even know why I took it. I've never fired a gun, honest! Well, only in the army, o' course, an' cadets and that... well, you 'ave ter, don'tcher?'

He went on to say again that he had gone to the house to ask Bessie for money. He'd been there days before looking over the wall. When he'd realised there was a big party going on that night he had hung around outside. He couldn't climb the wall with everyone walking about, and then, seeing guys going in carrying boxes, he had realised that they were waiters and he had grabbed a box and slipped in with them. He said he had then stolen a dress suit that was hanging in a room near the kitchen and he was planning to mingle with the guests looking for Bess, but had then had the thought he would get found out, and so he had gone into the kitchen and got a tray and started to serve drinks. He'd found Bess, and she had threatened to call the police, and it was then that he had threatened her with the gun and demanded some money.

He went on talking to Detective Baker. 'She said she 'adn't got no money but I knew she 'ad, cause she'd sent me a cheque in the post some months ago, and I'd seen 'er go to the safe when I was looking over the wall. And then she was jest gonna give me some greenbacks when suddenly she was fallin' at me feet! Well, I'd 'eard a loud bang, didn't realise it were a gunshot – well, not right away, like. Well,' – he raised his shoulders – 'it took me breaf away, an' I was jest gonna go down on me knees to 'er, when the door burst open, and this geezer was comin' in, so I scarpered, didn't I? But I didn't kill 'er, honest! Honest, it weren't me!' He was shaking his head vigorously. 'I didn't kill 'er, *honest!*'

Reggie Nichols was jailed for being in the country illegally, and was held for further questioning, and if found not guilty of murder he would later be deported back to the UK.

CHAPTER SIXTEEN

The police had searched Amber's garden several times, looking for the weapon that had killed Bessie. It was some weeks after Bessie's death that they eventually found the rifle. It was hidden high up in the branches of a tree; mostly they had been digging in the ground. It was then that forensics matched the rifling marks on the bullet taken from Bessie's body to the barrel of the rifle.

The film unit had moved on from LA to San Diego. Some of the cast were staying in a small and comfortable hotel away from the press; a large house had been rented for Amber and Steve, with good staff. The shooting was to take place on the large private estate and so far all was going well, but the days were long. Most evenings Amber and Steve returned to the house tired and after an evening meal they went to their rooms. This evening the two of them had been out to dinner, but they were not out late as they both had to be on the set early in the morning.

Amber's thoughts were still on Bessie; she missed her most at night. When she had come back to Sunny Hill House, after a dinner or a party, or sometimes working late, Bessie had always been there waiting, and they'd had a quiet coffee together, and Bessie had been anxious to know how the day or the evening had been. But now, when Amber came back to *this* house, it was quiet. And now in her room all she could do was think of Bessie. It had really hit her hard; she just couldn't get it off her mind.

At home it was Delilah who now came in the mornings to open the curtains and call her. She was getting up early for the studio, but life was not the same. The staff were getting along all right without Bessie's guidance, but Amber was now thinking she would have to get a new housekeeper; yes, she needed someone who could run the place when she was away on location, but then things could never be the same. Bessie was more than just a housekeeper; she was a friend, a mother, someone to confide in. Now nothing would ever be the same.

The thoughts brought tears to her eyes. The tears flowed. Who would want to kill poor Bessie? She hoped the police would soon find out. And could Detective Collins be right? Was it really meant to be her? The thought scared her. She wondered now just how many of her guests had carried guns at the party. People didn't carry guns to parties in England, did they? Or did they? Perhaps she was out of touch; perhaps they did now in London. The world had changed.

She yawned; she was tired. She got into bed. She would have to be up early again in the morning.

After breakfast and with Steve driving they left the house early on Tuesday morning for the studio near San Diego. Today rehearsals were to continue in a studio and a set-up car park, or parking lot, as the Americans called them, and office building.

Amber had been in makeup for an hour, and was now making her way to the appropriate studio. It was a bright sunny morning, and there were a lot of actors, all in costume, walking here and there. Most said, 'Good morning,' with bright smiles as they made their way to or from different studios. Some studios after earlier hours of working had a notice in red lights over the door saying, *NO ENTRY! RECORDING – DO NOT DISTURB.*

Amber reached her destination and pulled open the heavy studio door. Elliot was there, of course, sitting in his canvas chair marked *DIRECTOR*; Steve was also there now, and Byron Morrow, who had replaced Jerome. The camera, lighting and sound crews were still setting up, and Annie Shepherd, choreographer, sat waiting, then the sound was being tested as it was every morning. And soon Elliot was shouting, 'Places, please!' and they were about to start on another busy day.

They were now into hours of rehearsals; it was the middle of the morning and they had gone over the script several times, and it was time for the first real takes. Following Sarah's murder there was to be a police investigation, with Salvettini as the handsome hero detective, trying to protect the lovely heroine Camilla Carstairs from a killer, desperate criminal Henry Banks, played by Byron Morrow. Today they were filming a chase through a multi-story building with shouting and gunfire and police actors everywhere, men falling in pain as a bullet hit a car and there was an explosion and flames rose high. Off-camera the firemen came with extinguishers, this making a lot of smoke, and Byron Morrow was just about to grab Amber and hold her as a shield, and then above all the noisy excitement there were shouts of, '*Stop!* Stop the production!' coming from somewhere at the back of the studio.

Elliot shouted, '*Cut!*' He then turned and stood up with annoyance at the interruption. 'Didn't you see the red light? We're recording!'

Everything went suddenly quiet and everyone stood like statues with guns in hand, looking at each other with bated breath, confused, their eyes saying *what's going on?* as they saw Detective Lieutenant Mike Collins, his sergeant and two uniformed police officers coming onto the set.

At first Elliot thought they were actors and had come into the wrong studio. 'You guys lost? We don't need extras.'

Then there was more confusion and disbelief and shock, which seemed to shudder the whole building, as Detective Collins made a bold statement: '*Elliot Stirling*, you are under arrest for the murder of Elizabeth Nichols. Anything you say will be taken down, and may be used in evidence against you.' He then nodded to a police officer. 'Cuff him.'

His voice was strong, loud and commanding; it echoed around the whole studio. A sort of hushed disbelief went through everyone's mind. The silence was electric. Then there was a slight shuffling as everyone looked at everyone else with deep frowns and a silent, '*What?*' escaped from most of their lips; it was almost like a loud silent scream. It was a joke, wasn't it?

Amber was stunned. She couldn't believe her ears. She stood a few feet from Steve, and Byron Morrow was very close and had been just about to grab her, but now all three were frozen in action, both Salvettini and Morrow with raised guns still in their hands. As Morrow relaxed Amber gave a loud gasp; he saw her sway and took one step closer, putting an arm around her for support as she leaned heavily on him, just as Steve moved quickly to her side. She seemed about to collapse. There was a car nearby; Steve opened the front door and they both sat her down, her feet still on the ground, and held her hands. Of course Byron Morrow knew nothing of Elizabeth Nichols; he just thought that the police being here had shocked Amber, and she was about to faint. And he frowned; had he heard right? Elliot was under arrest?

No one uttered a word; they were all dumbfounded as Elliot was roughly jerked around, his eyes wide with surprise. He said nothing as he was being handcuffed, and then was quickly marched away.

The studio door clanged loudly as it was opened, and was still clanging loudly through the studio as it shut behind them. The stunned silence continued. It was like a film. And it had all happened so quickly, no one could believe it. Then somebody moved, and then the whole of the cast lowered their guns and relaxed; the cameramen, the lighting, the sound, the whole of the studio was then alive and mumbling in amazement...

Amber sat in utter disbelief, one hand clamped tightly over her mouth, Steve still holding her hand, Byron still standing close at her side. All were bewildered. Elliot Stirling? Murderer?

Amber sat just staring at the studio door. 'Elliot?' she muttered, looking up at Steve. '*Elliot?*' Her head was shaking but barely moving. 'I can't believe it! Elliot? It must be a mistake! It must be, mustn't it, Steve?'

Byron gave Steve a puzzled look, and then Steve explained briefly about Elizabeth Nichols.

For the rest of that day and for the next five days all production stopped. Ronald Tappener had been in touch.

Amber had flown back home to LA. She walked around in a state of shock. *Elliot* had killed Bessie? Thinking that it was *her*? She'd had a lot of arguments with him, but... did Elliot really hate her that much? It was frightening!

Three days had gone by, and Steve had come to Sunny Hill House, and they were sitting on the patio having coffee together.

'Really, Steve, I can't believe it!' She shook her head and clasped her hands tightly together. 'Do you think he really thought it was *me*? What have *I* done?' Every nerve in her body was tense. 'Oh, I know we've not seen eye to eye on many occasions, him directing, and me arguing and thinking I felt more comfortable doing things my way, but surely I never gave him cause to *kill*? Did I? *Why* would he want to shoot me? Do you think he's on drugs? You don't think that he killed Bessie so as to hurt me, do you?'

Tears welled in her eyes, and Steve put a large bronze hand across the table and covered hers. He, really, like her, was at a loss for words; he squeezed her hand. 'I'm sure it's all a mistake! God knows why he had a rifle anyway; maybe it was an accident? But it's done! And nothing is going to bring Bessie back, and you must try to get over it. I know it's hard, but I'm sure the police will contact you with an explanation when they find out the truth. It is hard, darling,' he said sympathetically; coming around the coffee table, he took her in his arms and hugged her, 'but life has to go on.'

She sobbed bitterly on his shoulder, clinging tightly to him. Then sniffed and pulled away, nodded and grabbed a handful of tissues that were in a box on the table. 'I know, I know you're right, life does have to go on.' She choked back the tears. 'I know what you are saying, but we have been friends for so long. We had nothing, Steve, either of us. I felt I worked for her, giving her a better life; I had the opportunities she didn't, and to think that *Elliot... Elliot!* Of all people, *Elliot?*' She squealed his name. 'I just can't believe it! I just can't!' She was shaking her head in despair. 'He mistook her for me, just because we both had red dresses.' She took a deep breath, and sniffed. 'Poor Bessie, she did look so lovely.' She kind of half-smiled. 'She'd never had much of a life; it was the first time that she had ever worn an evening dress... and she was so proud... oh, Steve.' She took a deep and faltering breath. 'I can't help it; I do miss her. And *fancy*, Elliot had the nerve to come here and visit the day after it had happened! Oh, Steve, what kind of a man is he?'

She swallowed. 'I keep thinking now that it was my fault for bringing her here to America. But she was so happy here; she'd had a rotten life in London and a bad marriage. And what about her writing cheques and keeping Reggie going with money? Why on earth didn't she say something to me? I'd have paid him off, enough to keep him away for the rest of his life. I just can't believe it... I wonder if Reggie had anything to do with the killing. He's been in jail, you know, for violence. You don't think it was him that fired the gun, do you?' She turned to Steve. 'Maybe *Elliot*

234

hired him to shoot me. He needed the money, didn't he? And maybe *he* shot Bessie by mistake.'

'No!' Steve had the slightest smile. 'No, I don't think so, but there could have been a fight and the gun went off by mistake?' He squeezed her shoulders. 'Come on, Amber, cheer up. Life really does have to go on.'

At police headquarters, Elliot, sitting across the table from police officer Detective Baker, had a completely different story to tell. It had all started when Stacey Devlin had fallen into the water in Guyana. He had felt responsible for her and had sat with her all night in the hospital in Guyana, and the next day Tappener had sent an air ambulance, and she had gone straight into the hospital in LA. He said he had visited her at the hospital for two days; he admitted holding her hand for comfort.

'She had asked me not to inform her family, as it would worry them, and so I respected her wishes. Then Ronald Tappener phoned asking how things were going, and of course I explained the situation.'

The hospital released her after the two days, Elliot went on to say, and then, of course, still being concerned for her health, he had visited her a few times at her apartment and things had got a little more involved. She had been so grateful to him for looking after her and for paying for medical care, and, feeling a little better, she had come to the studio to watch the shooting, because he'd now had to put Diana Whitlock in her role.

'Well,' he said, 'Stacey's a good little actress, I think an up-and-coming star, and I guess when you get to that stage, you don't like to miss out, or you could soon be forgotten.'

He went on, 'And then we had to go on location to Miami, and she wanted to come too. I didn't think she was well enough but I didn't like to stop her; there was no harm in her coming to watch, but the next thing I knew we were sharing a trailer. I hadn't planned this... I hadn't planned on leaving Elaine; I've been happily married for forty-three years, and still am. I'd never done anything like this before, and then I was afraid that Elaine would find out. I'm ashamed to say that for me, this thing with Stacey was just a fling.' He dipped his head, shaking it in disgust.

'I knew that Amber had seen us together, sneaking into a hotel room,' he said, 'but that was just for a drink, nothing happened, although I suppose it did look a bit suspicious, and then again she saw us at the trailer park and I did feel ashamed. Amber never mentioned it, though, and I felt sure she wouldn't say anything to Elaine. But it did worry me.'

He went on to say that, weeks after the filming was finished, he had taken Stacey out for dinner and when he had taken her back to her apartment she'd told him that she was pregnant. He said his first thought was Elaine, and he had gone into a rage and hit out at Stacey and she had lost her balance and toppled down a flight of stone steps. 'It isn't like me to hit women, it was just a quick reaction, I felt terrible, and I went down the steps after her and helped her up apologising, but she didn't seem hurt. But after that night we drifted apart, and I didn't see her until the night of Amber's party.'

The two of them had ended up drinking with a group of friends, and Stacey had said to Elliot quietly that she wanted to speak to him in private. They had arranged to meet in a quiet part of the garden, and he had guessed that she was going to ask him for money, and he knew after *this* it would not stop. She would threaten to tell Elaine. It would go on for years! He knew he had been stupid and the last thing he wanted was for Elaine to find out.

He'd had far too much to drink at the party and, for some unknown reason, on his way to the darker part of the garden where they had intended to meet, he had somehow wandered into the house. In his drunken state, not knowing why or how he had really got there, he found himself in a room. His head was dizzy. Seeing a rifle on the wall over the fireplace, he stood looking at it; he didn't remember taking it down, but it was in his hand. He remembered stumbling about, and bumping into furniture, and there were bullets right there in front of him. He took them; they were in his hand; he didn't know where he had got them from; he must have loaded the gun but had no recollection of doing it.

'And I just don't know why.' He was shaking his head. 'I'm not used to handling guns. I'm sure I didn't intend to use it, probably had thoughts of just threatening Stacey Devlin, *if* she was going to blackmail me. I didn't know where I was or why I was there. I do remember thinking *Stacey*, and *blackmail*.'

He went on to say that the next thing he knew there were a lot of people but he didn't recognise any faces, it was very loud, and then he was seeing trees, the music was distant, and he must have been in a quiet part of the garden. Through hazy vision he saw a red dress coming down the darkened path, and there was a man, and he remembered quickly jumping into the bushes. Blackmail came to mind again; she had brought a man with her to negotiate some sort of deal.

He had watched from the shrubbery as they went into the room. It had looked like a heated argument, and he guessed they were discussing him and the deal. It was hazy and so he eyed them through the gun sight, but things still looked fuzzy and he couldn't focus properly, and then the gun fired!

'The jerk of the rifle against my shoulder sobered me up a bit; it surprised me. I didn't realise what had happened,' he said. 'I was not thinking clearly, and the red dress was on the floor, and then I suddenly realised what I'd done. I'd pulled the trigger – not knowingly, but I'd shot Stacey. I put my head in my hands; I was shocked and aghast, and still dizzy from the drink, but then realised that I had to get out of there, and I flung the gun up into the air and made my way as quickly as I could, stumbling blindly through the bushes. I could hear the music, but didn't know where it was coming from, and then I was back at the party, and I was at the bar with Elaine when the police showed up! I was still dizzy and trying to focus; I remember Elaine saying, "Elliot, you've had too much to drink," and I caught hold of the bar to keep my balance. It was then that I saw Stacey. I blinked; it shocked me; who had I shot? I really didn't know.'

Stacey Devlin, when interviewed again by the police, had a different story to tell. She said that she had seen Elliot at the party; they hadn't seen each other for some time; he was drunk but she had asked him to meet her privately, and he'd suggested a quiet part of the garden. She said that she was going to tell him that she had lost the baby and he had nothing to worry about, it was over and his secret was safe, his wife would never know. It was the fall, of course, but she was glad because she didn't want a child right then to interfere with her career. And she was going to ask him not to forget her the next time a good part came up. She said he had told her several times that she was beautiful and a good actress and that he would make her a star, like Amber De Carla.

She went on to say that she'd left the bright lights of the party and was making her way down to the quieter and darker part of the garden when she saw Bessie. Of course, then, Stacey didn't really know who she was, but she was being bustled along by a man. They were talking in whispers but Stacey couldn't hear a word, and then they were turning the corner of the house. She didn't want to be caught nearby, as they might think she was spying on them, and so she had stepped back into the shadows, waiting for Elliot.

Of course she'd heard the shot, but had seen nothing, and then a man had run past her as she was standing in the shadows, but she couldn't identify him; it was too dark and he had been too quick.

She had waited and all had seemed quiet; no one came, and Elliot had not shown up. She assumed that he couldn't get away from his wife, and so she made her way back to the party. With all the noise and excitement, everything looked normal; no one seemed to have heard a shot. And then she had thought maybe it wasn't a shot. She began looking for Jerome, who she had come to the party with, but she couldn't find him. Elliot was at the bar with his wife;

she remembered him giving her a strange look, and then the police were gatecrashing the party and saying that there had been a murder.

'Why, then, didn't you say that you'd heard the shot and seen a man running?' asked the interviewing officer Baker.

'Well, when the police came in it was all confusion, and to be honest, I was scared to say anything. I didn't want to get involved even though I'd seen nothing.'

The police officer nodded understanding and said she would be remanded in custody for interfering with police inquiries by withholding vital evidence. She burst into tears as she was led away.

CHAPTER SEVENTEEN

Amber sat thinking back to Bessie's funeral. It had been a small and sad affair; it had drizzled with rain all day, and even after all the years together, she hadn't known any family to contact. All the staff had stood forlorn at the graveside, under black umbrellas, Downs standing very tall, a sad look in his eyes. Bella was in floods of tears; she and Bessie had enjoyed coffee every morning in the kitchen. Bessie had been so caring, so kind and so motherly, and the house would never be the same without her.

Steve and Jonah wore dark suits and black ties, Louise in deep purple. Elaine had come alone, and Ben Adams, the man that Bessie had been seeing, stood in the background, looking very grim.

After leaving the graveyard, they had gone back to the house, where Bella had provided a light buffet lunch and drinks for the mourners. Amber had told Downs to ask Ben Adams to join them, but Ben Adams had refused.

Elaine, in tears, was apologising to Amber for Elliot, saying that he'd always been a good husband; he had obviously met so many young women through the years, but nothing like this had ever happened before. She couldn't think what had got into him, and she was waiting now for him to tell her the whole story as she hadn't seen him since he had been arrested; she really hadn't heard it all, yet. And

Amber thought the same; she was waiting to hear Elliot tell the court what had really happened.

Thinking back on seeing Elliot at the trailer park with Stacey, Amber had clear pictures in her mind of how lovingly he had looked at her and of so many times he had touched her hand or put an arm around her. But she said nothing to Elaine; it was just as big a trauma for Elaine as it was for herself.

The flowers at the graveside had been beautiful. Amber had sent a wreath of red roses, but it had seemed so little a contribution for the life of a good woman and a good friend. Through glistening tears she particularly remembered the daisy-like flowers trembling as the raindrops fell on their open yellow petals; they had been like a ray of sunshine on such a sad and dull day. They didn't get many dull days like that; it seemed the rain had come in sympathy.

She felt Steve's arm tighten around her shoulders and the tears rolled slowly down her cheeks...

CHAPTER EIGHTEEN

Another month went by very quickly and Amber couldn't shake the sadness from herself. No one knew how much she missed Bessie; she felt half her life had been taken away. She had refused several parts, not wanting to work, and one day while sitting quietly by the pool she had called Mary Anne to bring her a pad and a pen. It was then that she had started recalling the events in her life and writing them down. Well, it really started with the events of Bessie's life. The more she thought about it the more the story developed, and she was scribbling fast.

The new film, *Shadowed Figures*, was produced once again by Ronald Tappener, and was now being directed by Jonathan Parks; he was a lot younger than Elliot and had new ideas. Amber was a lot quieter and somewhat subdued and certainly not so demanding; everyone had seen a great change in her. She learned her lines, and followed Jonathan Parks' directions. And then after a day's shooting her driver John picked her up and she came home alone.

She now sat many nights in a trance-like reverie, just thinking about Bessie, and feeling even more devastated knowing that it had been Elliot. Each night and any free time she had, she wrote a little more into her life story; the book was beginning to take shape.

She was sitting one morning by the pool, pen and pad in hand, when Downs came to inform her that there was a Mr

Ryan to see her; he had said he was an old friend. Amber was puzzled; she knew no one of that name, but told Downs to show him down here to the pool.

Amber stood up, tightening the belt on her short flowery beach cover-up, as Downs came again followed by a stockily built man, about five feet nine inches tall, with slightly greying curly hair; he was smartly dressed in a dark grey suit, white shirt and a red tie. He came forth with a big smile and hand out ready to shake. 'Kitty! It's good to see you.'

Amber felt her heart jerk, she was so surprised. 'Matt Ryan!' she said, shaking his hand. 'Well, this is a surprise; fancy seeing *you*!'

She indicated a chair and they sat by a glass coffee table, under a large green umbrella, both now a little speechless. He smiled and then said, 'You look different.'

'Yes, I've grown up since the theatre days.'

'And become a star.' He smiled again. 'I always thought you'd make it. Knew you had a lot of drive, ever since you took over from Melanie Corfield.' They chuckled together. 'Oh, what a night that was.'

Downs had brought them a bottle of champagne in an ice bucket. Matt talked of her success in films, and he said that he was now working for a television company, and he had given up directing over two years ago. They laughed about the theatre days, and then he was asking if she still kept in contact with Bessie... Of course this saddened her and she told him what had happened. It brought sadness to their happy reunion.

'I'm writing a book,' Amber said, changing the subject.

'Really?' said Matt. 'What's it about?'

'My life, right from the start, meeting Bessie. You're in it.' She smiled. 'But at the moment it's just a few notes.'

He grinned. 'I should like to read it.'

'It's not finished yet, but when it is I'll send you a copy.'

They talked on, and she asked him to stay for lunch, but he had another appointment. He left after a while, and Amber settled down again, scribbling notes on her pad now that she had met up again with Matt Ryan. She would add that into her book.

That evening Steve took her out for dinner, and of course she was telling all the exciting news of meeting Matt Ryan again and explaining that he had directed her very first performance. 'He was very surprised to hear about Bessie,' she said. 'I guess he was shocked.'

They were in a small restaurant, hoping to hide away from the press. The headline publicity over the killing had now died down, but when caught by the press she was still asked questions, which she tried not to answer. She still flaunted the glamour which kind of made the news boys forget what they were supposed to be talking about, but she was not as flamboyant now as she had been. Whether she was working or dining out or even going to flashy parties, she had not got that usual flair. Bessie was forever on her mind, and the thought pulled her down.

She told Steve she saw Bessie everywhere, standing in the room, or coming through the doorway; it was all so real. She even spoke to her, and had conversations with her. She had said, 'Steve is taking me to a party tonight,' and Bessie had answered, 'What gown will yer be wearin', luv?' and had disappeared.

Steve's handsome face crinkled into a disbelieving grin.

She saw the look. 'Bessie always said that! It's true, Steve.' She smiled to herself. 'I know you don't believe me. But I said, "I'll wear green tonight." '

He grinned again.

'It's true.' She fluttered her long lashes. 'And when I went up to my room, the gown had been laid out on the bed, and the shoes and bag beside it, just as Bessie used to do it. I called Delilah to come and zip up the back of the gown. It was a night I was at a party with you. It was a glamorous evening as usual, but I'd found it tiring and, coming in late, I missed Bessie being there to have coffee, which always seemed to slow me down a bit after a late night drinking. And before going to bed, you know, we just used to talk quietly about the evening's events. And then, so, when I went up to my room, I struggled with the zip before taking off the gown, and then I threw the gown over a chair, and went to bed. The next thing I knew was Delilah was pulling the drapes and letting in the sunlight, and she came back with the breakfast tray. After breakfast, I got up and showered, and went to the closet. The green gown was hanging up. I thought Delilah had hung it up, but it appeared that she hadn't.'

Steve looked puzzled. 'And you think it's a ghost?'

'Well, it does seem weird, doesn't it?'

He grimaced, and then went on to talking about the studio, to take her mind off weird things like ghosts. She was upset enough about Bessie. Ghosts were the last thing she needed.

It was some weeks later, after another one of those late nights, when Amber had gone to bed and fallen into a deep sleep again, and the next thing she knew was Delilah pulling the drapes and calling her early, as she was to be at the studio by seven o'clock. She got up, showered and put on her makeup and this morning went down onto the patio for breakfast; it was a lovely morning, blue sky with a cool breeze. Mary Anne came to the table to take a few quick notes, and just as she was about to go back to her office, Amber suddenly said, 'Oh, by the way, thank Delilah for putting my gown away again last night, and my jewellery. I was really too tired and I always relied so much on Bessie.' She half-smiled.

Mary Anne looked surprised. Amber really had changed now, thanking and apologising; it was not like her. She made a note to tell Delilah, and then left just as John arrived to take Amber to the studio.

During the course of the morning, the staff gathered as usual in the staff room for coffee, and Mary Anne conveyed the message.

'Goodness, she's changed since Bessie's been gone,' Delilah said, raising her eyebrows, 'sending *me* thanks... but I didn't put the dress or the jewellery away; she must have done it herself before she went to bed. Guess she had a few drinks as usual, and forgot. She's not the same, though, is she? She was even talking to herself the other evening.'

'Yes, I took her in a drink the other evening,' said Downs, 'and she was chatting away. I thought I was interrupting something, but there was no one else there.'

'Perhaps she was reciting her lines,' Mary Anne said with a smile, 'but you're right; she's certainly changed. But then I guess Bessie's death was a real shock to her... well, I suppose it was for all of us, but they'd known each other for years, so I understand.'

Bella added, 'Yes, Bessie told me that she knew Miss De Carla before she became famous. And she used to call her Kitty, so I guess that's her real name...'

Chapter Nineteen

Amber often moved about the house in a daze; everywhere she looked, she could see Bessie standing in the doorway or sitting in a chair, and she imagined her smile and her cockney voice, as she said, "'Ello, luv, 'ad a good day, 'ave yer?'

Amber rarely sat at the desk in the library, but now she sat with her elbows on the antique desk, her chin resting on one hand, deep in thought. She added these cockney words to her book.

She'd had dinner alone, and Downs had brought her another glass of wine and wished her a good night; he was retiring. She had turned. 'Good night, Downs...' Then elbows on the desk again, hands clasped under her chin.

It had been a long day at the studio and it was still a hot and sticky night outside. The lights were low in the library; it was quiet, the purring of the ceiling fan the only sound. She was deep in thought about Bessie, and added more writing into the book. It was in the evenings that she missed her most. She tried not to get tearful, but she just couldn't get the whole dreadful thing out of her mind. She could hear Steve's words: *And nothing's going to bring her back. And life has to go on.* Of course he was right – she scribbled his words down – and of course she knew that, and life was going on, but there was a sadness in the air; she felt it would never be the same again. She supposed that as the years went on it would all come right in time, but at the moment? She shook her head.

She had thoughts now on getting a new housekeeper; she scribbled on a notepad to remind herself to tell Mary Anne in the morning. She rubbed her arms – the room was gradually getting cold – and she stood up; she felt tired and was going to bed.

She just reached the library door, and a quiet voice said, 'Kit?'

She turned from the door quickly, her eyes searching the room; it was her imagination. Bessie was strong in her mind, but... no, it couldn't be; it *was* all imagination. But she felt a little uneasy, and glanced around the room. All was deathly silent. She put her hand on the door, and opened it an inch or so, and the whisper came again: '*Kit!*'

She turned quickly again, scanning the room. Was it a voice, or was it a draught of air or a squeak of the door as she opened it? It had sounded like a whispering voice. She just couldn't get Bessie out of her mind; she could see her grey uniform dress, and flashes before her eyes of the red evening gown.

She held her breath, her eyes scanning the empty room, and then very nervously she whispered, 'Bessie? Bessie! Is that you, are you here?' Her own voice had a strange and ghostly echo and she felt goosebumps run up her arms.

The silence that followed seemed to have that high-pitched hissing sound; her ears were strained for the slightest sound or movement, anything. No, she was being silly, but she thought she could feel a presence, something that she couldn't define; she wasn't alone. It was uncanny, it was scary, but it was all in her mind, just imagination, wasn't it? She and Bessie had often sat here in the early evening, chatting, and now she was imagining the feeling that she was still here.

She didn't dare to call Bessie's name again. She switched off the ceiling fan; it slowed with a soft purring sound and the silence seemed even more intense. She scanned the room again with a shiver, before turning off the light and going quickly out of the library, closing the door quietly.

In the spacious hall the house was silent, and the softness of her footsteps on the pink marble floor seemed to clatter; she had walked this marble hall so many times, but now it was like being suspended in space. The low light from the chandelier made shadows and she looked behind her nervously. She mounted the sweeping marble staircase, and stopped to look back again; she had a feeling of being watched. She mounted two more steps and stopped again, turning nervously. Her hand gripped the brass handrail hard; she swayed a bit; there was a sort of nervous buzzing in her head. There was nothing there behind her. It was the wine; she'd had two glasses with dinner and Downs had brought another one into the library. Or was there something there? As much as she missed Bessie and wanted it to *be* Bessie, the very thought frightened the life out of her, and she turned and ran the rest of the way up the stairs and along the upper hallway and into her room, closing the door quickly behind her and holding her breath, waiting. Waiting for what?

CHAPTER TWENTY

Amber thought of more writing in her book, and of the ghost of Bessie; she had found the experience somewhat tearful, and somewhat fearful, and yet exciting. She recalled the time when she had first started at the theatre and met Bessie, the bus rides after the show, going to the Three Whistles. The day she had rented the apartment in Belgravia (she saw Bessie's amazement in her mind's eye), and the day they had both been stunned on arrival here at Sunny Hill; what a day that was, meeting Downs for the first time, and Bessie's words sounded loudly in her head: *Blimey! Bloody hell!*

She grinned and closed her eyes, shaking her head. 'Oh, Bessie.' She took a breath. 'Bessie, what a character you were,' and tears filled her eyes.

Mary Anne had tracked down three women wanting the job as housekeeper, and it was on Friday morning, after Amber had gone to the studio, that she was interviewing Mirabel Hastings. She seemed suitable; she was English, which Mary Anne thought Miss De Carla would like. Mrs Hastings seemed frumpy, not a bit like Bessie; she was painfully thin, aged about sixty. Her eyes were blue, hard and piecing as she looked down her long thin pointed nose at Mary Anne, but she seemed efficient enough, and of course Miss De Carla would want someone who was capable and whom she could trust to do her job just the way Miss De Carla wanted it. But, of course, before Mary Anne signed her up, she would have to be approved by Miss De Carla herself. And so Mary Anne checked with Miss De Carla first, and then made Mrs Hastings an appointment to see her, on Monday morning, at eight o'clock.

Three days had gone by and it was Monday morning, and Mrs Hastings arrived right on time. Downs let her in; at first sight he didn't like her, but of course he kept his opinion to himself.

Mary Anne showed her into the office.

Amber looked up from behind the desk, and felt a bit of a jolt. She was not impressed as the painfully thin and scraggy woman with a flat chest marched through her office door, dressed in a blue chequered dress, her thin lips tight in a hard straight line. The long sharp nose sniffed as the beady dark eyes took in the surroundings. The look said it all; it wasn't good enough.

Amber thought, *This woman is arrogant, and very superior!* 'Sit down, Mrs Hastings!' Amber didn't stand up. And Amber never said 'please'.

In conversation the women were clashing with every word that passed between them. Amber could see that they would never get along, and she also wanted to keep her other staff happy. She had known she had no intention of taking this woman on the very minute that she had walked into the office, but she told her that she would be in touch. The minute that Downs had shown Mrs Hastings out, Amber phoned Mary Anne to say, 'No way! Was it a woman? She'd make a good prison guard.'

Mary Anne grinned. 'Sorry.'

Two weeks had gone by, and there had been five women for the housekeeper job, and Amber, with her pernickety ways, had pooh-poohed them all except one, Maria Gonzalez. Maria Gonzalez was Mexican and spoke English with a Spanish accent. She was desperate for a job. A widow aged forty-three, with two children, a girl, twelve, and a boy, ten, she had been a housekeeper for twelve years, but her employers had closed the house and moved away. She of course could not live in, but she would come in every morning at seven o'clock. Mary Anne had thought her the least likely for the position, but Amber felt satisfied.

The days and the weeks went on, and Maria was proving to be efficient, and running the house as Amber had wanted. And for once, Mary Anne thought Amber was pleased.

CHAPTER TWENTY-ONE

Amber and Steve were starring together again, in a film called *Dangerous Lovers*. It was about a brother and sister who fell in love and of course had to be kept apart, and there were dark mysterious corridors and secret love affairs. It was another Tappener production, and a box office success; it seemed he just couldn't go wrong.

Of course there was a red carpet premiere, and for Amber much glamour once again, and then award ceremonies where she and Steve both won, and then to follow there were celebrations all round, with parties and dinner parties and cocktail parties. Amber eventually got back into the swing of things, with her glamorous gowns, and thrilling her fans and blowing kisses. She was never out of the press, which she found intimidating, but of course she secretly loved all the publicity and the attention, and where would she be without the press?

Her book had taken a long time to write. Matt Ryan had been interested to receive the manuscript, and had taken it to an editor in London, who of course had taken some time to look it over, and, being busy by that time, Amber had almost forgotten all about it.

It was some time later, while she was sitting by the pool, when Downs brought her the morning's mail and there was a letter from Matt Ryan. He said that the weekly series of her book was now showing on TV in the UK and seemed to be becoming a great success; he had also included a disc.

That evening she phoned Steve and asked him to dinner, and afterwards they sat in the TV room with drinks watching the video of *Rags to Riches*, sometimes laughing, especially about the Guyana trip. And then the cockney woman who was representing Bessie brought a tear to Amber's eye, and Steve put an arm around her, trying to cheer her up.

It had been a nice evening, and Steve had given her a friendly kiss and had left at midnight, and then Amber went to bed. She had been wearing a stylish but simple red dress this evening, and as usual she flung it over a chair, then got into a silk nightdress and then got into bed.

She turned out the light, slithering down into the cool pink satin sheets with a slight smile, the video still clear in her mind. The memory of the mosquito net in Guyana made her grin even more; it had been a nightmare, but she'd come through it. Well, hadn't they all? And now she was glad to have Steve as a friend again.

A pale moon shone through a gap in the drapes, giving a dim light into the room. She closed her eyes, surrounded by the soft satin and the smell of lavender that Delilah sprayed on her pillow every night to help give her a peaceful sleep, and with the smile still on her lips she began drifting away...

It was then she heard a scraping sound. She opened her eyes; the room was quiet. Her first thought was of a spider, then that she'd been dreaming. But then it came again, a sort of rustling sound like someone moving about.

She widened her eyes, scanning the room in the dimness of the pale moonlight coming through the gap in the curtains. Was it the soft purr of the ceiling fan that flickered across the room and caught in the thin pale beam of moonlight? Yes, of course it was, or perhaps something outside?

Then she thought she saw a shadow crossing the room. She sat up quickly and put on the light. There was nothing. She was sure that she'd seen a shadow, but it was just a trick of the dim lighting; it had probably been just the shadow of the trees outside playing on the curtains.

She turned off the bedside lamp and snuggled down again, and then it happened again: the rustling sound. She sat bolt upright again, straining her eyes in the dimness, and there was the shadow crossing the room again. She quickly put on the light. There was nothing, but she'd seen it, and this time she was in no doubt she was not dreaming. She'd had a few drinks, but no, it wasn't the drink either. She felt a little unsettled, and a bit scared to switch off the light.

'Is anyone there?' Her whispered voice echoed around the room; it was a bit scary, and she could see there was no one there. She whispered nervously again, a little bolder, 'Is anyone there?' It sounded stupid; if anyone was snooping around, who was going to answer and own up anyway? Then, hesitating, she got up and went into the sitting room, thinking that whoever it was would by now be creeping out into the hallway, but on switching on the sitting room light all was still. She checked the outer door; the key was still there and it was still locked. She went into the bathroom and then checked the dressing room, but there was no one.

She remembered being followed up the stairs; that was a creepy feeling. Was it Bessie? The thought frightened her; she'd never been afraid of Bessie, but *now*?

She felt a presence in the room, or was it that she was just imagining things, with the thought of the video earlier? She whispered, 'Bessie, are you there?' Hoping, and yet *not* hoping, for an answer.

The silence was intense; she listened; it was eerie. 'Bessie?'

She went back to the bedroom, her eyes scanning everywhere. She sat on the side of the bed and turned out the light, and as her eyes got accustomed to the dim light coming from a small gap in the curtains, she had a nervous intake of breath as there in the corner was a shadow. 'Bessie?' she said quite sharply but cautiously. The shadow moved very slightly. '*Bessie!*' Her voice was louder now and more enquiring, then a whisper came back to her; it sounded like, 'Yeah?'

Panic rose within her. She quickly switched on the light; the shadow had gone. She stared hard into the corner, trying to imagine Bessie, but she couldn't even picture her face; there was just nothing. She had imagined it all, she told herself, but she wasn't sure, and wished she could get rid of the loud shushing silence that was ringing in her ears. Was it a voice? Had she heard something?

She felt shaky, frowning and cringing, her shoulders scrunched up, holding her breath and gripping her hands together so tightly it hurt; she missed Bessie terribly, but now the thought that Bessie could be here terrified her more than she could say. But then she couldn't resist trying again.

'Bessie!' she said boldly, in her normal sharp and demanding manner. 'Bessie, you're frightening me. If you're here, show yourself or say something, or even move something! Bessie! I just have to know!'

The silence was deathly, and a chill filled the room, or did it? The air seemed to be swirling cold around her arms and bare shoulders, and she was trying to hear beyond the loud rushing deathly silence, but it was all imagination, wasn't it?

She turned her head quickly, hearing a rustling sound, and her eyes opened wide; the red dress moved on the chair. She clapped a hand over her mouth and stood frozen. *Did it move? It did, didn't it?* She couldn't believe her eyes. She stood for a moment with a feeling that she couldn't describe, like a sort of buzzing inside, but all was still and quiet.

'Bessie?' It was a disbelieving frightened whisper. She stared hard at the red dress, willing it to move again, and then her eyes scanned the room for the slightest shadowed movement.

She sat down now on the side of the bed again, gripping the sheet and knowing that if she stood up her legs would give way under her. She felt very scared, and yet somehow within her was a bubbling of excitement, feeling that Bessie *was* there. But she couldn't be, could she? Her eyes were wide, waiting, but nothing moved.

Amber woke to find herself lying flat on her back across the bed. Her eyes opened, looking up at the ceiling; the sun was streaming in through the gap in the top of the curtains, the fan still spinning, and the bedside light was still on, then, suddenly remembering the night, she sat bolt upright and stared into the corner. Had it happened? Or had it all been a dream? It had all seemed so real. She felt a little dazed, then held her breath; the red dress had gone!

She went into the dressing room; the dress was hanging in the closet, her shoes put away. She stood, one hand clapped hard over her mouth, just looking. Had it happened? She swayed a little at the thought. Or had she had too much to drink? She must have hung the dress up herself. Or perhaps Delilah had been in?

She came out of the shower wearing a white towelling robe, just as Delilah was coming through the door.

'Oh, you're up. Good morning, Miss De Carla.' She swished back the drapes, letting in the bright golden sunshine.

'Morning, Delilah.'

Delilah turned her head, a little surprised; it wasn't often that she got a pleasant 'good morning' from Madam.

'Thanks for hanging my dress up again.' Amber was waiting for her reaction.

Delilah looked startled. 'Oh! Er...'

'Delilah!' Amber cut her short, lifting her chin haughtily as usual, half-closing her eyelids, but of course this morning there were no false lashes to flash. 'You *didn't* hang up the dress, did you? And you *didn't* hang up the green gown the other night either, did you?'

'N-n-no, ma'am, I'm sorry, ma'am, I—'

'Delilah! Do you believe in ghosts?' She saw the look on Delilah's face; the big brown eyes showed white and the small black face seemed to pale.

'*Ghosts?* Ma'am!' Delilah was a little flustered. 'I don't know... no!' She was shaking her head, her brown eyes still wide. 'No, I don't think so.'

Amber, seeing the wide-eyed enquiring look, twitched her lips, not knowing whether to say anything, and then

260

decided not to. 'Oh, never mind, Delilah; it was just a thought, that's all. It's a film I'm doing. I'll be down for breakfast in about ten minutes.'

'Yes, ma'am.' Delilah dipped her head. 'Yes, ma'am,' and she went away quickly down the stairs with a deep frown. *Ghosts?* She went into the kitchen.

Bella looked up as the door flew open with great gusto. 'What's the matter? You look as if you've seen a ghost!'

'Oh! *Don't!*' Delilah exclaimed, then, seeing Bella frown, 'Oh, it's nothing.' She shook her head. 'Miss De Carla will be down for breakfast in ten minutes. I was surprised she was up and showered when I went in; she even said good morning.' Then she added, '*Pleasantly.*'

Bella nodded. 'Gosh! Oh, is that what's upset you?' She switched on the coffee machine in readiness.

Amber did her makeup, fixing the long false eyelashes as usual, and did her hair in a ponytail and tied it with a bright pink ribbon. She was not going to the studio today. She put on a bikini and a smart, stylish, very short sea-green chiffon beach cover-up, and slipped into white four-inch stiletto sandals, and went daintily down to the breakfast that was laid out on the patio. She sipped hot coffee deep in thought.

After breakfast she made her way to the pool, and lounged back on a deck bed with a script, but she couldn't concentrate; her eyes closed behind the large white-framed sunglasses, her thoughts were back on the night before. Was it Bessie? She felt sure it was... but it couldn't have been, could it? Or could it? The thought was eerily frightening.

It certainly wasn't a dream. But had the red dress moved? No, it was all her imagination. Delilah certainly

261

hadn't hung up the dress, so she must have hung it up herself. Maybe she had been sleepwalking? No! No! She had never done that in her life.

Her thoughts were suddenly startled as a feeling of cold breath came close to her ear, and a voice whispered, 'Kitty?'

She sat up quickly, whipping off the sunglasses and looking behind her; her heart was pounding. Downs was just coming across the garden with a tray of coffee. 'What's the time?' she blurted out.

'Eleven o'clock, ma'am.' He frowned. 'Excuse me, ma'am, but are you all right? You look as if you've seen a ghost.'

'Bloody cheek.'

The voice made Amber jump and she loudly blurted out, '*Eoh!*' and looked very quickly behind her. She was aware of Downs staring at her for a minute, and she saw him look over her head, and then he poured the coffee.

As Downs walked away, he hesitated and was tempted to turn and look back, but he didn't.

Amber, still feeling frozen, sat holding her breath. Was it Bessie? It was her voice, or had she imagined it again? Downs obviously hadn't heard it, although he had been looking at her curiously.

'Bessie, are you here?'

Downs was way across the garden as she spoke, looking around her. She saw him turn and hesitated again.

'Did you call, ma'am?'

She was a little flustered. 'Er... er, no, Downs! No! No, it's all right!' she called back, as he disappeared behind the bushes, and up the steps into the house. She felt

262

embarrassed; had he seen her talking to herself? But now he had gone.

She very quietly said, 'Bessie? Bessie? Are you there? Where are you?'

There was no reply; she felt alone, and then lifted the silver coffee pot. For a moment she held it as if suspended in time, about to pour the coffee, then saw that Downs had already poured it. Her mind must have been blank; she had not seen him pour it. What was wrong with her?

Her eyes now were searching around the whole garden. She put down the silver coffee pot and picked up the cup of black coffee on its saucer, her eyes still wide and searching as she took a sip and sat deep in thought.

It was all in her head, wasn't it, because she had Bessie on her mind, or was she going a bit mad? Had she really felt a breath close to her ear? Had she really heard Bessie's voice saying, 'Bloody cheek'? It was so typical of her. She *had* heard it, hadn't she? There really was no question. But Downs had never flinched, so he had not heard anything; of course he hadn't. It was all in her head, wasn't it? Wasn't it?

It was all nonsense; her mind was arguing with her mind, and only she could shake it off. She was still mourning Bessie, so it had to be just a reaction, didn't it? She felt that she would never get over the shock of it all. Well, if it had been a normal death, then perhaps she could have come to terms with it, but *murder*! And *Elliot*! *Elliot*, of all people; it was unthinkable.

She was muttering to herself. 'We never really did get on too well with you directing, did we?' She shook her head, then thought, *He did get angry! But then so did I. But I never thought of him as violent. Well, not enough to kill, anyway...*

She wonder now just how Stacey Devlin was coping, thinking that he loved her, and then knowing how close she had come to death. *But then you never know about people, do you?*

She sipped the coffee, still deep in thought, and then put it down and sat back on the deck bed, putting her feet up and her sunglasses on. She closed her eyes, still with Bessie on her mind, and, listening to the twittering of the birds, she drifted off, dozing in the warm sunshine...

She woke with a start, as a shadow blotted out the sunlight and Downs was there, calling her for lunch.

After lunch she went into the library; it was always cooler there. She had set her laptop up on the big antique desk, and she checked through a few emails and made a few notes for Mary Anne.

The phone rang. Downs' voice came through: 'There's a Mr Ryan on the phone, madam.'

Amber pushed a button and said, 'Hello.'

Matt Ryan's voice came down the line. 'Hello, Kitty... Amber. I'm sorry. I'm back here in the States. How are you? Did you see the disc?'

'Yes.' She smiled into the receiver. 'It's very good. I tried to ring you.'

'Sorry, had a problem with my phone.' He said he'd been travelling around the States, and was due to leave the day after tomorrow, and then he was asking if she would like to go out for dinner tonight, and she accepted.

Matt Ryan picked her up at seven thirty; she was very pleased to see him, and she found him very pleasant company even if he was a few years older than her, twelve to be exact. With him she kept up her fancy image, but felt much more relaxed. They talked again about the old days, he remembering how she had saved the day when Melanie Corfield had come in drunk, and he had fired her.

'I don't think she ever really made it,' said Matt. 'I think she just let herself go, and I don't think it was so much the drink; I think it was drugs.'

Amber nodded, thinking back on that night when she first performed. 'Well, thanks for giving me the chance.' She smiled. 'It's only through you that I'm where I am today.

'Well, I gave you a chance, but you've worked very hard to get to this stage. And, well, I can't say I wasn't worried,' Matt said, with a laugh, 'but at the time, I was desperate.' They chuckled happily together. 'Have you ever been married, Kitty?'

'No.' He had called her Kitty again. It made her feel a little sad; no one had called her that for years, only Bessie. 'Are you married, Matt?'

'No.' He chuckled, shaking his head, a bit hesitant. 'Never had the time. I'm just as busy now as I ever was, but I might settle down one day.' He had an odd smile. 'Perhaps we both will...'

There was a slight pause for a second as their eyes met. His had a strange twinkle; it was a question, and yet it wasn't, and then he said, 'Are you filming at the moment?'

She took a breath. 'Well, no, not right now. Ronald Tappener, who has produced all of my films with Steve, is looking for a new script, which is a surprise; he usually has a script ready as soon as one film is finished. Jeff Caruso phoned a few days ago with a script; he's a producer. I don't really know him; I just met him at a cocktail party. I might consider it,' – she grimaced – 'but it's a musical. I haven't sung and danced for years.'

'You were great,' he butted in with a smile.

She went on, 'I work a lot with Steve Salvettini, as you know, and you get used to one person, and we work well together, but I wouldn't be opposite him if I took the role. To be honest, I'm glad to have a few weeks off. Losing Bessie has really upset me; I can't really concentrate on anything.'

He kind of half-grinned, nodding sympathetically with understanding. 'You gonna marry him?'

'Who, Steve?' Her voice rose with a smile. 'No, don't believe all you read in the papers; we are just good friends.'

He smiled with that strange look again as the waiter poured them more red wine.

CHAPTER TWENTY-TWO

The weeks went on, and Amber was reading the part of Ella Bay for *Dreamer*; this was the musical. She had told Jeff Caruso she would let him know her decision. If she accepted the role, she was to co-star with Raphael Garcia, a lesser-known star, singer and excellent dancer; they had met on several occasions, and this evening she had asked him to dinner at Sunny Hill, knowing that it was a much more private way for them to discuss the scenes than going out.

Raphael arrived at seven thirty; Downs served them wine on the patio. Raphael came originally from Madrid; he was slim and of medium height. His skin was dark-tanned, his hair jet black and he had a thin black moustache. His eyes were very dark brown and they glittered in the candlelight, his brows heavy and black, his forehead furrowed. He was not unattractive, but not the handsomest of men. He spoke English with an accent and sometimes his words were not so clear. He was aged thirty-seven, but he had heavy wrinkles around his eyes that aged him; he had made several films but most of his work had been in stage musical productions; he was casually dressed in black trousers, a light grey jacket and an open-necked white shirt.

Raphael had brought her a bouquet of red roses. He was the romantic type, telling her she was beautiful and how the candlelight made her blue eyes shine. There was a moment when he seemed to be acting and she thought he was going to kiss her; she moved away and then mentioned the script. He said he had brought a copy with him, and she said they should get back to it.

The musical was to be about a Spanish song and dance man who, from singing and dancing in the street in Spain, made it to the top after being spotted by a millionaire and taken to New York. There he became a great success, until he broke a leg and found himself unable to perform dance routines. But he had a wonderful voice and there were to be some beautiful duets.

They discussed the script, and they had a nice evening enjoying each other's company.

After a few days of reading Amber decided not to take the musical part with Raphael, and she phoned Jeff Caruso. He was disappointed and tried to persuade her, but she said that she wasn't ready to be dancing and singing, and although she would have liked to have taken on the part, she could not do it at this time. She then explained that it was the anniversary of Bessie's death, and she felt that she couldn't go into a musical; it brought back too many memories. And her day went on much the same as usual, quietly sitting by the pool.

Steve phoned, asking how she was. She said, 'Feeling a little sad. I'm sorry, but I can't help it.' She knew he understood.

It was a few weeks later when Matt Ryan took her out for dinner again; they had a very enjoyable evening and they talked into the early hours of the morning about the old times. He told her of his job with the TV company and that he was now travelling the world; he would be leaving in the morning.

Sitting by the pool the next day, she supposed that he was at this moment on a plane to the UK, and then in two days' time he would be travelling to Holland, France and Germany.

The garden was quiet with just the twittering of the birds, and a warm breeze disturbed the foliage and gently swayed the tall palms. She closed her eyes. She still couldn't shake the thought that Bessie was after all this time still here in the house; she had felt a presence, but she couldn't define the feeling. It was scary but somehow she felt comforted. Nevertheless, of course, it was weird, and she'd not mentioned it to anyone.

The new script from Ronald Tappener was called *Romance and the Island*; it was a film about a tropical island, and would mean going away on location again, but it was to be filmed mostly on Miami Beach and down in the British Virgin Islands. It was about a yacht that got marooned on an island, supposedly miles from anywhere. There was no food or water, but a romantic love story of survival. Steve was keen, and he'd said it would be nice to get away for a while.

Amber was reading through the script with interest, and as she moved some of the pages fell onto the tiles and a page almost went into the pool. This brought back the memory of Guyana, the wind taking the pages, Stacey falling in the water. And then her thoughts went to Elliot, and she wondered how he was faring in prison. She had not seen Elaine, and she wondered how she was coping. She gathered the papers up, and put them back in the folder.

It had been a really bad time for her, and with each new role she still found it hard to concentrate, but she had enjoyed the glamorous limelight, the parties and the photos that the press snapped of her and Steve. They had both been out of the public eye for some months, but she was still pleased to be queen of the screen. She and Steve were still free to pick and choose the work they preferred, and they were both considering this new Tappener production, *Romance and the Island*. They had chuckled about it, saying being marooned on a Caribbean island couldn't be worse than Guyana. And they were guaranteed to have a yacht on hand for dinners in the evening.

CHAPTER TWENTY-THREE

Steve was at the studio when she arrived. They had been reading and rehearsing and filming for a few weeks, under the direction of Jonathan Parks, and it was all going well. The film was a true story of survival, written by Michael Atkins, of the time some years ago when his yacht had run aground, and he and his wife had been stuck on a remote island for weeks.

They were to be on location for two months. A private flight had been arranged for the whole crew of twenty-five to fly to Union Island in the Caribbean, and they left early Saturday morning: the camera team (led by Ed Bennett), the sound and lighting teams (led by George), Annie Sherman, choreographer, Mary Lou Steel and Sheena May, makeup artists, and Simon, always good with wardrobe, although it would mostly be shorts and T-shirts and beachwear.

Amber and Steve were to leave Sunday afternoon, on another private flight with Jonathan Parks, and Ronald Tappener was to accompany them. Jonathan had rented a large house with staff, for Steve and Amber and himself to share, and Ronald Tappener was to stay for just one day and just one night. For the technicians trailers had been hired and a catering team on the island had also been arranged for them.

The flight for the crew was good, and, on arrival, a truck was there to take all the equipment. It took an hour to load the truck and then it set off, the whole crew following behind in a coach.

They had been driving for about forty-five minutes on a narrow road, on their way to the trailer park, when the truck in front with the equipment on was hit by a fast-moving truck coming towards it, in a head-on collision. The coach driver swerved dangerously and pulled over to the side of the road, and the technicians stood helplessly watching as all of their expensive equipment went up in flames.

Ed Bennett, who never went anywhere without his camera, watched and filmed the disaster as firemen were now fighting the blaze, and then the police came quickly onto the scene.

Ed then phoned Jonathan Parks, describing the disaster, and the death of both drivers and one passenger.

Jonathan Parks phoned Ronald Tappener, and arrangements were made for the two of them to fly down alone. Then Jonathan Parks phoned Steve Salvettini saying that their trip was cancelled, and that he would let them know when they would resume filming.

It was the next day that Jonathan phoned Amber, telling her of the disaster and saying that there was to be no more filming for some time. And so, at home, Amber wandered down to the pool. She lazily untied her belt and let the pink flowery cover-up slip from her shoulders; it was all done with great flamboyance as if posing for a movie. The pink flowery bikini beneath covered very little of her shapely and very slightly tanned body; she never dared to sit in the sun, afraid to get even one wrinkle. She sat and daintily kicked off her white stiletto-heeled sandals, and her long shapely legs curled up under her as she made herself comfortable on the green mattress of the poolside lounger, shaded by the large green umbrella.

She had a book, but soon lost interest, and was daydreaming away. The garden was quiet and peaceful as usual with just the twittering of the birds; a slight cool breeze wafted over the garden, disturbing the bushes and wavering the tall palms, and suddenly, Bessie's cockney voice whispered in her ear, 'Why don't you go back to London, luv, for an 'oliday? Do you good, it would, to 'ave an 'oliday, get away from it all for a bit...'

Amber's eyes shot open as she sat up quickly with alarm, and looked around her anxiously; there was no one there, at least not Bessie. But it was all so clear. Had she dozed off? She didn't think she had, but she must have done. It was imagination; it was a dream. But it was all so real.

It was very hot; maybe the sun was getting to her. She stood up, and decided to take a dip in the pool, feeling the cool water caressing her flawless body.

After doing a few lengths, she came out of the pool and wrapped herself in a large white towel, the sound of Bessie's voice still ringing in her ears: *'oliday, luv, do you good to get away for a bit.* She snuggled into the large, thick white towel hugging her body, and decided right there and then that it was a good idea and that was just what she would do.

CHAPTER TWENTY-FOUR

The flight to London Heathrow had been good, and now she was following the porter outside, where he transferred her luggage to the waiting limousine that she had arranged to meet her. The driver, very smart in a black suit and peaked cap, smiled pleasantly and very politely, opening the door for her; before getting in she took a deep breath, thinking, *London! Home!* The London sky was the usual drab grey; although the weather was mild, it was the first time in years that she had worn a warm jacket and a silk scarf.

The limousine started off and joined the usual hubbub. The London traffic was busy as ever. A mixture of heavy lorries moving slowly and the familiar old red double-decker buses brought back memories, and the shiny black London cabs dodging in and out; there were no taxis in the world like London taxis, and they usually had chatty cabbies.

The limousine engine purred gently as they stopped and started with the rest of the traffic, and after a while the driver turned to the left, driving around the shrubbery and small flowered garden, and then into the semi-circular drive to stop outside the Dorchester Hotel. She felt overwhelmed as a uniformed doorman with shiny brass buttons and a top hat quickly opened the car door, then, recognising her, bade her, 'Good morning, Miss De Carla, and welcome to the Dorchester Hotel.'

She smiled sweetly, flashing the long black false eyelashes. He smiled in return; it was a look he'd seen so many times in the cinema. He then stood aside, and she went through into the spacious marble foyer and to the desk, where a young and handsome man welcomed her with a big smile, again with recognition, and took her credit card. She signed in and he wished her a pleasant stay, and the bell boy then showed her up to her suite, which she found was enormous. It was all so new to her; she had never imagined that London could be like this...

The sitting room had thick Persian carpet and easy deep comfortable armchairs, and two large beige sofas that could seat six. In the centre of the room between the sofas there was a glass-topped coffee table that held a huge arrangement of red roses and a silver ice bucket of champagne; the card said, *Have a great vacation, Love Steve*. At one end of the room there was a polished oak dining table with eight chairs; on the table were a vase of flowers and a complimentary bottle of red wine and a welcome card from the manager.

A door led through into the bedroom, which was equally spacious, with a king-size bed and two dressing tables and a whole wall of closet space. The en-suite bathroom was also enormous, with plenty of space to put a makeup bag and plenty of light. Most of the hotels that she had stayed in had no room and dull lighting; the Dorchester was exceptional. The bell boy went away with a big smile, clutching a big tip.

There were two big bay windows in the lounge, with heavy drapes and large golden tassels; she was looking out on to Hyde Park when the porter arrived with her luggage.

She settled in and unpacked, then, lying on the bed, rested for the afternoon to recover from the flight. Then, after showering and dressing, she went down for a drink at the bar before dinner.

She took a seat on a high stool at the bar; there were a lot of people but it was not crowded. The handsome black barman beamed a very white toothy smile at her. 'Good evening, Miss De Carla.'

Her glossy red lips parted in a smile, pleased again with the recognition.

'What can I get you, ma'am?'

'Dry Martini with an olive, please.'

He smiled and mixed the drink, and began to shake the typical American cocktail. 'Hope you like it shaken and not stirred,' he joked, and they chuckled pleasantly together. He set the drink before her on a small paper napkin. He noticed the long red fingernails as they clasped the delicate glass, and smiled again, saying, 'You don't remember me, do you? I come from Barbados.'

'Oh, I've been there,' she said, enthusiastically.

'I know.' He had a broad grin. 'I'm Basil; I'm the taxi driver that sat outside your house. I was hoping to be a star.' His grin became, impossibly, even broader. 'But I did get into the picture, just a quick flash.' He chuckled. 'I saw *The Tiger's Eye* twice. I thought I was *great*.'

They chuckled again, and she was beginning to feel that she wasn't quite alone in London.

CHAPTER TWENTY-FIVE

After enjoying the cocktail and thanking Basil – it had been pleasant conversation – she left the bar and made her way to the dining room, and the maître d' showed her to a secluded table in the corner, where she enjoyed a beautifully cooked meal and a half-bottle of white wine. After this she went back to the suite, and slept soundly.

She awoke refreshed, showered and dressed, and then phoned for breakfast. It came quickly, pushed into the room on a wheeled table that had a snow-white tablecloth: water, orange juice, fruit, toast and coffee as she had ordered. The very pleasant young waiter put a chair to the table for her and poured her coffee. He went away smiling, pocketing the tip, and eager to tell his colleagues that he had served Amber De Carla.

After breakfast Amber made a few phone calls, first to Mary Anne, and then to Steve, thanking him for the roses and champagne. He asked about the flight. She then phoned Matt Ryan, but his secretary Jenny said that Mr Ryan was in the north of England and she would let him know that she had called.

Amber came out of the hotel; the sky was grey as usual in the UK. Even though the weather was mild, she wore a warm jacket. The doorman greeted her warmly and called a cab, and she took the short journey to Harrods. This was the first time that she had ever been into this large store; when she was living here in London she could never have afforded to shop in such luxury. Now she could afford to buy the whole store, but she bought very little: a lipstick and eyeshadow, in a pretty shade of lavender.

She had lunch at Walton's fish restaurant, and then took a taxi to the London Theatre; she thought it would be nice to go back and take a trip down memory lane.

The cabbie was chatty and asked if it was her first time in London, and of course she said no, and that she had been born in the East End. 'It hasn't changed,' she said, looking out on the traffic with the cars and taxis and red double-decker buses all crammed together in a slow-moving mass, motorbikes weaving in and out.

This part of London she recognised, and they were nearing the Three Whistles pub; she asked the driver to stop. He pulled into the small car park, just off the main road. She got out and asked him to wait for her. He watched, a little surprised, as she pushed open the pub door, and he wondered why a smart, posh, well-groomed lady would want to stop for a drink in a tatty pub. Or maybe she had to find the ladies' room. He lit a cigarette.

The pub door swung to with a squeak, shutting out the loud buzzing sound of the ever-moving traffic. The strong familiar smell of stale beer tickled her nostrils; it seemed nothing had changed. The man behind the bar in a blue striped shirt had his back to her; he was arranging bottles on a mirrored glass shelf. He'd heard the door open and shut, and turned his balding head expecting to see a man, but there was this glamorous blonde with a glossy magazine smile expensively dressed in a bright red jacket and black smart trousers and boots. He smiled automatically, and was obviously a bit stunned and delighted.

'Hello, Bill.'

The red glossy lips made his name sound magical, and he had a double-take: *Kitty!* He leaned forward over the bar. '*Kitty?*' His voice rose to almost a squeak.

'Yeah, hi!' She smiled. 'Surprised?' She raised her well-groomed eyebrows.

'*Surprised?* I'll say. Surprised, yeah! How are yer?' He leaned across the bar, hand out, eager to shake.

'Oh, I'm fine.' Still smiling, she took a seat on a high stool at the end of the bar, where she had sat so many times with Bessie.

'Yer look good. Yer gonna 'ave a drink?' He reached for the gin and put a glass in front of her.

'Oh, no, thanks, Bill, it's a bit too early for me. I've only just had lunch.'

He smiled and nodded in agreement. 'Yer look well,' he said, a bit lost for words. 'Are you still acting? Where you livin' now? Went to Belgravia of all places, didn'tcher? I remember Bessie telling me. Do you ever 'ear anything from 'er?'

A saddened feeling came over her, although it didn't show. 'Bessie died, Bill.'

'Oh, I'm sorry to 'ear that.' He seemed concerned. 'What happened? Was she ill?' He was expecting her to say cancer.

'Murdered.'

'*Murdered?*' It stopped him in his tracks. His eyes opened wide; his head shook in disbelief. 'Did they catch the bloke who did it?'

'Yes!' She had a slight smile at his reaction, but she didn't go into detail. And then she went on to tell him that they had gone to America six years ago, and about the circumstances of Bessie's death. 'I must say it has really shaken me; I can't concentrate on working.'

'Well, you look as if you're doing well. Still on the stage, are you?'

She smiled. 'No, I'm now into films.'

'*Films?* Wow! Good for you. What, in 'ollywood, like?' He nodded with raised eyebrows and a grin, expecting her to say no.

'Yes.' She chuckled; it was obvious that Bill did not go to the cinema. 'I'm not Kitty any more, Bill; I'm now Amber De Carla.'

'*Blimey!*' He jumped back as if he'd been struck, and then scratched his head. 'My missus is always talking 'bout you.' He pointed a finger with a look of amazement. 'You're a *star*.'

She chuckled again. 'Yes, I finally made it, Bill. And I'd better be going; just popped in to say hello. I've got a taxi waiting outside.' She shook Bill by the hand, and slid down off the stool, and he came around the bar and walked with her to the door. She waved a hand to him as she got into the taxi.

Bill felt a bit mesmerised, smiling to himself as he walked back into the bar. *Blimey, Amber De Carla. Wait 'til I tell Millie.* He picked up the phone.

'Where to, lady?' The cabbie half-turned his head as he pulled out of the car park into the traffic.

'The London Theatre,' and once again they joined the noisy moving throng.

The taxi stopped; she paid him and got out and he drove off. Standing now in front of the theatre, she looked up, seeing the billing: *MY FAIR LADY, starring Catharine Maxwell*. She smiled to herself, her mind's eye seeing her name, *Kathy Hutchinson*, as she was then. She felt a twinge in her stomach, and lifted her shoulders, still smiling; it had been such a thrill, but she had come a long way since then.

The photos on the easel board were of the said Catharine Maxwell, looking very glamorous in a white Edwardian gown and a large white hat. Amber wondered if she was a newcomer and making her name. There was also a handsome, grey-haired gentleman in a morning suit, Gerald Clifford; neither actor was known to her.

The doors were closed. She walked around to her right and into the alley. The so-familiar stage door still needed a coat of green paint; she pulled it open and stepped inside as she had done so many times, sadly, now, without Bessie.

Old Sam was not at his cubby hole as normal to grumpily greet all who entered; he had been known to all the actors as 'the miserable old devil'. There was no one about and the whole place seemed dead. She imagined the normal excited hubbub of whispered voices, as the cast rushed about quickly for a costume change. The silence was eerie, but then she supposed that it was too early for rehearsals.

She made her way to the stage and stood in the wings; this was where she had stood on that very first night. It gave her a tingling feeling all over, as she relived getting hustled along with the group of young people; it was all so clear in her mind. It was also the first night that she had met Bessie...

She walked out to the centre of the stage, reliving that very first night of being the leading lady. She had felt so proud, taking a bow and hearing the enthusiastic audience clapping, knowing that they had liked her performance. All now was in darkness, there were no shadowed faces or movement, and then suddenly she was in full spotlight, and from the even more darkened auditorium, a rough voice shouted, '*Oi!* What yer doin' up there?'

She could see no one. 'Sorry,' she called back. 'There was no one at the stage door when I came in.'

There was no reply, and then suddenly a man was rushing towards her from the right side of the stage. ''Ey, 'ow did you git in 'ere anyway, eh?'

The spotlight went out. She turned to the man now in the semi-light. 'I came in the stage door, and old Sam wasn't there.'

'Well, 'e ain't 'ere any more; 'e's dead, died last year.'

'Oh, I'm sorry to hear that.'

'Did you know old Sam, then?'

'Yes.' She smiled. 'This is where I first started. I was just reminiscing, that's all.'

'Oh, yeah?' He grimaced, lifting his head and flipping up his eyebrows with an inward grin; he'd heard it all before. Another one trying to be a star? He looked at the expensive clothes and the thick makeup, thinking she was a bit dolled up. 'Who are yer, then, bloody Amber De Carla?'

'Yes!' She smiled again with a slight nod, looking at him, pleased at the recognition, but then knew from that look that he didn't believe her. 'I started here, and gave my first leading lady performance right here.' She pointed a finger to her feet.

He frowned, looking at her; he didn't believe a word of it. But she was quite cultured; she certainly wasn't the average bird prancing around the stage and looking for fame. If he'd been at his post at the stage door, she certainly wouldn't have got in here anyway. 'You bin actin' long, then?'

'Yes, some years now,' nodding, 'filming.'

'Oh, *yeah*?' he said casually, a slight comical chuckle in his tone, surprised eyebrows raised again. 'Where? *'Ollywood*, I s'pose?'

It was then they both turned as Matt Ryan walked quickly from the left side of the stage. 'I thought I'd find you here.' He was beaming, arms out wide as he gave her a big hug. 'Hi, Dan, you met the great Amber De Carla, then?' He looked at Amber. 'Jenny gave me the message and I came back quickly in a helicopter. I've been up in the north for a couple of days.' They chuckled together. 'What are you doing in London?'

Dan Greenford stood aside, mouth open, staring hard, the stage still in semi-darkness. He couldn't believe it; she really *was* bloody Amber De Carla? It took his breath away, then he said, 'I'm sorry, Miss De Carla, I really didn't recognise you, I really thought you were just 'avin' me on. I've seen a lot of gels come through 'ere, all 'oping to be stars. I've seen a lot of your films. 'Ere, what's that Steve Salvettini like, is 'e a nice bloke? Coo, I never thought I'd be 'avin' a conversation with you... especially not right 'ere in this theatre.'

'This is where Amber started.' Matt put an arm around her and gave her a slight friendly squeeze, and they smiled at each other. 'She brought the house down. Haven't you got any light in here?'

'Oh, yeah.' Dan, still feeling flummoxed, fumbled with his phone, taking it from his pocket, and said, 'Jim, turn the stage lights on.'

In a second a glow from the back of the stage lit up a park-like scene of trees and pathways and sunshine. Both Matt and Amber turned to look at it and smiled at each other again.

Dan felt a little in the way and made the excuse that he should get back to the stage door, or he would have more people just wandering in. 'So nice to have met you, Miss De Carla, it's bin a real pleasure.' He smiled and exited quickly into the wings on the right, the same way that he had come up onto the stage.

'You still come here, then?' Amber looked at Matt, a bit surprised.

'Yes, I pop in from time to time, to see how things are going. It was me that got Dan the job after old Sam died. And when Jenny said you were in London, I just knew you would be here. Have you met Pete Owens? He's the director here now, nice guy. So what are you doing in London? Filming?'

'No, we – that is, Steve and I – were supposed to go on location, to the Caribbean islands, for a new Tappener production, and all the equipment got burned up in a road accident.'

'Oh, anyone get hurt?'

'No, luckily just the equipment, and then of course everything stopped for a while and so I thought I would like a break. Nice to get away for a break. Since Bessie, I find it hard to concentrate, even now.'

'Yeah, guess it takes a long time.' He shook his head in amazement; where *had* the time gone? 'How long you here for?'

'*Eoh*, just ten days.' She raised her eyebrows. 'I only arrived yesterday. I still have the script to read; I'm hoping to get to grips with it. My manager James Avery said the Tappener production will probably start back up in a couple of weeks; I'm hoping to be word perfect by then.' She smiled.

'Where you staying? What you doing for dinner tonight?'

She smiled. 'Nothing much. I'm at the Dorchester.'

'I'll pick you up at seven thirty, OK?'

'Yes.' Her smile broadened. 'Nothing fancy. What I'd like is some good old fish and chips.'

'I know just the place.' They left the stage arm in arm, and he drove her back to the Dorchester.

During the week she hired a limousine, and she went to Max Milner's office. He was surprised to see her and took her out for lunch.

She and Matt had been sightseeing. They drove around Buckingham Palace, and past where she used to live in Belgravia; they visited the museums, and the Tate art gallery; they dined in the very best restaurants, and it was nice to be free of the press.

Steve phoned her, saying that he was getting more into the script and it was good, and that he was looking forward to starting up work on it again. She was pleased to hear his voice, and said that she was coming back the day after tomorrow.

CHAPTER TWENTY-SIX

Amber had settled in again back home at Sunny Hill House, and Steve had come for dinner. They now sat on the patio over the pool, with glasses of wine. The night as usual was warm under a starlit sky, and oh, so different from the UK, and she was telling him that she had been to the London Theatre. 'That's where I first performed, and I met Matt Ryan, and he was good company; we went out for dinner, and we had sightseeing days. I really never knew there was so much to see in London; well, I suppose I've never seen it.' She chuckled. 'Back then, I never had the time or the money.'

He saw the tears welling in her eyes.

'I really did enjoy it, Steve, but...'

He took her in his arms and kissed her, and she clung to him. 'Oh, Steve, it brought back good and bad memories, but now it really is so good to be back.'

He left just after midnight, and they met again in the studio next week. Everyone welcomed her back, even Ed Bennett, although he knew just what he was in for; the nightmare would start all over again.

Over the months the filming went well, despite the usual ups and downs, and Amber was glad to get back into the swing of things. Jonathan Parks, being a lot younger than

Elliot, was strict but could take all her nonsense; they did things *his* way, or not at all.

Amber loved this glamorous part; it was a fast-moving story of gambling and rich society, luxury yachts and ski boats and hidden sapphires, a story of survival, and filmed mostly in the Caribbean islands. They also had a lot of laughs during rehearsals, and for the first time in a year or so, she felt relaxed, wearing the most beautiful evening gowns and feeling glamorous, as was her usual role.

She was in the limelight once again, the cameras flashing everywhere she went, she and Steve making headlines in the press, and she loved still being the queen of Hollywood; this was right where she wanted to be. She had always worked hard, right from the beginning, and it had paid off generously.

On location in Miami the evenings were full of the usual buzz and excitement of the city and the nightclubs and drinks parties and dinners, as they had all been before, and then, after three months of hectic filming, she returned home to Sunny Hill House.

CHAPTER TWENTY-SEVEN

Even though Amber enjoyed and needed friends, she craved the glamorous lifestyle, the bright lights, the filming, the showbiz world; she never wanted it to change, but she also needed the peace and quiet of her own home. It was nice to get away from the hubbub for a while.

It was peaceful just sitting here now on the patio over the pool. A bright moon shone from a light blue-grey sky, turning the green of the garden to soft shades of grey, and she now felt relaxed for the first time in months. She had dined alone, and now, deep in thought, she reached out to clasp the stem of the wine glass on the glass-topped coffee table that held a single candle in a hurricane shade, a group of small gnats hovering above the flame. It brought back thoughts of Guyana; it had been peaceful there, too. *Too* peaceful.

She smiled and put the glass to her shiny red lips and sipped the red wine, then took a deep breath and heaved a sigh of relief, feeling the tension draining from her body. It was calming just hearing the gentle patter of water running in the fountain. As the sound of the last bird call faded into the night it seemed all was just switched off, and the thought of Guyana was again so clear in her mind; it had been just like that, the last bird calls, and the last monkey call, and the clicking and buzzing of the insects that came out in force at night. How she had survived that week she would never know. She smiled; she must have looked a mess... she had felt a mess... and the spiders, even more scary than the snakes and crocodiles. She shivered at the thought. They must have been creeping around all night in the darkness, who knew where? Probably clinging to the underside of the bed, and where were they hiding during the day? She rubbed her arms, feeling the shiver go right through her body remembering the bright and shining eyes of the one that lived in the bathroom that had watched her every day.

She sipped the wine, and took a deep breath; it was warming, and then her thoughts went back to London, hearing in her mind the rumble of the traffic and the hissing of air brakes on lorries, and the red double-decker buses and the black taxi cabs. That was London.

She smiled, seeing in her mind the Three Whistles, with its heavy dark wood and old-world charm, breathing in and imagining the strong smell of beer that seemed to tickle her nose. It had been great to be back, and to see Bill. Like London, he hadn't changed a bit, still the same old Bill pulling pints for the local East End barrow boys that gathered there every evening, but since the strong drinking and driving and no-smoking laws had come in the English pubs had lost their happy atmosphere. She agreed they were good laws, but pubs had to have that beery smoky smell; that was what the English pub was all about, and it put a damper on the people's carefree socialisation, everyone worrying about how much they should drink, and one too many and they would lose their driving licence.

She sipped the wine, again reliving the red double-decker buses and hearing the hubbub of traffic and the newspaper man shouting, 'Read all abart it!' on the corner near the London Theatre, quite often in the drizzling rain; it hadn't changed in years. Then there was the sudden silence as the stage door closed with that familiar heavy thud behind her when she stepped inside and the London buzz was just switched off; it was a different world. Yes, that was London's East End; it had a certain charm, and would always be home...

She suddenly felt a shiver and rubbed her arms as a chilled breath whispered close to her ear, 'You all right, luv?'

Amber turned slightly to her left, feeling a goosy shiver run right through her body as she saw a misty red dress, then she smiled and thought *gouwn*. 'Yes, Bessie, I'm all right.' She took a deep breath and sighed. 'It was lovely to be back in London; we missed such a lot, you and I. I just wish you'd been there.'

'Oh, I was there, luv! I was! I was right there with yer, every step of the way. It *was* nice to be 'ome, wasn't it? Nufin' like it, eh?'

A tear pricked Kitty's eye, imagining Bessie's smile. She smiled back. 'I went to the Three Whistles; Bill's still there. We had some good times together, didn't we?'

'Yeah.'

'But now I'd never turn back, would you?'

'No, luv, not now, *never...*'

Lightning Source UK Ltd.
Milton Keynes UK
UKOW06f2304200815